shannon
stacey

taken with
you

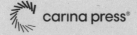

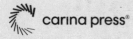

Recycling programs for this product may not exist in your area.

ISBN-13: 978-0-373-00228-3

TAKEN WITH YOU

Copyright © 2014 by Shannon Stacey

Edited by: Angela James

www.CarinaPress.com

Printed in U.S.A.

taken with
you

Acknowledgments

I'd like to acknowledge the men and women
of the New Hampshire Fish and Game Department, as
well as the Maine Warden Service for their dedication to
the preservation of nature and the New England way of
life. As lovers of both wildlife and OHRVs,
my family holds these officers in the highest respect,
and we're grateful for their service.

Dedication

For Mary Ahlgren,
who made our library a place my boys loved to visit.

New York Times and *USA TODAY* bestselling author **Shannon Stacey** lives with her husband and two sons in New England, where her two favorite activities are writing stories of happily ever after and riding her four-wheeler. From May to November, the Stacey family spends their weekends on their ATVs, making loads of muddy laundry to keep Shannon busy when she's not at her computer. She prefers writing to laundry, however, and considers herself lucky she got to be an author when she grew up.

You can contact Shannon through her website, www.shannonstacey.com, where she maintains an almost daily blog, or visit her on Twitter, @shannonstacey, her Facebook page, or email her at shannon@shannonstacey.com.

Dear Reader,

Over the course of writing the last four books in the Kowalski series, a character who was first introduced as a friend of Paige Sullivan in *All He Ever Needed* grew on me. Hailey Genest, Whitford's librarian, was fun and smart and had a great sense of humor, and it wasn't long before I started receiving questions from readers asking about her story.

Well, *Taken With You* is finally Hailey's story, but her road to happily ever after will be a rocky one. Matt Barnett is everything she thinks she's *not* looking for in a man, and the sexy game warden is going to turn everything she believed about love and relationships upside down.

I hope you enjoy this return visit to Whitford, Maine, and happy reading!

Shannon

ONE

THE SNARLING, POSSIBLY rabid, five hundred pound grizzly bear lurking in the trees was the final straw.

Hailey Genest stopped in her tracks, staring at the area of the forest where she'd heard the rustling. Okay, so maybe it wasn't a grizzly bear. She didn't think Maine had grizzlies, even deep in the woods. It was probably only a black bear, but it was a *really* big one.

"I think it was a chipmunk," her buddy system partner said.

Hailey turned her stare on Tori Burns, who'd talked her into this stupid wilderness adventure. "I hate you so much right now."

Tori grinned. "Your mascara's smudging."

"Why are we friends again?"

"Because you came into the diner during my shift and whined about being the last single woman on the entire planet because all of your friends have found their soul mates. When I pointed out I'm single, you decided *we* should be friends."

She hadn't been whining. She'd just had a rough day and hadn't felt like she could call her friends to vent because they were all probably greeting their menfolk at the door. And, yes, she had imagined them in aprons and pearls just because she could.

"First Paige married Mitch, then Lauren ran off to Massachusetts and married Ryan, and Katie's living with Josh." Hailey snorted and crossed her arms. "Those damn Kowalski men stole all my women."

Tori sighed. "And now *I'm* friends with a woman who wears makeup and new hiking boots on a wilderness adventure."

"The better I look, the better I feel and I thought I'd need the boost." She looked down at her feet, trying not to wince. "Pretty sure my blisters are reaching horror movie proportions, though."

"I told you it would be better to wear sneakers than brand-new hiking boots."

"I wanted to be fashionable."

"Yes, because limping is totally the new black."

Hailey took a few steps, trying to ignore how much her feet, calves and every other part of her body hurt, but then she stopped. "Listen."

After several seconds, Tori frowned. "I can't hear the others anymore."

"Not even the woman who sounds like she has a built-in megaphone and sucked helium for breakfast. They left us behind." Even as she said the words, which should have been cause for concern, Hailey felt a pang of relief.

If the group had left them behind, there was no pressure to keep up, which was something she'd been failing at miserably for at least a mile. She considered herself to be in good shape, but hiking for miles over uneven ground in the woods was kicking her butt. And they still had paddling canoes to look forward to, just to make sure her arms and back ached as much as her legs tomorrow.

Since her usual daily workout was pushing a cart of books from the night drop box back into the library, she could only wonder what she'd been thinking. Or drinking.

"If we hurry, we can catch them." Tori cast a doubtful glance at Hailey's feet. "If it helps, we get to *sit* in the canoes."

The thought of being off her feet did help a little, so Hailey did her best to keep up with her new friend. Tori wasn't very tall, but she walked with a long, confident stride that was hard to match. Trying to ignore how her impending blisters and the muscles in the backs of her calves were having a contest to see which could burn the worst, Hailey put one foot in front of the other and tried not to stumble over roots.

After what felt like miles, Tori stopped in a clearing and shook her head. There were several paths in front of them and they all looked the same degree of disturbed. No matter how hard she looked, Hailey couldn't tell which one their group had taken.

"Aren't they supposed to break off tree branches or something to point the way?" she asked.

"We weren't kidnapped by Magua. We just didn't

keep up. I think if the tour guides noticed they'd lost us, they would have waited rather than leave signs for us to interpret."

Hailey slapped herself in the face, then grimaced. "I'm going to need a blood transfusion before we get out of these woods."

"I have some Deep Woods Off in my pack. You want it?"

"No. I already have bug repellent on." She waved at a particularly persistent blackfly. "It's all natural and it nourishes my skin. It smells good, too."

"Too bad it doesn't keep the bugs away."

"The comments on Pinterest said it wasn't *quite* as effective as the chemical versions, but did I mention it's nourishing?"

Tori snorted. "And now you're nourishing the blackflies."

"I suck at being outside."

"You *are* surprisingly bad at it for somebody born and raised in rural Maine."

"Whitford's rural, but it's not *this* rural." Hailey wanted to point out her parents had chosen Whitford, not her, but a bug almost flew into her mouth, so she closed it.

"Well." Tori put her hands on her hips. "We're lost."

MATT BARNETT LEANED against a tree trunk and imagined himself at a crossroads. To the left was the low road. He could continue his walk in peace, making his way back to camp. Crack a beer with his old man. Drop a line in the river.

To the right was the high road, which meant approaching the two women whose voices carried through the trees like sirens. The fire truck kind, not the beautiful women luring sailors onto the rocks. They were lost, and rescuing damsels in distress wasn't on his vacation agenda.

Then again, vacations weren't supposed to have agendas. And as much as he wanted to kick back in his favorite fishing chair with a beer, it wasn't in his nature to leave two women alone in the woods. Unless, of course, they'd done it on purpose and it didn't sound like that was the case here.

With a weary sigh, he pushed off the tree and made his way to the women. He stepped out onto the path in front of them and had to give them credit for not screaming. They both yelped a little and the brunette dug her fingernails into the blonde's arm, but no full-blown hysterics.

He couldn't really blame them for being startled. Being on the downside of a two week vacation, Matt was looking more than a little rough. The jeans and flannel shirt were common enough, but his lucky fishing hat was nothing short of disgusting after years of wear. His hair had been overdue for a cut before the vacation even started, and he hadn't shaved since the last day he worked. If he'd been holding an axe, the women probably would have fainted.

"You ladies lost?"

"Nope." It was the brunette who spoke. She looked him straight in the eye while she lied. "We're all set, but thanks."

"Where you heading?"

This time it was the blonde who spoke, and she pointed at a spot over his shoulder. "Since we're facing that way, probably that way. Now if you'll excuse us, we—"

"Sound carries in the woods, so I know you're lost." He had a cabin and a dwindling vacation to get back to. "I'm Matt Barnett. I have a cabin a couple miles from here. I've been coming here my whole life and I haven't buried a single body in the woods yet."

"We totally believe you," the brunette said. "Because serial killers always start the conversation with how many bodies they've disposed of."

Even though there was a touch of humor in her voice, he noticed neither of them relaxed, which was good. Women shouldn't trust strange men who popped out of the tree line. But he also wanted to get this show on the road. If he had to tell them he was a game warden, he would, but he'd try to avoid it if he could. That, more often than not, led to questions and complaints and friends of friends who'd been cited and could he just look into that? He didn't want to go there, if possible.

"Let's go with the theory I'm *not* a serial killer for a few minutes," he said. "I'm not leaving you stranded in the woods, so the way I see it you ladies have two options. You can let me lead, which means I'll be in front of you and you can keep an eye on me, or I can shadow you, which means you won't be able to see me, but I'll be able to see you. That would be creepy."

"Or we could run," the blonde said.

He'd always been partial to brunettes in the past, and this one should have caught his eye. She was cute and had the potential to be a real firecracker, but for some reason it was the blonde who kept snagging his attention. Nothing about her—from the makeup she'd put on her face for a trek through the woods to the brand-new boots on her feet—was his type.

And she was looking at him like he'd just crawled out from behind a Dumpster. He'd seen that look before and he tended to not like women who aimed it his way.

She could probably run. The jeans and the form-fitting fleece zip-up she was wearing accented the fact she was in nice shape. But those boots had to be hurting her and the way her makeup was smearing around her pretty brown eyes told him she'd been sweating. If walking through the woods was an effort for her, running would be a joke.

"Pretty sure I could catch you."

The brunette snickered. "Of course you'd catch

her. I'm faster than her, plus everybody knows the blondes always die first."

"You guys are hilarious," her friend muttered.

"I'm Tori," the brunette said. "And this is Hailey. We've gotten separated from our group and, at the rate we're going, I'm not sure we'll ever catch up."

Progress, finally. "Which outfit are you with?"

"Dagneau Adventure Tours."

Keeping a straight face was one of the hardest things he'd ever done. Those boys had moments of competence, but they'd inherited the business from their father and were in it solely to thumb their noses at nine-to-five jobs. He thought they were idiots, personally. "Did you research Dagneau Adventure Tours before you signed up?"

"They had a great website," Hailey said.

Tori nodded. "And they offered the specific package we were looking for."

"What package was that?"

He watched Hailey try to jam her friend's ribs with her elbow, but Tori easily evaded it. "We wanted an adventure geared toward celebrating being single. Like, no couples stuff."

So the pretty blonde was single. Not that it mattered, but it was a tidbit of information his brain seemed to want to file away, just in case.

"In the future, you should get referrals and ask for references," he said. "You shouldn't take the company's word for it when it comes to your safety. Especially when it comes to the outdoors. Nature's pretty, but can be a real bitch at times."

"Thank you, Jeremiah Johnson," Hailey muttered, and when she blushed under his hard look, he assumed she hadn't meant for him to hear it.

"Tell me what the itinerary was, starting with where you parked," he said to Tori, choosing to ignore the implication he was some kind of hermit backwoodsman.

Once she'd laid out the plan for the day, Matt was faced with another decision. It was really six of one, half dozen of another as to whether it made more sense to help them find their group or take them out of the woods. But Hailey looked as if she'd had enough adventure for the day and, even though she didn't seem to like him very much, it went against his nature to see a woman miserable and not try to make it better.

"I think it's closer to head back to your car than to try to meet up with your group. Especially since your car won't be moving away from us while we're trying to catch it."

Tori waved her hand. "Lead on, then."

Hailey hesitated. "It seems wrong to just leave. What if they come back to look for us?"

"They deserve it," Tori said. "For leaving us."

"Maybe the idiots in charge do, but not the rest of the women."

Matt sighed. Leave it to the Dagneau boys to come

up with a way to get a bunch of single women into the woods. He made a mental note to have a closer look at their business and maybe rustle through their paperwork as he pulled his satellite phone out of the holster on his hip.

"Your phone works out here?"

"It's a satellite phone." It was a personal phone, in addition to the work cell phone he'd been issued. "My family spends a lot of time up here and I don't like being cut off from the world."

He started walking as he called into dispatch and asked them to relay to the Dagneau brothers that two of their guests had been lost and found. When he was done, he put the phone away and then looked over his shoulder to see how the women were faring.

They were still where he'd left them, and he was already too far away to make out their expressions. He held up his hands in a *what are you waiting for* motion and then had to wait while they caught up.

"We weren't sure if you wanted privacy for your phone call," Hailey explained. "Sorry."

He hadn't missed her wincing as she approached, but there wasn't much he could do about it. He certainly wasn't carrying her back to her car and he couldn't get his truck close enough to where they were to make a difference. By ATV he could, but it would take longer to go get it, get back and make individual trips with the women than it was worth. She'd have to suck it up.

"Let's go, ladies." He set off down the path, keeping a slightly slower than moderate pace and pointing out rocks and roots in the path.

HAILEY WAS NEVER going on an adventure again. Okay, maybe not *never,* but it would be a while and next time it wouldn't involve hiking boots or bug repellant.

Only by sheer force of will did she bite back the complaints about her feet hurting. And the bug bites. And the fact she was starving. For reasons she couldn't even begin to explain, she didn't want their flannel-clad hero to think any less of her than he already did.

But she didn't do a very good job of killing the sigh of relief when Matt stopped and gestured toward a fallen log. "Sit a few minutes. Have a drink. You *do* have water, right?"

Nodding, Tori pulled a bottle from the small backpack she was wearing and offered it to Hailey. They sat side-by-side on the log and shared the water bottle back and forth, and she arched an eyebrow when Matt pulled a flask out of his back pocket. If the guy was drinking, maybe they shouldn't be following him around the woods.

"Just water," he said, amusement evident in the set of his mouth. "I promise."

Hailey groaned as tiny bugs seemed to realize she'd stopped moving and invited hundreds of their closest friends to the party. She tried waving them away, but she knew it was futile. "The blackflies aren't supposed to be bad yet."

"You can blame the winter we had."

Hailey wasn't sure what winter had to do with getting the blackflies riled up earlier than usual, and she suspected if she asked, she'd get a long and boring science lesson. Instead, she pushed herself up and then hauled Tori to her feet. "Let's keep moving."

At least the view wasn't bad while they were walking, Hailey had to admit to herself. Matt Barnett might be *way* too scruffy from the neck up, but his lower eighty percent was a treat. Tall and nicely built without being bulky, he had the kind of broad shoulders she found attractive in a man.

The flannel shirt he was wearing over what looked like a T-shirt didn't allow her to see his torso, but she'd bet it was as nicely firm as his legs. And his ass. Sometimes the shirt would lift and she could make out the bulges in his back pockets. One she now knew was his water flask and she assumed the other was his wallet. He was wearing things on his belt, too. She could make out shapes under the shirt, but not enough to tell what they were. One was presumably a holster for his satellite phone. What he had on the other hip, she couldn't guess. Probably some kind of super Boy Scout rescue kit.

"I recognize that pile of rocks," Tori said after a while. "We're almost back to the parking lot."

As much as watching Matt walk didn't suck, Hailey was glad to hear it. "I'm going to soak in a hot bubble bath for an hour. I can't believe we're missing movie night for this."

Tori shook her head. "We talked about this. We're sick of watching movies about women who are only happy in the end if they've found a man who loves them. We're out in the woods, embracing being strong, fun, single women. Or we were supposed to be, anyway."

If only there was buffalo chicken dip in the woods. "How did we come to the conclusion going on an adventure tour in the wilderness was the best way to embrace being single women?"

"It made sense after the second glass of wine."

"Wouldn't watching whatever movie we wanted illustrate a happy single woman more than walking in the woods?"

"Maybe it was the third glass." Tori leaned closer, dropping her voice to just above a whisper. "He's kind of hot, and he looks at you a lot. You should ask him out."

"He looks at us both a lot since, you know, we're the only two other people here and it would be weird to look at trees while he's talking to us. Besides, the whole Grizzly Adams thing he has going on does nothing for me."

"Who's Grizzly Adams?"

Hailey shook her head. "Further evidence you're too young to be my friend."

"Hey, you picked me. And speaking of, who's Jeremiah Johnson?"

"For crap's sake, Tori. Really? They're from TV and movies. Famous scruffy mountain men hermit types."

"I don't think Matt's a hermit. He has a satellite phone."

That might impress Tori, but Hailey wasn't looking for a guy who spent enough time in the middle of nowhere to need a satellite phone. She wanted a man who wore suits and didn't roll his eyes at the thought of museums or operas. He'd have the kind of job that brought not only big paychecks, but benefits and Christmas parties Hailey could dress up for.

That guy wasn't in Whitford, or if he was, he was hiding from Hailey. She'd joked a few times about moving to the city to find her Prince Charming, but she couldn't bring herself to actually do it. She loved her job and her house. And the people of Whitford. She loved her life.

She just wanted somebody to share it with and, no matter how good Matt looked from the back, he had no chance of being that guy.

Hailey almost cried when they broke out of the tree line and she saw Tori's car in the parking lot. Padded seats, climate control and no blackflies.

"Thank you for making sure we got back okay," Tori said, shaking Matt's hand.

"It was my pleasure." Hailey wasn't so sure, but she smiled anyway when he turned to shake her hand. "Make sure you put something on those blisters when you get home."

"I thought I hid the limping better than that." His hand felt huge and hard, but the firm squeeze had just the right amount of pressure.

"I was starting to wonder if I'd have to give you a piggyback ride out of the woods."

Shaking his hand was one thing, but jumping on this man's back and wrapping her legs around his waist? Strangely heat-inducing but was never going to happen. "Well we're out now. Thanks."

It didn't escape Hailey's attention that Matt stood at the edge of the parking lot, where the dirt met the trees, and watched them until the car was started and they were on their way. Probably because she was watching him in the mirror.

"You should have asked for his satellite phone number," Tori said, nudging Hailey with her elbow.

She groaned. "No."

"If you got laid, this day wouldn't have been a waste."

"I'm not going to talk about my sex life." There wasn't anything to talk about. "At least the gossips in Whitford will have something to talk about for a while."

Tori's mouth turned down at the corners. "We don't *have* to tell them."

"We skipped out on movie night for this, so they'll ask about it."

On the first Saturday of every month, some of the women gathered without men or kids to watch a movie and, since it had been Hailey's turn to host, she hadn't been able to simply skip it. She'd had to explain about the adventure tour and how the first weekend in May was the only opening they had, thanks to a cancellation.

"We don't have to tell them every single detail," Tori said.

"The fact you believe that is proof enough you weren't born and raised in Whitford. Trust me. We're going to be famous."

TWO

BY THE TIME Matt got back to the family's cabin on the river, the light was starting to change. His dad would probably be tracking the time, wondering if it was time to worry yet.

Bear met him at the edge of the porch and he leaned down to give his black Lab a good neck scratch. "Be glad you stayed behind, buddy. It was a *long* walk."

Bear's tail thumped against the wooden planks for a few seconds before he walked back to his favorite spot under the double swing. Dogs were a man's best friend until a long nap in the shade was on the flip side of the coin.

"Was thinking about starting up a search party." His dad held up a can. "Just as soon as I finished this beer."

Matt grabbed one of his own and plopped down in the other chair. "Had to rescue a couple of damsels in distress."

"Only you would find women in need of help out here in the middle of nowhere."

"It's a gift." He drained a quarter of the can, fighting the grimace. He was thirsty, but he wasn't a big fan of beer. It was a tradition tied up with the camp and fishing and his old man, but at the moment he would have swapped it for a tall glass of lemonade in a heartbeat.

"Tourists?"

"I don't think so." He realized now he'd never asked the women where they were from, other than where they'd parked their car. "Based on the accents, I'd say they're both from Maine, though I can't pinpoint where exactly. Got separated from their adventure tour."

"Which one?"

"The Dagneau boys."

That garnered a throaty sound of derision that, in Matt's experience, only old men from New England could master. "Those two morons would be lucky to find a hooker in a whorehouse."

"I think I'll stop in and have a talk with them next week."

"Somebody needs to."

Policing local business practices wasn't necessarily part of his job as a game warden, but he'd always found if a man looked and sounded official enough, nobody would question him. And since it was guys like Matt who'd get called out to find the people jerks like the Dagneaus lost, he figured that gave him the right to speak up.

"I got the house," he told his dad after a few minutes. "Called the owner while I was out for a walk. Good price and they don't have a problem with Bear."

The dog raised his head at the sound of his name, his expression full of joyful expectation. When Matt just smiled at him without getting out of his chair, Bear sighed and dropped his head back onto his paws.

His dad shook his head. "Why rent a house when you can stay here? It's only forty minutes to Whitford."

This was ground they'd only covered half a dozen times already. "No, it's forty minutes from the main road. From here to the main road, if it hasn't rained and you don't mind your coffee bouncing right up out of your travel mug, is a good twenty minutes."

"Lots of people commute an hour to work. No sense in wasting money."

"You know I get called out at all hours. It can't take me almost half an hour just to get on the road. And this isn't a home, Dad. It's a camp. I'd have to find a house in a few months, anyway. Moving twice would also be a waste of money."

On the list of traits Charlie Barnett liked in a person, frugality ranked right up there with patriotism and being able to drive a stick shift. Even his old man had to admit Matt couldn't winter in a cabin that had no indoor plumbing after Columbus Day.

"Your mother's hoping this is temporary. That there won't be enough going on to merit a full-time warden in the area, after all, and you'll go back to your usual area."

Which was close enough to his parents' house on the outskirts of Augusta, Maine so he could pop in for supper a couple nights per week. "We're close enough to the big lake here so I'll be kept busy even if everybody on the ATV trails behaves. And it makes sense that it's me. I don't know Whitford or the new trails, but I'm familiar with most of the area since we've been coming here my whole life."

"She says it's too far away."

"Did Mom write this down for you, or are you winging it?"

"You spend almost forty years with the same woman and tell me if you need a script."

Matt wasn't even capable of spending two years with the same woman, though not for a lack of trying. "It's not like I'm an only child. She has two daughters, a son-in-law and grandchildren to fuss over."

"You know your mother. Until you find a wife, she's terrified you're going to starve to death wearing dirty clothes."

"Maybe Whitford's where I'll find a woman who won't spend our entire relationship trying to change me into the version of me she wants."

His dad's chair creaked as he shifted sideways to get a better look at him. "They're not all like Ciara, son. And, to be honest, there were warning signs right from the beginning. You just didn't want to see them."

That was probably the truth. It had been easy to ignore the jabs at his wardrobe and the way she'd steered him toward doing activities she wanted to do. But over the nearly two years they'd been together, Ciara's hints about things she wanted changed had gone from subtle to big neon signs flashing her dissatisfaction with him.

They'd been arguing about his job a lot toward the end. At the beginning, Ciara hadn't minded a boyfriend who wore a uniform, carried a gun, made decent money and—according to her—was hotter than any of her friends' boyfriends—but it wasn't enough. The long and erratic hours made her unhappy. The questionable odors that often accompanied him home made her face screw up in a way he found really unattractive. And stripping to his boxer briefs in the yard and spraying himself off with the garden hose before he could go into his own home had made *him* unhappy.

Still, he'd clung to the relationship. When things were good between him and Ciara, they were really good. Until the company Christmas party for the bank where she was a teller. He'd put on the suit she told him to wear and did his best to make his tie straight, but he could feel the judgment rolling off her like toxic waves.

He was getting her a glass of punch when he overheard her talking to a couple of her coworkers about the engagement ring she was sure he'd bought her for Christmas. "Knowing Matt, he'll hide it in a pile of moose poop and make me hunt for it. I just hope he's wearing a decent shirt for once so I won't be embarrassed to put a picture of us on Facebook."

Breaking it off with her two weeks before Christmas wasn't something he was proud of, but he couldn't look at her without feeling a burn of shame that really pissed him off. And he couldn't stomach the thought of her spending another holiday with his family.

"I've dated a few times since Ciara, Dad. I know they're not all like her."

"We liked Wendy."

"She wasn't cut out to be a game warden's wife."

His dad snorted again. "We heard about that and don't think we're too stupid to see you're testing these poor women."

"It's not testing. It's making sure we're right for each other."

"Really? So you just happened to, during the course of one shift, roll around in mud, get bear shit on you *and* get sprayed by a skunk?"

Okay, so that might have been a test. And Wendy had failed. "I bet when you were dating mom, she never looked at you like you were something she needed to scrape off her shoe."

"You'd lose that bet."

Matt seriously doubted that. His mom gave her husband some good-natured ribbing after a day of fishing or a trip to camp like the one they were on now, but Connie Barnett was never ashamed of the man she'd married.

Someday he'd find a woman who didn't wrinkle her nose at him or nag him because he'd rather wear a T-shirt that came free with a case of beef jerky than a fancy button-up shirt from the mall.

Whether or not he'd find her in Whitford remained to be seen.

BY THE TIME Tori pulled onto Hailey's street, she wasn't sure she'd be able to get out of the car. The new hiking boots had been tossed onto the floor of the backseat, but her muscles were already protesting the day's adventure by stiffening up on her.

"You going to make it?" Tori put the car in park and grinned at her. "I'd offer a piggyback ride, but you're a lot taller than me, so it would just be awkward."

"The test will be getting out of the car. After that, I can crawl if I have to."

"We should have invited our rescuer home with us. I bet he could have carried you inside without even breaking a sweat."

With a body like that, he probably could. Unfortunately, the package as a whole didn't do much for her. "What is it with you and trying to hook me up with that guy? He probably collects roadkill in his freezer."

Tori frowned. "Who would do that?"

"Exactly."

"Hailey, just because a guy is hairy, smells a little bad and has a hat so gross even a ten-year-old boy wouldn't touch it doesn't mean he's not marriage material."

She actually shuddered. "Then you marry him."

"Oh, no. I'm never getting married. You're the one who's on the hunt for Prince Charming."

"And that guy wasn't him." She reached into the backseat for her boots, wincing. "Next time, let's go to a nightclub."

"Whitford doesn't have a nightclub."

"Katie and I went to a great club on the Valentine's Day before last. We'd have to spend the night at a motel, but we wouldn't be in the woods."

"Nice places?"

"Of course." Hailey paused halfway out of the car. "Okay, not really. But they meet the minimum requirements of being a nightclub and motel."

"Gee, I can hardly wait."

Hailey managed to get out of the car without falling on her face. "I'll call you tomorrow if I don't drown in the tub."

Boots in hand, she walked to her front door in her stocking feet. She'd never been so glad to see her house, and that was saying something. She was crazy about the little Cape and coming home at the end of the day was one of her greatest pleasures. It was also one of the reasons, besides loving her job, that kept her from leaving Whitford and moving someplace with a little more variety in its men.

There was a ranch-style house to her left and a young family lived there, but she couldn't really see or hear them thanks to a strip of woods along the property line. On the other side was a smaller version of her own house. It was closer than she would have liked, but a couple whose only child had already moved out had lived there when Hailey bought her house. A few months ago, the couple had moved away in search of work.

The house hadn't sold, though. Fran Benoit, who owned the Whitford General Store and was ground zero for all things gossip related, told her they never even got a nibble, so they were trying to rent it instead. While Hailey didn't mind the lack of interest because new neighbors were always a crap shoot, she was starting to have reservations about it sitting empty. It would start going downhill and she didn't want it dragging her property value down with it.

Ignoring the front door, with its sidelights and hanging pots, she let herself into the door she usually used, which opened into a mudroom between the garage and kitchen. After tossing the boots into the corner, knowing there was a good chance she'd never wear them again, she went into the kitchen. A bright room, with lemon walls and white cabinets and woodwork, it was devoid of clutter while still being warm and welcoming. It usually cheered her up after a long day at the library which, despite her best efforts, still had a lot of dark-stained oak going on, but right now she just wanted to grab a glass of iced tea and collapse.

Her living room wasn't quite as bright as the kitchen, with pale mint walls and beige leather loveseats, and the master bedroom was more neutral with soft blues and peach tones, but overall her home was decorated in colors that made her happy. Most of the accent furnishings were white rather than wood, and she kept redecorating limited to a slight throw pillow fetish. Some women bought shoes. She bought colorful throw pillows.

Throwing herself onto a loveseat, Hailey sent a text to Paige Kowalski. Paige had only been in Whitford a few years, but they'd become almost immediate friends and she was still the person Hailey went to when she had something on her mind.

Are you busy/sleeping/covered in baby poop?

Within seconds, the cell phone rang in her hand and Paige's name flashed on the screen. Hailey swallowed some iced tea and answered it. "Hey, new mommy. How's it going?"

"Right now, it's quiet. Which means right now is the greatest moment of my life."

Hailey laughed. "Oh, come on. Sarah's almost

seven weeks old now. You don't have the hang of it yet?"

"What I *have* figured out is that little Sarah Rose loves to sleep on her daddy's chest. Poor Mitch has been trying to signal to me he has to pee for a half hour now, so I'm avoiding eye contact."

"Didn't you tell me he has to start traveling again next week?"

Paige's sigh was loud over the phone. "He's trying to keep it to a minimum but yeah, he has to go out of town next week."

"Maybe you could get one of those man dolls people use to cheat their way into carpool lanes."

"Mitch would probably like to think it wouldn't be the same. Hey, aren't you supposed to be paddling around in a canoe or something right now? I remember something about Liz covering for Tori because Tori and you were going on some kind of adventure hike. Then I was wondering if I hallucinated that because I only sleep five minutes a day now and I'd never heard your name and hiking used in the same sentence before, but I know Liz worked today."

"Let's pretend it was a postpartum hallucination."

"Ooh, that good? Tell me. And tell me every single detail very, very slowly because Mitch won't interrupt me while I'm on the phone. As soon as I hang up, quiet time's over."

Hailey told her every detail she remembered, pausing every once in a while so Paige could laugh at her or lecture her about new boots and trusting homemade concoctions from internet sites.

"Wait, tell me again about the guy that found you? Do you think he lived in the woods?"

Hailey realized she might have overplayed the poor guy's *Deliverance* factor a little. Or a lot. "He said it was a camp, I think. And he said his family goes there."

"So he wasn't a weird hermit guy, then?"

"He had a satellite phone."

"Oh, well then. There you go."

"That's what Tori said. I have no idea if hermits have satellite phones. But he heard me call him Jeremiah Johnson."

"Jeremiah Johnson was kind of hot."

Hailey rolled her eyes, even though Paige couldn't see her. "No. Robert Redford, playing him in the movie, was kind of hot. In real life, I think Jeremiah Johnson was probably pretty gross."

"In the movies, the guy who comes to the rescue is never pretty gross."

Gross was a bit harsh. So the guy needed to be reacquainted with hot, soapy water and a razor blade. And laundry detergent. Those were all things that could be fixed. Underneath all that, he'd had a great body, a voice she could imagine would make reading the phone book out loud sexy, and there was something about his eyes. He had really pretty eyes. Brown, but lighter than hers, and thick eyelashes.

In the background, Hailey could hear Sarah start winding up to a full shriek and Paige sighed. "I bet he woke her up on purpose."

"Go kiss Sarah for me and let your husband pee. Call me if you get bored or you need a break while Mitch is on the road, okay?"

They hung up and Hailey finished the rest of her iced tea. Next up was a long soak in a hot bubble bath.

And she'd put on an audiobook, too, to keep her mind from straying yet again to how jealous she was of her best friend. All of her friends, actually. They were all living happily ever after, while she was still waiting for her prince to come.

She wished she could be more like Tori. Tori had no interest in being anybody's wife and intended to live the rest of her life having torrid and temporary love affairs with any guy who tickled her fancy, and then moving on before the fancy-tickling turned sour.

While Hailey figured Tori just hadn't met the guy who'd change her mind yet, she admired the principle. Even a torrid and temporary love affair would be enough at this point in her life.

But it had been so long since a man tickled her fancy, she was starting to wonder if her fancy simply wasn't ticklish anymore.

IT WAS STILL dark enough for the truck's headlights to be on when Matt drove into town on Saturday morning. It had taken him over an hour the previous evening to clean himself up, but now he was in uniform, fairly well caffeinated, and ready to start the day.

As small towns went, Whitford was pretty typical of many in Maine. Tourists drove through on their way to the lakes or to a ski resort or the mountains, but rarely stopped. The town had some appeal, but it existed more out of habit than anything else.

Until recently. In an attempt to save their snowmobile lodge, the Kowalski family had worked with a nearby ATV club and the state to get access from the trail system to the lodge. From there, riders had access to Whitford, and business had definitely picked up for places that offered food, lodging and gas. That trickled into the rest of the town's economy and the residents went out of their way to welcome the four-wheeling crowd.

It had been more successful than even Josh Kowalski—the youngest brother, who ran the Northern Star Lodge and had spearheaded the effort—had imagined, and that was where Matt came in. Even with a department ATV that Whitford police chief Drew Miller had managed to finagle a grant for, the local law enforcement couldn't keep up with the increase in off-road traffic.

His first job in Whitford would be leading an ATV safety course. Once kids reached ten years old, they could take the course and hit the trails. In the past, Whitford parents had had to travel to the nearest class they could find, but Josh had pushed to have one right in town to serve the surrounding area.

Thanks to the early hour, Matt had no trouble finding a parking spot in front of the police station and he could smell the coffee as soon as he walked inside. A guy about his own age stepped through an office door and extended his hand.

"Drew Miller," he said as they shook.

"Matt Barnett. Nice to meet you."

"Help yourself to some coffee if you want."

After he'd made himself a cup, he followed the chief into his office and took a seat. "I have a feeling running this safety class today's going to require a lot of coffee."

"I'd be right there with you, but I'm having Dave Camden do it. He's the school resource officer, so he knows the kids." Miller smiled. "Plus, I'm the chief, so I don't have to do it if I don't want to."

Matt had a feeling he'd like this guy. "I appreciate you coming in early on a Saturday so we could meet. This will be a crazy week with a lot of driving time. I can't move into the house I rented until next Saturday, so I'll be commuting from my current apartment."

"Wasn't a problem. My wife works the early shift at the diner, so I use the time to catch up on paperwork. Or to chase it, anyway. I never seem to actually catch up."

"I know what you mean." Paperwork was the

bane of any law enforcement officer's existence. "I'm looking forward to making Whitford home."

"I think it's a great town, but I'm biased, of course. Got a nice small-town feel to it."

"Hell, on my way in, I saw the barber shop has one of those old-fashioned poles. Brings to mind old men and hot lather shaves and listening to the ball-game on the radio."

"Good chance a game will be on, but Katie Davis isn't old or a man. Gives a mean hot lather shave, but a word of advice. No matter where you're from or who you root for, when you walk into the barber shop in Whitford, you're a New England sports fan. Don't piss off the woman with the electric trimmer in one hand and scissors in the other."

A woman who loved sports and knew her way around hot lather? "Is she single?"

Drew gave him an amused look. "She's engaged to Josh Kowalski."

Toes Matt wouldn't step on even if he were the type to poach another guy's woman, which he wasn't. "Lucky guy. Looking forward to meeting him."

They'd be working together a lot. Once the ATV club that oversaw the original trail system helped connect to Whitford and a neighboring town and a system on the far side, they realized they didn't have the manpower to run the entire thing. Over the win-ter, word had spread on the internet there would be great riding in the area come spring, and it was clear they'd need more volunteers.

The people of Whitford, obviously seeing the financial benefit, had heeded Josh's call, and the Northern Star ATV Club was born. Since Josh Kowalski was the president and Matt would be the game warden, they'd be getting to know each other well. Along with a guy named Andy Miller, who was the trail administrator.

"Hey, Andy Miller," Matt said. "Any relation to you?"

"He's my dad. And he lives at the lodge with Rose Davis, who's the housekeeper, Katie's mom, and the woman who basically raised the Kowalskis after their mom died."

Matt rocked back in his chair, trying to absorb that info and sort it into some kind of mental visual. "Well, that's…close-knit. Hopefully a little more Mayberry than *Flowers in the Attic.*"

"*Flowers in the Attic,* huh? I remember that title from when I was a kid and *all* the girls were reading it."

Ouch. "Hey, my sisters were always bringing books home from the library, but if my old man saw me reading, it meant he hadn't given me enough to do. I had to sneak-read whatever books I could."

"Since you're doing the safety class at the library today, I should warn you if Hailey Genest finds out you're moving to town, she won't let you leave without a library card. Budget committee gets really hung up on the number of patrons, so it's not really optional where she's concerned."

"Good to know." The name popped out at him, but he wrote it off as a coincidence. Hailey wasn't exactly a rare name, and what were the chances a woman he'd stumbled across in the woods was the librarian in his new town?

They talked about the town for a while, and the chief shared some of his concerns about the new ATV trails. And Matt did his best to pay attention, but his mind kept wandering back to the Hailey he'd met in the woods. It had been doing that a lot since he'd watched them drive away, which made no sense to him.

He could never date a woman who wore makeup to go on a hike in the woods. The new boots were simply a rookie mistake, but the makeup and the fact she'd sacrificed effectiveness for a pretty smell in her insect repellant told him she probably didn't spend a lot of time outdoors. Matt practically lived outside.

Hell, she'd probably never even baited her own hook. A man like him had no business thinking about a woman like her.

THREE

THE WHITFORD PUBLIC Library was usually open from ten in the morning until five o'clock on Mondays through Fridays—the board having recently agreed it no longer made sense to be open until eight on Fridays—and three hours every other Saturday afternoon, but on this particular Saturday Hailey was there at seven-thirty to unlock the door and turn the lights on.

When Drew Miller had stopped by and asked her if they could hold the six-hour ATV safety class at the library, she hadn't hesitated even a second before saying yes. She was all for anything that brought kids through those doors.

They had the two computers, as well as board games and jigsaw puzzles, and she allowed the kids to hang out and use the Wi-Fi without giving them sideways glances. Whitford didn't offer a lot for children, so she made sure the library was a relaxed place with heat in the winter, air-conditioning in the summer and lots of comfortable places to sit. She built her displays carefully and every time a kid paused to look at a book, she mentally high-fived herself. When the book was actually checked out and brought home, she did a butt-wiggle dance in her chair.

Her predecessor had been one of those scary women who peered at people over her reading glasses and shushed them for breathing. When she'd retired, Hailey had been given the job because she'd been the only applicant, and she'd thrown herself into turning the library's reputation around.

She'd gotten to know her patrons' tastes and built the collection around what they wanted to read, but always kept her eye out for a book that might surprise them. In a long battle with the trustees, she'd fought to build the audiobook collection. A lot of people had to make long commutes to find jobs and she could barely keep the popular titles on the shelves. She hadn't won the digital book battle yet, but she'd educated herself and was able to offer tech help to her patrons. Even with more and more residents turning to ebooks, the library remained valuable to them because Hailey worked her ass off to make sure it did.

She'd knocked on every single door in Whitford until she got the donations and volunteers she needed to rehab the interior. Not a lot. She had a strong respect for the history of the building. But she'd brightened the paint and replaced the ancient, dark carpet with colorful tile and rugs.

Sometimes it was discouraging, all the battling against video games and the budget committee. But in Whitford, the library was a cool place to hang out and reading was a cool thing to do. As far as Hailey was concerned, she was winning the war.

She went into the oversized closet masquerading as her break room and started a pot of coffee. Josh was supposed to show up, since he was the president of the new Northern Star ATV Club, and she hoped he'd be carrying a basket of baked goods from Rose. Rosie Davis may have been the housekeeper for the Northern Star Lodge for as long as any of them could remember, but she'd managed to spoil the entire town with her cooking.

With her eye on the clock, Hailey opened the package of paper hot cups she'd bought and set a stack next to the coffeemaker. The sugar bowl was full, and they'd figure out there was milk in the minifridge.

At fifteen minutes before eight, the door opened and Josh walked in, carrying a big basket covered with a checked towel. Hailey's mouth started watering and she didn't want to share with the other guys filing in after him, all of whom she knew except for the game warden who entered about a minute after the others.

There was something about men in uniforms, she thought. Dave Camden, the newest member of the WPD and the school resource officer, didn't do much for her, which was good since he was also too young. Sam Jensen, who was a volunteer fireman and pretty much the sum total of the Whitford rescue squad, was wearing his WFD polo shirt and black pants. They'd dated twice, shortly after Hailey returned from college, but there hadn't been any chemistry between them.

The game warden, though, was a strong possibility. His crisp green uniform showed off one hell of a body, which she'd had a chance to check out at her leisure while he was introducing himself to the other guys. His hair was buzzed pretty short and his jawline was so clean-shaven she wanted to run her fingertips down the rugged lines of his face.

A man with a career, good grooming habits and a great ass right here in Whitford. Maybe it was her lucky day.

"Where should I put these, Hailey?" Josh called, holding up the basket.

"In my car."

He laughed, the sound echoing through the building. "Nice try. Rose said I have to share, which means you have to share, too."

"Fine. I set you guys up at the big tables in the reference section. You'll have to go in the break room to get coffee, though. This building suffers from a serious lack of electrical outlets."

It had taken her two years to get the okay to have some electrical work done and the amount they'd approved was ridiculously low. She'd settled for upgrading the outlets they used for the computers and adding outlets to the seating areas where people liked to plug their chargers in.

She realized the hot guy in the game warden uniform was staring at her, but kids started arriving with their parents in tow and she was too busy getting everybody settled in to make eye contact with him.

Even during regular business hours, the noise level wouldn't have bothered her. They'd quiet down a little once the actual education part of the class started, and she usually put a notice in the weekly paper and always put a sign on the door. If you were looking for quiet time at the library, the hour two dozen preschoolers were watching a story time puppet show wasn't it.

Once the library officially opened at ten, she knew Josh would try to keep the kids down to a dull roar, and she might have to hand out some sympathetic, if not entirely sincere, apologies to patrons who missed the sign, but it was one day. Everybody would survive.

When the game warden bent over to pull the handbooks out of a cardboard box and his uniform stretched over his back and behind, she decided to give him a hand.

"I'll help you pass those around," she said, holding out her hand for a stack. He smelled delicious and she moved a little closer.

"Thanks. If you don't mind, there's a box of Warden Service pencils there, too. If you could make sure each kid has one, that would be great."

"Not a problem."

His voice certainly tickled her very-much-still-ticklish fancy, and Hailey frowned as she moved around the tables, passing out workbooks and pencils. There was something about his voice that seemed familiar, but she couldn't quite place it.

She snuck a few more looks at him, but she would remember that jaw if she'd seen it. And that mouth.

"Hey," Josh said, "Matt marked a few of those workbooks as instructors' copies because they have the answers in them. Did you see them anywhere?"

"You afraid you'll flunk ATV Riding 101 without a cheat sheet, Kowalski?" Dave Camden asked, smirking.

Hailey frowned. "Matt?"

"Yeah, Matt Barnett. The game warden?"

She turned to face the guy with the smooth jaw and crisp uniform. "His name is Matt?"

It clicked. The lines of his back. The ass. The voice. He saw her staring and stared back. With those light brown eyes framed by dark, full lashes.

Wow. Tori was never going to believe this. And she was never, ever going to let Hailey live this one down.

MATT WAS GLAD he hadn't seen the town's librarian until after he'd introduced himself to the other guys because he'd been struck speechless when he realized this Hailey was, in fact, the same Hailey he'd helped find her way out of the woods. He wasn't sure what the chances were of that happening, but he felt like he should buy a lottery ticket or bet on a horse race.

She looked different today. Her hair was in a ponytail again and she had makeup on, but just a touch and it was accenting her pretty face rather than making her look like a raccoon. Her T-shirt had something to do with some computer game all the kids, including his niece and nephews, were playing, and jeans. And she had on sneakers. She didn't really look like a lot of librarians he'd known, which might go a long way toward explaining why the kids were so comfortable there.

He'd had some reservations when the police chief told them they'd be holding the class in a library, but Hailey didn't seem to mind the noise or the banana bread crumbs coating the tables.

She minded him, though. He wasn't used to women not being happy to see him, and he wasn't quite sure what to make of it. It's not like he'd deliberately disguised himself to fool her into believing he was some kind of forest hermit.

He suspected he knew what her problem was. She'd been checking him out since he walked into the building, and finding out he was the same guy she'd turned her nose up at in the woods had thrown her for a loop.

It was too bad, really. Hailey the librarian might rev his engine, but he didn't need to get sprayed by a skunk to know she wasn't for him.

He'd seen recognition strike, her expression turning sour, and then she'd mumbled something about having work to do and walked away. Rather than follow and ask what her problem was, he dug the instructors' workbooks out of the bottom of the box so he could stop thinking about her and get to work.

They had a lot to cover in six hours. Besides the actual safe operation of ATVs and snowmobiles, they had to teach them the laws, some basic survival and emergency stuff, first aid and how to respect the land, wildlife and—most importantly—the landowners.

Nothing said he couldn't have a little fun with it, though.

"Okay, kids, let's see how much you know about being out in the woods." He was deliberately loud, knowing his voice would carry to Hailey. "How many of you make sure you wear bug spray every time you're going to spend time outside?"

Less than half of them raised their hands, which didn't surprise him. Where they were in the state, there wasn't a lot of concern about mosquito-borne illnesses. Yet. He'd work on that. "And should you use an insect repellant with DEET or one that smells pretty?"

They all shouted *DEET* at the same time. He looked toward the circulation desk and was rewarded with a very black look from the pretty librarian.

"That's right. Next question is true or false. You should wear brand-new hiking boots if you're going on a long hike in the woods."

Most of them got that one right, too, though he couldn't say which kids did and which didn't since he was looking over their heads. Hailey wasn't even attempting to mask her annoyance. With her arms crossed, she would have set him on fire with her eyes if she could.

"One more. If you're going into the woods with a group of people, you don't need to know where you are or have a map or compass. True or false?"

"False!" a kid yelled, loudly enough so all of the adults flinched out of habit. They were in a library. "You might get separated from them and then you'll be lost."

"That's right. And how old are you, buddy?"

"Ten!"

Hailey lifted her hand above the desk, then paused before closing it into a fist and lowering it again. Why, he did believe the librarian was going to flip him the bird.

"Good job," he told the group. "Okay, guys, we're going to break for five minutes to finish that banana bread and refill my coffee cup, and then I'm going to talk laws for a little while before turning it over to Mr. Kowalski here for the riding basics."

He hadn't planned to take a break at all, but he knew if he didn't move, he was eventually going to lose his train of thought and embarrass himself. Having Hailey in his line of sight would play hell on his concentration.

He was starting another pot of coffee to brew when Josh Kowalski squeezed into the small break room. "I'm going to take a wild guess and say two plus two equals you being the guy who found Hailey and Tori in the woods last weekend."

"Heard about that, did you?"

"This is Whitford, so everybody's heard about it. In the version I heard, though, you were very hairy, smelled bad and, depending on who you asked, were wearing a fresh bear skin like a coat."

"That sounds like Hailey's version. Her friend Tori seemed a little less...dramatic."

Josh laughed. "I don't know Tori as well as I do Hailey, but I think you're probably right about that. And, based on the looks she's been giving you, it's probably a good thing you're going to work in the area, but live somewhere else, with your own library."

Not for long, Matt thought, but he didn't say it. Apparently the people of Whitford didn't know *ev-*

erything. As far as he knew, only Drew Miller and the home's owners knew that he was moving to town.

He could almost picture the look of shock on Hailey's face when he showed up to get his library card. Because, yes, he could read.

"A word of warning," Josh said in a low voice. "The women in this town have been on a husband hunt for Hailey Genest for a while now, so brace yourself."

"If you think I'm husband material for that woman, you don't know her as well as you think."

"I know you've both had your eyes on each other more than the work you're supposed to be doing."

Yeah, Matt was going to have to work on not doing that.

MATT FROM THE woods is IN MY LIBRARY. She sent the text to Tori, even though she was working the morning shift at the diner. Her friend could juggle plates and a cell phone like magic and, since the owner of the diner was at home juggling a newborn, there was nobody to yell at her. Except Carl, the cook, but he was more of a silent glare kind of guy.

OMG. 911?

That would be overreacting. *He's the game warden. And he's hot.*

Matt from the woods is a hot game warden? At library? Stalking you?

He's doing the OHRV safety class. Coincidence!

It took a couple of minutes for Tori to reply, no doubt waylaid by customers. *Send pic!*

Hailey looked over and was thankful Matt had his back to her. Not only because that was a particularly nice view of him, but because he couldn't see her looking. She didn't see any way, even with her phone on silent as it always was at work, to get a picture of him without him knowing.

Then inspiration struck and she walked over to the group, taking pictures with her phone as she moved around. When Matt stopped talking and gave her a questioning look, she gave him a tight smile.

"I always take pictures of events to put on our bulletin board," she explained. "Pretend I'm not here."

He held the eye contact until the seconds stretched into just shy of awkward, and then he turned back to the kids and resumed talking.

By taking more than a dozen photos from all different angles, she was able to sneak a full-on shot of the game warden. Once she was back at her desk, she cropped it down a bit to focus on his upper body and face, then sent it to Tori.

Holy shit.

That's pretty much what Hailey had thought, too. *Right?*

The answer was immediate. *Get his number this time. Ask him out.*

That's not what Hailey had thought at all. Not going to happen. *Patrons. Have to go.*

Liar. Not open yet. Also, you're chickenshit.

Hailey rolled her eyes and closed the message thread. She wasn't asking Matt for his number. Or a date. If she had her way, she was never going to see him again after this class was over.

To be fair, the man hadn't done anything wrong. Maybe he'd taken a few cheap shots at her, but she was the one who'd gone on a hiking and canoe trip in makeup and new boots. Her sense of humor usually extended to laughing at herself when the situation warranted.

But she'd been waiting for what seemed like forever for that sizzle of sexual awareness. The guy who'd walked into her library this morning was one she wanted to flirt with. She wanted to make eye contact and see her desire reflected back at her. The first touch. First kiss.

For a few wonderful minutes, there was hope. There was a man right here in Whitford she might have gotten naked for. And where there was dinner and kisses and mutual nudity, there was a chance at more.

Then it was all snatched away. He might have shined himself up for work, but she'd seen him in his natural habitat and she didn't want to get naked with that guy. She'd wanted to run from him. That, unfortunately, didn't bode well for a chance at more.

Fair or not, that disappointment and inflamed sense of dissatisfaction had his name all over it.

With a sigh, she pulled out a small stack of papers and made herself get to work. Shortly after becoming the police chief, Drew had reached out to the local businesses for help in a program he wanted to start in Whitford. It was sort of a pre-community service program for youth who committed very minor offenses and just needed a little nudge back on track. Hailey had jumped all over that.

Her most recent "volunteer" had been assigned a task she'd been putting off for far too long. He'd matched books on the shelves to books in the system and listed any books they were missing in middle grade and young adult series. Now Hailey had to analyze the stats for each series and decide whether or not to replace the missing books for each.

It was tedious work, but it kept her mind busy. The hands on the clock moved, a few patrons came and went, and she managed to mostly ignore the class going on at the other end of the floor. It wasn't easy with nine kids, eight parents and the instructors, but she managed to burn through a good chunk of the morning's to-do list.

At eleven, there was a rush past her desk and she laughed at the kids trying to run outside without technically running.

Josh stopped. "We're taking an hour for lunch. Do you want anything while I'm out?"

"I brought a lunch, but thanks."

They all filed out, except for Matt Barnett. He

took the time to sweep banana bread crumbs from the tables into a trash can and then tossed the empty coffee cups in after. Hailey tried not to allow any mushy feelings in as he dampened a paper towel and actually washed the table, too. She was a sucker for men who picked up after themselves.

She was surprised, though, when he stopped at the circulation desk on his way out. He leaned against the tall counter, close enough so she could smell that aftershave or cologne or whatever it was again.

"You get a lunch break?"

She wasn't sure what to make of that. Was it a prelude to asking her to join him, or just a point of information? "I bring my lunches and eat at my desk. One of the joys of being a one-woman show."

"So you never get a break?"

"I'm not exactly a gerbil in a wheel here. And every once in a while I put a *be right back* sign on the door and meet my friends for lunch."

"I guess that's both the good and the bad of a small town."

"Mmm-hmm."

The conversation seemed a little surreal to Hailey. Because he was in a library, he did what everybody always did and talked in a low voice. His low voice was husky, and it was all too easy to imagine him leaning close and whispering sexy things.

"How are those blisters?"

So much for sexy. "They're fine, thanks. And thank you again for bringing us back to our car."

"No problem."

"I guess it's kind of your job, isn't it?"

He smiled, and her fingers tightened around her pen. No matter how much she tried to imagine him with unkempt hair and beard, his smile was devastating. "I'm usually a decent guy even if I'm not getting paid for it."

"Hey, at least I was able to be fodder for your safety class." It came out a little less self-deprecating humor and more snippy than she'd intended.

"I shouldn't have poked fun at you. I'm sorry. But it was all in fun." A horn sounded outside and Matt stood up straight. "I'm grabbing lunch with Dave, so I've got to run. You want me to grab you anything?"

"No, thanks."

Once she heard the door close, Hailey sighed and dropped her head to her desk with a thump that sounded very loud in the suddenly very quiet library. She had no idea what she'd done in a past life to deserve being tormented by a scruffy mountain man disguised as a smoking hot guy in a uniform, but she wanted this day to be over.

She ate her lunch at her desk, skimming review sites for the upcoming must-have books, and she was busy helping a patron with a genealogy site when the safety class group poured back in. Glancing up, she saw Matt looking for her and she dropped her gaze before their eyes met.

Time crawled by, and she kept herself as busy as possible. The class moved outside when Sam Jensen started the first aid portion of the class because they had a few patrons on the computer and reading periodicals. According to Matt, kids tended to get a little loud when they were pretend splinting each other's body parts. Other than that, she had to do her best to ignore the group and the low timbre of Matt's voice.

Once the usual closing time had come and gone, things got really slow. A few people saw cars in the lot and stopped in, but most of Whitford assumed the library was closed as usual. Then the door opened and Tori walked in.

Hailey realized she should have seen that coming. She shook her head, but Tori just grinned and kept walking until she reached the circulation desk. Then she turned so she could see the class.

"Aw. His back's to us."

"You need to go away."

"Not without seeing the new and improved Matt-the-hot-game-warden."

Hailey sighed, praying Tori's voice was low enough so they wouldn't be overheard. Old buildings tended to have acoustic quirks. "Work Matt might be hot, but we've seen not-at-work Matt. Not hot."

"That's called potential."

No matter what Tori had said before, Hailey found

herself wondering if Tori had stopped by out of curiosity, or if she was interested in him herself. Not
that she cared. "I'm working."

"I'm not leaving until he turns around."

"*He's* working."

"That's okay. You guys can keep working."

"While you stand there and stare at him?"

Tori nodded. "He'll turn around eventually. You
can feel when somebody's staring at you and, since
he's law enforcement, it probably won't take very
long."

Hailey blew out an exasperated breath. "I can't
let you stalk people in my library."

"Okay." Tori started to move and Hailey figured
she was giving up.

She should have known better. Her friend headed
straight for the class and there was no way to stop
her without making a spectacle of themselves. Instead, she watched while Tori interrupted and had a
few words with the game warden. There were smiles
and nods, along with a laugh from Matt, and then
they shook hands.

Tori made an *OMG* face at Hailey as she walked
back to the desk, her back safely to the class group.
"The picture doesn't do him justice."

"Since I was trying not to be obvious, I'm not
surprised."

"You need to claim him before somebody else
does."

Hailey rolled her eyes. "I don't *want* him."

"Bullshit. Who wouldn't want him? Get that *Property of Whitford Public Library* stamp and stamp it right on his forehead. Then cross out the library's name and write yours."

"Go away."

"If you don't want to keep him, then pretend he's a book. Enjoy him for two weeks, then return him."

That wasn't an unappealing idea. Enjoy this Matt and throw him back before he had enough time off to regress to his previous condition. But that's not what she was after at this point in her life. "I'm not looking for a fling, Tori. If I'm going to find a husband and a father for the kids I'm running out of time to have, I can't be distracted by a guy who's all wrong for me."

"What's *wrong* is that you can look at that man down there and not see the possibilities."

Tori winked and walked out the door before Hailey could further her argument that the possibility she saw was the possibility he would turn back into scruffy, smelly Matt and stay that way. She didn't think a little sophistication in a man was too much to ask for.

When three o'clock rolled around and the safety certificates were handed out, the class practically exploded out of the library. It was a beautiful day and there were plenty of daylight hours left to burn.

The men packed up their stuff and cleaned up before heading out.

"Thank you for letting us use the library," Matt told her, because of course he had to stop and torment her a little more before he left. "I saw the hours on the door, so I know you went out of your way for us."

"Remember that if you ever catch me fishing without a license." She realized her mistake as soon as his face registered interest.

"Do you fish, Hailey?"

She laughed. "God, no. Worms. Bugs. *Fish*. It was a joke."

"Oh." He shifted the box in his arms. "Maybe I'll see you around."

She was *not* going to be able to keep her eyes on the bigger picture if Matt kept popping up to tempt her. "I doubt it. Really, since I don't plan on going out in the woods again anytime soon, what are the chances we'll run into each other again?"

The game warden left, but not before giving her a *we'll see about that* smile that she turned over and over in her mind for hours. What was *that* supposed to mean?

FOUR

HAILEY WOKE UP on the following Saturday—which was her Saturday off—well before she intended to. She even tried to burrow under the blanket and go back to sleep, but it wasn't going to happen.

There was a truck idling outside. And whatever it was, she knew it was bigger than the UPS truck, which shouldn't be there on a Saturday morning anyway, because she could hear it over the white noise of the fan running in the corner of her room.

With an annoyed growl rumbling in her throat, she got out of bed and walked to the window. Peeking through the gap in her curtains, she frowned. There was a moving truck parked in front of the house next door.

It wasn't remotely possible somebody had bought her neighbors' house without her knowing anything about it. She'd just been in the general store yesterday and if anybody knew why a moving truck might park in front of the house, it would be Fran. And Fran would have tripped all over herself trying to be the first person to tell Hailey what was happening on her own street.

Since she wasn't going to be able to sleep again,

she went downstairs and brewed herself a mug of coffee. By the time it was ready, they'd shut the truck off and she heard the bang of the back door being opened. She could hear a faint murmur of male voices and the less faint rattle of dollies being rolled up and down the truck's ramps. Moving was a loud process and they'd just started.

At some point she'd have to put on some clothes, her brightest smile, and go welcome her surprise neighbors to the neighborhood. If nothing else, she'd coerce them into getting library cards, since they had to be from out of town or she'd have known they were coming.

Maybe it was some kind of witness protection thing, she mused. That was the only thing that could explain the Whitford grapevine dropping the ball. Taking her coffee with her, she wandered into the living room, where the huge windows offered better views of both the front and backyards. She could see the truck and part of the front yard from there, but no people.

Unfortunately, with the way the sun was facing, she couldn't really see into the truck, either. She could make out some cardboard boxes, but nothing that would give her some clues about her new neighbors. She didn't see any toys or bicycles, but that didn't mean there weren't kids.

She finished her first cup of coffee, then had another while she ate a microwaveable breakfast sandwich. It was early and she was too lazy to make a real breakfast for herself. After a quick shower, she got dressed and tried to ignore the noise from next door.

Curiosity got the better of her, though, and she found herself putting off mopping the kitchen floor in favor of peeking out the living room window. Two guys were trying to muscle a huge, beat-up brown leather sofa off the truck. They weren't wearing any kind of a uniform, so she wasn't sure if they were a moving company or her new neighbors or friends they'd roped into helping.

"Put some muscle into it," she heard another male voice say, and then the guy laughed.

Hailey froze. It couldn't be. There was no way in hell it was even possible. Then the owner of the voice stepped into view and her hands curled into fists. Matt Barnett was moving in next door.

Oh, hell no.

She went out the door and headed across the lawn. "Hey!"

He turned and there was no doubt he recognized her. His back stiffened and he rolled his head to the side. "You have got to be kidding me."

"What are you doing?" Maybe he was helping a friend move in, which would still be a weird *small world* coincidence, but not too bad.

"I'm moving in."

Damn. He was close enough to her now so she

didn't have to yell. "Since when? How did I not know this?"

"In a weird coincidence, I talked to the owners and finalized the details over the phone right before I met you and Tori in the woods. Have I mentioned how nice and polite and normal your friend is? Anyway, maybe you didn't know because it's none of your business."

This was bad. "You're stalking me."

"Excuse me?"

"The woods? The library? Now you're going to live next to me?"

He shook his head. "You are quite possibly the most irrational person I've ever met. And I've met some doozies in my line of work."

"So it's just a coincidence that you keep popping up in my life?"

"Honey, the last thing I need in my life is a woman like you."

Even though she didn't *want* him to want her, that pissed her off on principle. "You'd be lucky to have a woman like me. If you ever call me honey like that again, you'd better be running away at the time."

"We both know I could just walk fast and you still wouldn't catch me."

She wanted to say something that would cut him to the bone, but her sense of humor was beating out her panic that she was going to have a hot neighbor who'd already caused her all kinds of turmoil, and she couldn't hold back the smile.

Before she actually laughed out loud, she turned and walked back toward her house. Dignity in defeat.

"Hey, aren't you supposed to bring me a pie?" he called after her. "Or a casserole?"

She didn't slam her door, but she wanted to. Just having him in her library for six hours had caused an epic struggle between her head and the parts of her body below the neck. And now he was going to be right next door.

With a sigh, Hailey decided to burn off her sexual frustration with some house cleaning. Spotless floors and sparkling toilets were almost as satisfying as an orgasm. Almost.

MATT HAD THOUGHT it was funny that in this supposedly gossip-filled town, Hailey hadn't known there was a game warden moving to town, but now he saw the joke was on him. Nobody had told him he'd be living next door to the town's librarian. Who just happened to not like him very much and now thought he was stalking her.

Perfect. Welcome to Whitford, Warden Barnett.

The house had seemed perfect. The pictures they'd sent him had shown the garage, which he needed. A nice backyard. And they didn't mind if he cut in a dog door for Bear, which was necessary because of Matt's unpredictable hours, as long as he replaced the door when he left. But they conveniently hadn't mentioned the neighbor was a pain in the ass.

Maybe that was something she saved just for him.

"Who was that?"

Matt turned to his brother-in-law, Jeff, who he had strong-armed into helping him move.

"Remember the lost princess in the woods-slash-librarian I told you all about at dinner a few nights ago?"

"No shit. That's her?"

"That's her."

Jeff nodded and looked toward Hailey's house. "I don't think she's going to bring us a pie."

"Pie?" Their friend Donny rounded out the moving party, and he never passed up food.

"Sorry, dude. The neighbor lady doesn't like our friend Matt, here. No pie for us. Or casserole."

"Did you try smiling at her?"

Matt shook his head and pulled the work gloves from his back pocket. "Let's finish getting this truck unloaded."

A person didn't realize how much crap he owned until it was time to move it all. He lost track of how many trips they made, but he was thankful he'd taken the time to write an overview of the contents on each box.

"It's time," Jeff told him in a voice that should have been accompanied by an ominous soundtrack.

"Did Donny measure the doors?"

"Yeah. And when I saw him trying to figure out if he was holding the tape measure upside-down or not, I went back and measured them again."

Matt laughed and shook his head. "He gives new meaning to the expression measure twice, cut once."

"That he does. It's going to be tight and it's gotta be sideways, but it should go in that study or whatever you're calling it, where you want it."

Matt eyed the gun safe sitting in the back of the moving truck. Even emptied out, the thing weighed a ton. Taking it out of a ground floor studio-type apartment that had French doors hadn't been too bad, especially since he'd had a couple more guys. Now the three of them had to get it up steps and through narrow interior doors to the room the previous owners had used as a dining room. He didn't really want to have the thing sitting in the living room, though that was Plan B. Ideally it would have gone in his bedroom, but they weren't getting it up the staircase without more guys and a better plan, so he had a smaller biometric safe to go next to his bed.

"Are you trying to move it with your mind or what?" Jeff asked. "Because staring at it doesn't seem to be doing much."

"Smart-ass." Matt pulled his T-shirt over his head and tossed it onto a pile of boxes.

It took them almost twenty minutes just to get the safe secured on the dolly with ratchet straps to Matt's satisfaction. During those twenty minutes, he lost count of the number of times he glanced toward his neighbor's house. And two or three times, he was sure he saw her curtains twitch.

He wasn't sure why he annoyed Hailey so much. It had to be more than the fact he'd witnessed her misguided attempt to go hiking, but he couldn't quite wrap his head around it. There were glimpses, though, of humor and he was looking forward to getting to know her once she'd calmed down. Which, admittedly, she'd probably do faster if he didn't push her buttons. He couldn't seem to help himself.

When they took a breather before starting the process of getting the safe down the ramp, Matt was thankful he'd sent Bear home with his dad for the week. He missed his dog, but Bear was neither underfoot nor running loose in a new neighborhood, so it was worth it.

He wondered idly if Hailey liked dogs, or if Bear would be another entry in her list of reasons Matt annoyed the crap out of her.

"Hey, Casanova," Jeff said. "You're not getting any of her pie. Let's go."

Matt looked next door in time to see the curtain jerk and smiled. It was too early to tell how that was going to go. "Come on. Donny, you take the heavy end."

Donny looked at the rectangular safe, then looked at them and back again. "Which end is that?"

Matt and Jeff laughed, and then Hailey was forgotten while Matt tried to keep himself and his friends from being crushed.

EVEN IN WHITFORD, there had to be something better to do than peek out her windows and watch a shirtless, sweaty Matt Barnett carry boxes.

Scrubbing her overactive hormones into submission hadn't worked as well as she'd hoped. One, she had a strict housekeeping regime that meant there wasn't very much to do beyond the floors, which she always did on her Saturdays off. And, two, she wasn't going to accomplish anything while looking out her window every five minutes.

She thought about texting Tori, who wasn't working this morning, but the last time she'd done that, her friend had shown up at the library. There was no way Tori showing up at her house to watch Matt move in would be anything but conspicuous and the last thing Hailey needed was more awkwardness.

Finally, she grabbed her purse and her keys. Even driving around in circles, listening to the radio, was better than mooning over a man she didn't even like.

She ended up at the Trailside Diner simply because driving around Whitford was boring and not worth burning the gas. Tori wouldn't be working, but Liz would be and Hailey had enjoyed getting to know her better. Liz Kowalski had moved to New Mexico with a guy after high school, but she'd moved back alone almost a year before. Now she was Liz

Kowalski Miller, married to the chief of police, and the entire town was on pins and needles, waiting for baby news.

Hailey took a spot at the counter because it was easier to chat there, and nodded when Liz held up the coffeepot. Liz had the Kowalskis' dark hair—hers long and pulled into a ponytail—and blue eyes, and she was wearing the new Trailside Diner tees that had the Northern Star ATV Club logo on the back.

"I hear the safety certification class at the library went well," Liz said, setting a mug of coffee in front of Hailey.

"In other words, you want to hear about the hot game warden."

"Of course."

"At this very second, he's moving in to the house next to mine."

Liz's jaw dropped. "You're not serious."

"Totally serious." She added cream and sugar to her coffee, debating on whether or not to have a second breakfast. Although, it wasn't like a microwaveable breakfast sandwich really counted as a first breakfast. More of a pre-breakfast snack. And it was heading toward lunch, so brunch would work.

"That's really weird."

Hailey looked up at her. "I accused him of stalking me."

"That's more weird."

"He makes me crazy and I don't know why."

There was just something about the man that set her on edge.

Liz grinned. "We know what that means."

"I should have driven the hour to McDonald's." She glanced at the specials board, then wrinkled her nose. "I just want a side of fries, I think."

"Awesome breakfast."

"Brunch. And I'm not really that hungry."

"Of course not. You're only here to hide from your hunky neighbor."

Before Hailey could come up with a response, Liz walked away to give her order to the kitchen and check on her other customers. Hailey drank her coffee and fumed. She wasn't hiding.

It was only a few minutes before Liz brought her fries and Hailey drenched them in vinegar and salt before popping one in her mouth.

"Tori says you two have great chemistry," Liz said.

Hailey almost choked on the fry. "What? The only time Tori's seen us speak to each other was in the woods and I wasn't exactly at my best."

"Neither of you are in the woods now, so you're not limping around with raccoon eyes and he doesn't look like something out of a horror flick, so what's stopping you from having a good time?"

"I gather no detail was spared in that story." Hailey dabbed a fry in pooled vinegar. "And I'm not looking for a good time. I'm looking for forever. A husband, you know?"

"You have to give a guy a chance before you know if he's husband material."

"But if I already know he's not, what's the point?"

Liz frowned. "You know he's not husband material because he doesn't shave when he's on vacation?"

"No. I know he and I aren't compatible in the long term because he's the rugged outdoors type. I'm…not."

"Yeah, well Drew didn't think I was wife material and look where we ended up."

Hailey smiled when Liz made a big production of showing off her wedding ring while refilling her coffee. "I heard you're pregnant with septuplets."

Liz snorted as she set the carafe back on the burner. "That's what I get for eating too much of Rosie's pie and stopping at the general store on the way home. I was so full, I rested my hand on my stomach for a split second. Did you see the picture on Facebook?"

"Of course I did. Fran's turning into a one-woman, Whitford version of TMZ."

"I thought Paige having Sarah would take some of the pressure off, but it's gotten so bad, I'm waiting for somebody to pass me a pregnancy test under the bathroom stall door."

"So, off the record…"

Liz laughed. "No, I'm not pregnant. And, even

further off the record, we haven't been trying yet.
Soon, but we wanted to enjoy being married—just
the two of us—for a little while first. But we've been
talking about it a lot lately, so not too much longer.
And when it *does* happen, Rose will know before
Fran."

Since Rose had practically raised the Kowalskis,
helping their dad after their mom died, that was a
must. And Rose lived with Drew's dad, so as a couple they definitely ranked higher on the totem pole
than Fran.

The bell dinged, signaling food ready for Liz to
deliver, so Hailey was left alone with her fries and
her simmering envy.

She was genuinely happy for her friends. She really was. They'd found men who loved them and they
were married or heading in that direction, and Paige
had a baby. Wanting that for herself didn't take away
from her joy for them.

A couple of times over the last several years, she'd
gone so far as to watch the employment market in
more urban areas, even though it would mean more
bureaucracy in her job. Shaking up her life didn't
seem like a bad idea when it came with a dating pool
that included more than the guys she'd grown up
with. Fine dining, a movie theater and other places
to actually *go* on a date didn't sound so bad, either.

But when push came to shove, she loved her job,
her house and this town. And she didn't simply love

being a librarian. She loved *her* library, and she was afraid if she left, her replacement wouldn't fight for it the way she did. When the economy was rough, it took a lot of passion and chocolate to get through every budget review and town meeting. She loved the Whitford Public Library too much to walk away from it.

She just needed to find a GQ guy in the land of L.L.Bean.

FIVE

"THIS IS OUR new home, buddy." Bear was riding shotgun, sitting up and staring out the window after a long nap. He turned when Matt spoke, his tongue hanging out. "You'll like it. You'll have a bigger yard. And a pretty neighbor to look at."

He pulled the truck into the driveway and shut it off. The garage was so full he couldn't pull it in there if he wanted to, and that wasn't likely to change any time soon. It would take him a while to unpack the boxes of stuff he didn't need right away, plus he had an ATV, a snowmobile and his lawn mower, among other things. Having a two-bay garage would have been nice, but he probably would have filled that, too.

After snapping a leash onto Bear's collar, he went around the truck and opened the passenger door to let the dog out. He listened well, but Matt was aware a new neighborhood would be full of temptation for Bear and he needed to keep a close eye on him until he learned his boundaries. It wouldn't take long because he was a well-trained dog, but he didn't want to take any chances.

"Welcome home, Bear," he said after the dog had watered a bush and he'd unlocked the front door.

Once he'd closed it behind him, he unclipped the leash and let the Lab run.

Sinking onto his leather couch with a deep sigh of relief, he watched Bear make his way around the downstairs, sniffing every square inch and box.

It had been a hell of a day. Loading the truck, making the drive to Whitford, then unloading the truck. Then turning around and driving back to Augusta to return the truck and pick up his dog. Now it was almost dark and he felt like he was sitting down—besides in a truck seat—for the first time.

Judging by the sound, Bear had found his food and water dishes on the mat in the kitchen, so Matt leaned his head back and closed his eyes.

Woof.

That didn't take long. He hadn't started installing the doggy door for Bear yet, which meant he'd be playing canine doorman until he got it done. And he'd have to supervise the trips outside until Bear learned what was his yard and what wasn't.

"Gotta go out, boy?" Another woof, so he walked into the kitchen and opened the back door.

Bear shot out onto the small deck, sniffing as fast as his nose allowed, then ran into the yard like a maniac. Matt watched him for a minute, but then realized his neighbor was out in her backyard.

There was a garden shed at the back of the property, just before the tree line, and the doors were opened. It looked like she was checking garden hoses. She had a couple of them spread out on the ground, with one still coiled, and she kept bending over to check areas that had probably been kinked for leaks.

It wasn't a bad view. She was wearing jeans that hugged her curves and he found himself watching her progress down the first hose. Every time she bent over, he got a little more appreciation for living next door to the town's librarian.

When she walked back to start the other hose, he looked back to his own yard and realized his dog was gone.

"Bear!" Through the corner of his eye, he saw Hailey spin around, her head coming up. "Bear!"

She started to run and, before he could make sense of what was happening, she caught her foot in the garden hose and went ass over teakettle.

HAILEY STARED UP at the sky, trying to process how she'd ended up flat on her back in the grass with her head pounding, her breath coming up short in her chest, and her knee screaming in protest of whatever had just happened.

"Hailey!"

Hearing her name shouted killed any hope he was going to do the polite thing and pretend he hadn't seen her less than graceful fall. Sure enough, just a few seconds later, he was on his knees next to her.

"Are you hurt?"

"Just my dignity. And I'm not sure I had much to spare as it was." He chuckled, bending forward so she had no choice but to look into his face. Such a handsome face with concerned eyes. "I'm okay. I only see one of you, thank God. One of you is enough."

"Too bad you didn't damage that funny bone of yours when you fell. Why did you take off running like that?"

"When a game warden is yelling 'Bear!' like a maniac, normal people panic."

Matt sat back on his heels, a chagrined expression on his face. "Bear is my dog's name."

She turned her head and saw a big black Lab sitting at the edge of her yard, his head cocked to the side as if he was trying to figure out why a grown woman was lying in the grass. "How original."

"I found him when he was just a baby. He was a black fur ball with huge paws, stuck in some puckerbrush, and when I got him out, he nuzzled me for a few seconds and then tried to rip my coat to shreds to get to the crackers in my pocket. Name seemed to fit."

As if he knew they were talking about him, Bear walked over to sit next to Matt. Both of them staring at her was just weird, so Hailey pushed herself up until she was sitting, too. When she held out her hand, the dog skipped the sniffing and getting to know you stage and bumped his head under her palm for a good scratch.

"I didn't know you had a dog," she said.

"He's been with my dad this past week. The long commute meant being away longer hours than usual, plus I didn't want him to wander off in the chaos of moving." He ruffled the dog's fur, then wrapped his arms around him when Bear threw himself against his chest. "I missed you, too, buddy."

Hailey couldn't take it. The obvious love the man had for the dog he'd rescued as a puppy was too much. How was she supposed to keep her guard up when they were so damn adorable?

She managed to push herself to her feet, intending to put some distance between herself and the pair, but her knee protested her weight and she winced. Shifting her weight to her other foot, she eyeballed the distance to her door. Her backyard had never looked so big before.

"Let me help you."

"You never miss an opportunity to be the Good Samaritan, do you?"

"It's a gift. Although there have been a lot more opportunities than usual since I met you."

That was a statement she couldn't really deny with a straight face, so she shrugged. She expected him to offer her his shoulder. She even braced herself for the possibility of him putting his arm around her waist.

Matt did wrap his arm around her waist, moving

in so close her arm was forced over his shoulders, but she wasn't ready at all when his other arm slid behind her knees. As he lifted her off her feet, she made a squeaking sound and clung to him.

"You could have just let me lean on you," she hissed.

"Faster this way. Bear, stay outside."

Hailey tried to relax enough to enjoy the sensation of being carried by a man for the first time. It would have been even more enjoyable if he wasn't wearing a shirt and they were heading to her bedroom, but she'd settle for being cradled by hard muscles.

Matt managed to climb the back steps of her deck without hitting either her head or her feet on the railings, and then he paused while she reached out and opened the door. After successfully navigating the door frame, he kicked it closed behind them and carried her into the living room.

Now didn't seem like a good time to point out she preferred shoes be left on the mat by the door, so she kept her mouth shut while he lowered her onto the couch. When he stood back up, she was strangely flattered to see he didn't grimace or rub the small of his back. What a gentleman.

"Wow, you have a lot of throw pillows," he said. "Shove some of them under your leg while I get some ice."

It was strange seeing a man in her house, and she tried to remember the last time a guy had crossed her threshold. When she did go on a date, she took her own car and met him at their destination. She'd dated one man a few times, so he'd eventually picked her up at home and even kissed her goodnight on her front step. But inviting him in hadn't felt right and that had been the end of him.

The last man to stand in her living room was probably the guy who'd repaired her phone line. The phone guy had been taller than Matt and definitely more round, but it still seemed as if Matt took up more space in the room, as though he were somehow larger than life.

Naturally, he took the easy way out and grabbed a bag of frozen vegetables rather than making a real icepack, which he then plopped on her knee. "How bad is the pain?"

"It's honestly not that bad. I think I just tweaked it a bit and, if you didn't have a hero complex, I probably would have walked it off by now."

"Hero complex?" He walked behind her and adjusted the big pillow behind her back so she was more comfortable. "Hardly."

When he palmed the back of her head and gently pushed it forward, Hailey's breath caught in her throat. And when his other hand brushed the hair away from her neck, it released in a long, shaky exhale.

"What is this?" His voice was low and she felt the cushion shift as he leaned on the back of the couch.

What was that? That was a soft and lonely stretch of skin that loved to be kissed and had gone without for far too long. "What is what?"

His fingertip traced a gentle circle at the nape of her neck and all she could do was hope the low-grade tremor she felt on the inside didn't show on the outside. "This is a bad bite and you've been scratching it. A lot."

"I didn't realize I had a bite there until I was at work yesterday. The tag on my shirt rubbed against it all day and drove me nuts."

"You should put something on it."

His touch was working just fine, replacing the annoying itch with a rather pleasant tingling sensation. "I will."

"Do you have any hydrocortisone cream? I don't want to leave it like this."

"I think I have some in the junk drawer next to the stove." If her friendly neighborhood game warden wanted to give the back of her neck some tender loving care, who was she to stand in the way of him doing his duty?

When he pushed himself up off the back of the couch, a gust of Matt's breath blew across her exposed skin and she closed her eyes.

"Who keeps hydrocortisone cream in the kitchen junk drawer?"

"People who tend to cut themselves making salads keep antibiotic cream there, so it all goes in.

And it qualifies. Batteries and first aid creams and junk. In the junk drawer."

"Or aspirin and first aid creams and medicine. In the medicine cabinet."

Hailey could tell he was walking away from her, so she opened her eyes to watch him go. Even if she tried to put aside being under the influence of his touch on her neck, she had to admit he had a nice ass. Exceptional, even. It was probably all that walking he did in the woods, rescuing lost women.

She was in so much trouble.

If MATT NEEDED a reminder that making a move on Hailey would be like turning down a pothole-riddled dead-end dirt road, the inside of her house was more than enough. Light colors, white wood and no clutter implied this was a woman who wouldn't like her man coming home with mud—or worse—on his boots.

He found her meager first aid supplies in the junk drawer with a flashlight that—knowing her—would need batteries, a screwdriver, half a dozen bottles of nail polish and enough other debris so it took him two tries to close it. No wonder there was no clutter in her house. It was all shoved into one drawer.

When he walked back into the living room, she had the bag of frozen vegetables in her hand and was flexing her knee. It seemed to bend with no trouble, though she winced a little. When she saw him, she dropped the improvised ice pack back on her knee and smiled.

"I don't think the damage is too bad."

"Good. Now let's take care of that bite. Do I need to give you the lecture on the dangers of mosquito bites and how to properly protect against them?"

"No, Warden Barnett," she responded in a snippy voice. "I've learned my lesson. And I can do that myself. Honest."

"I've got it." If him touching her neck made her squirm, he wasn't going to pass up the opportunity. She wasn't the only one who could be contrary. "Tip your head forward."

With an exasperated sigh, she lowered her head to give him access to her neck.

"This might sting a little," he warned.

He took an antiseptic wipe out of its package and cleaned the inflamed bug bite thoroughly. Between her tag rubbing on it and her scratching it, she'd made it pretty raw and there were some dried blood flakes at the center of the bite. When he'd cleaned it to his satisfaction, the wipe leaving the area wet with antiseptic, he leaned close and blew gently on her skin.

Her body jerked and he watched as her fingers tightened around a throw pillow so tightly he was surprised her nails didn't pop through the fabric. She sucked in a breath, but didn't say anything.

"Did that sting?" he asked, knowing damn well that wasn't the problem.

"No. Are you almost done?"

"Almost."

He squeezed a dab of hydrocortisone cream on the tip of his finger and took his time applying it to the bite. Even though it only took one fingertip to apply the medicine, he let the others trail over her skin, enjoying her battle not to react to his touch.

Until his own body started reacting, too. Skimming his fingertips over her neck, feeling her respond to him, affected him more than he'd thought it would. If he didn't put some distance between them, he might be tempted to do something really stupid.

"That should do it." He put the cap on the tube and gathered the wipe and package to throw away. "Stop scratching it."

After tossing the garbage and wrestling with her junk drawer again, Matt washed his hands. Then he went back for a final check on his patient. "Do you want anything before I go? A drink? The TV remote?"

"No, thank you."

He tilted his head and grinned. "A neck rub?"

She growled and chucked a throw pillow at him. "Out!"

He was still laughing when he let himself out through her kitchen. Bear had been waiting for him, staring at the door, and Matt gave him a good scratch behind the ears. "Let's go, bud. We've got to make my bed and get yours upstairs. And I have to find the coffee filters or we'll have a rough morning."

Bear ran ahead of him, then stopped at the back door, looking utterly confused. Matt laughed at him and opened the door so the dog could go in.

"Tomorrow we'll install your door, okay? I have to dig my tools out of the garage and all that. But right now, beds and coffee are number one on the list, so we've got some work ahead of us."

Bear walked into the living room and jumped onto his end of the couch. After giving the cushion a good sniff to make sure nothing about it had changed, he curled up and closed his eyes.

Matt shook his head. "It's a good thing I didn't try to make you into a K-9. You'd give up the farm for a belly rub and a nap."

When his dog ignored him, Matt went out to the garage and looked at the stack of boxes. The coffee filters hadn't been in any of the boxes marked *kitchen*. So where would he have put them?

If push came to shove, he could probably borrow a few filters from his neighbor. She had a coffee machine similar to his on her counter. But he'd gotten her all wound up and he figured there was a good chance if he asked for a coffee filter, she'd probably go so far as to brew a pot and drink the whole thing in front of him out of spite.

Matt chuckled and dug into a box stupidly marked *miscellaneous*. He was probably going to enjoy living next to Hailey. She had a great laugh and it was easy to push her buttons. It was a great combination as long he remembered not to let *her* figure out how to wind *him up*.

That wouldn't be good at all.

SIX

HAILEY SAT AT her table, sipping her Sunday morning coffee and wondering if assaulting a law enforcement officer didn't count if the officer in question wasn't in uniform at the time.

Walking across the yard and heaving the saw or the drill at his head would still be assault, but it might be a misdemeanor if he wasn't on duty. Plus, if he was out of uniform, he was probably unarmed, which was something to consider. Chucking power tools at a guy with a gun wasn't a good idea.

And he'd only lived next door for twenty-four hours.

Today was not only Sunday, but it was the weekend before Memorial Day weekend. Yard day. Today was the day she traditionally cleaned up any remaining debris from winter and made sure her lawn mower and edger were running okay. Sometimes the pavers around her perennial beds were shifted by snow and ice, and she'd check those. She had a lot of perennials and bushes because gardening wasn't her favorite thing to do, but she liked her yard to look nice.

But Matt was out there. Sawing and drilling and

hammering and, in general, being noisy. And Bear didn't like the whiny pitch of the saw, so he'd bark like mad whenever it was running, and Matt would laugh.

And he had no shirt on again. The man seemed to have a serious problem with clothing and she wasn't sure how that would go once it was the middle of summer. Then would come shorts, if he bothered. Worse, she wasn't sure if she was dreading it or looking forward to it.

When a car pulled into her driveway, she frowned and went to the window. It was Paige's car and Hailey felt a pang of concern. She rarely showed up unannounced and she hadn't been out much at all since having the baby.

By the time she got outside, Paige had hung a massive diaper bag over her shoulder and was wrestling the car seat out of the backseat.

"Let me help you." Hailey took Sarah's seat while Paige kicked the car door closed.

"Are you busy?"

"Nope. Just drinking coffee and putting off my to-do list for the day."

"I can help you with both of those things. Only one cup of coffee for me, though. I shouldn't even have that because I had one this morning and I'm nursing, but I'm going to lose my mind if I don't."

Once they were inside, Hailey unbuckled Sarah,

who was looking at her with solemn blue eyes. "You are the most perfect baby girl I've ever seen."

"Don't let her fool you," Paige said, setting the diaper bag on a chair. "She's a Kowalski. That love comes with a whole helping of crazy-making."

Hailey lifted the baby out of her seat and cradled her, bouncing her gently. "I bet she's worth the crazy."

"She is." Paige sighed. "So is her daddy."

The saw started, Bear barked and Sarah startled in Hailey's arms. "Sorry, doll. The horrible man who lives next door doesn't care about us at all."

Paige went to the window and looked out. "Oh, my."

"He also doesn't like to wear shirts."

"Aunt Hailey's a lucky lady."

Hailey snorted. "Aunt Hailey was going to work in her yard today, but it sounds like a construction site now."

"But what a view."

"Hey, married lady. Come take your daughter and I'll sneak you some caffeine."

Paige laughed. "Ha. You keep my daughter and I'll make my own coffee. I had to grab a few things at Fran's and she fell asleep, so we've been driving around. I had the radio on and was singing and having a good time, but then she woke up and we were close, so we came to visit."

"How long did you drive around?"

Paige shrugged. "I might need gas."

"That's not a good long term plan for coping with Mitch being on the road."

"No, but it felt good to cruise around and sing for a while. And Rosie's so eager to get her hands on Sarah, she's pushing me to go back to work."

Hailey sat down at the table because tiny little bundles of joy got hard on the back rather quickly. "What does Mitch think about that?"

"Mitch is a very smart man and thinks I should do whatever makes me happy." Paige smiled and took a sip of the coffee she'd poured. "I don't really need to be at the diner. Between Ava, Liz and Tori, they've got it covered. But it's still my business. I might not wait tables, but I want to be there at least a few hours several days a week. I'll get out of the house and Rose gets her fill of Sarah."

Hailey looked into the baby's face, trying to ignore the way her insides turned all warm and fuzzy. "I don't know what I'd do if I had a baby."

"Take it to work with you."

She laughed. "Libraries are the perfect place for babies."

"I'm serious. Maybe you don't realize how much this town loves you, Hailey. You could bring a baby in a bassinet and nobody would mind. Cutting back the hours a little wouldn't hurt anybody, and you might get a few people turn cranky if the baby was crying, but overall you could make it work. By the time the baby's ready to need some running around room, you'd be ready to find child care."

"I almost believe you. Not that it matters. I've yet to meet the hypothetical child's father yet."

"Hypothetically, you need to come look out this window."

Hailey threw her a dark look. "Matt Barnett is not the father of my hypothetical child, even hypothetically. I have no desire to raise a little pack of forest urchins, running around barefoot with no shirts on in the mud."

"Forest urchins?" Paige returned the look. "Why are you being so hard on this guy?"

Hailey sighed. "Because he touched the back of my neck and I wanted to climb him like a horny monkey."

Coffee *almost* sprayed from Paige's mouth as she tried to choke down it and a startled laugh at the same time. "Seriously, Hailey?"

"Seriously. Just looking at him makes me want him. Then he put some cream on the bug bite on the back of my neck yesterday and…just that was almost enough, if you know what I mean. Oh, and that was *after* he carried me into the house."

"What? Why?"

Hailey told her the entire story, leaving nothing out because this was her best friend, after all. She could trust Paige to keep her best interests at heart.

"Hailey, you need to climb that man like the horny monkey you are."

Or not. "He looks good right now, especially with the whole sweat-glistening naked torso thing, but he's not my type."

"I didn't say to marry him. A horny monkey can climb a tree, then climb back down and choose another."

"I'm starting to regret the horny monkey thing."

"Yeah, it's not very sexy."

Sarah wriggled in Hailey's arms, making squeaking sounds. "What is she doing?"

"She's ready for breakfast. Again."

"Good. Then it's my turn for coffee." Hailey handed Sarah off to her mother. "After you feed her, you can take a nap if you want. I'll keep an eye on her."

"Thanks, but I'm going to head over to the lodge after. Business has picked up enough that we're going to go through the food budget. We're looking into the feasibility and legalities of purchasing their kitchen supplies through my suppliers." She went to the couch and grabbed throw pillows to make herself comfortable for feeding Sarah. "And, bonus, Rosie will get to fuss over her grandbaby."

Even though the Kowalskis weren't Rose's biologically, which was good considering Josh and Katie's relationship, she considered them as good as hers, and therefore their children were her grandchildren.

Johnny, Sean Kowalski's son with his wife, Emma, was about to have his first birthday, but they lived in New Hampshire, so Rose was ecstatic to have a baby close enough to smother with love.

Hailey curled up at the other end of the couch and drank her coffee while Paige nursed Sarah, making small talk about nothing. But her mind kept bouncing back and forth between thoughts of Matt and wishing she had a baby of her own. As much as the former sounded like a delicious treat, if she was going to ever get the latter, she couldn't afford to be sidetracked.

"I need to start going into the city on the Saturdays I have off," she said suddenly, and Paige rolled her eyes.

"And do what? You're just going to bump into Mr. Right by hanging out at the mall every other Saturday?"

"Or the movie theater or a bowling alley. I'm sure as hell not going to find him at the library, am I?"

The saw fired up again and Paige gave her a meaningful look. Hailey looked back at her coffee mug and ignored her. There would be no climbing of Matt Barnett.

It took Matt most of the day to put in the swinging door for Bear, between installing the frame itself and wiring the alarm. He'd taken a long break midmorning, then gone out for a run with the dog, which had eaten up more time than he'd anticipated. Bear still wanted to investigate his new surroundings more than exercise.

Once the construction was wrapped up, he'd put away his tools and had a very late lunch in the form of a small microwave pizza. He was going to need to make a run to a real grocery store soon and stock up on essentials. Thankfully, there was a chest freezer in the garage. It worked and barbecue season was coming, so he'd fill it with meat.

Now he was out in the grass, doing one of the more unpleasant chores that came with owning a dog. Especially a large dog who ate a lot. With a spade in one hand and a rake in the other, he moved through his yard.

Movement caught his eye and he turned to face his neighbor's house.

Hailey was perfectly framed in her big bay window and, with the sun behind clouds and the lights on in her living room, he had no trouble seeing her. She had one of those telescoping dusters and was cleaning her ceiling fan blades. Or that's what she was supposed to be doing, anyway.

Her hips were swaying and, as he watched, the slight moving with the music became a full-on dance. He could see the small mp3 player clipped to the neck of her shirt and the white wires leading up to her ears, and her eyes were closed.

Her mouth moved as she sang along with whatever

song had her moving like that, and his body hardened in response. It was a sexy song. He could tell by the way she moved and, even though he couldn't dance worth a damn, he wanted nothing more at that moment than to be in that room, his body moving in time with hers.

Then the cell phone in his pocket vibrated and he jerked his gaze away. It was probably creepy, watching Hailey dance when she didn't know he was there, and it was definitely something he couldn't make a habit of.

His mother's number showed on his screen, just to hammer home the vague sense of guilt and wrongdoing.

"Hi, Mom," he said, carrying the yard tools back to the deck. He leaned them against the side of the house and sat in one of the patio chairs that had also gone with the house.

"Are you busy?"

"Nope. Just finished up."

"Good. I miss you. You live so far away now."

Matt smiled. "I'm not *that* far away. Last Sunday I was there for Mother's Day and you saw me just yesterday."

"For fifteen minutes. And I hate not being able to picture where you're living."

"I showed you the pictures the owners sent me."

"It's not the same."

He sighed, giving in to the inevitable. "I've barely

started unpacking. This weekend the trails here open *and* it's Memorial Day weekend, which you know is crazy for me. But how about the following Saturday you and dad come over and visit?"

"That sounds wonderful. I bet your niece and nephews would like to see you, too."

"Bring everybody, Mom." She would anyway. "We'll have a cook-out."

"That sounds wonderful. I'm putting it on my calendar right now. How do you like your neighbors?"

An image of Hailey flashed through his mind, her hips swaying to a sensual rhythm he could feel even if he couldn't hear it. "The neighbors are fine."

"Really?"

Jeff must have run his mouth, and Matt made a mental note to make his brother-in-law pay somehow. "She's nice."

"I heard she called you a stalker."

"It was a joke, Mom." Bear brought him his rope, hoping to play, so Matt tossed it out into the yard. "It's a long story, but I'm not having problems with my neighbor."

"I'll probably get to meet her when we're there. You should invite her."

"Maybe. I have to run, Mom. It looks like it might rain and I've got tools outside." It was a lie, but a little one.

"Okay. I love you, honey, and we'll see you Saturday after next. I'll make my pasta salad."

"It wouldn't be a cookout without it. Love you, too, Mom."

Even after the call ended, Matt didn't get up. After pulling his T-shirt back on, he relaxed in the wrought iron chair. He was tired, and maybe a little afraid he'd succumb to the temptation of walking to the back of the yard again, where he could see Hailey. Bear wasn't the only one who needed to learn boundaries.

The dog brought him the rope and, after a game of tug, he tossed it into the yard again. Bear raced after it, almost tripping over his own feet in his rush to grab it and bring it back so he could refuse to drop it again.

He was hungry, the microwave pizza long since burned off, but he couldn't work up the ambition to go inside. It was a nice night and he didn't have anything in the fridge worth making. The diner was a possibility, but that also required a level of ambition he didn't feel.

"Five more minutes," he told Bear. Then he'd probably nuke another pizza, just because they were there. And easy.

HAILEY TUCKED HER phone between her cheek and her shoulder and pulled the baking dish of shepherd's pie out of the oven. The left oven mitt must have been damp, though, because her fingers started burning almost immediately, and she dropped it onto the stove surface with a hiss.

"What's happening?" Tori asked, interrupted in the middle of a sentence about a show they both watched.

Shifting the phone back to her hand, Hailey shoved the rack back in and closed the oven door. "I made shepherd's pie and burnt my fingers getting it out."

"Shepherd's pie, huh?

Distracted by getting to the sink so she could run cold water over her fingertips, Hailey spoke without thinking. "For my new neighbor."

"Your new neighbor the hot game warden?"

"How long was it between the time I left the diner and the time Liz called you?"

"About thirty seconds, probably. I was working, though, so she left a voice mail. I was waiting for you to bring it up and then you distracted me with television talk. So tell me everything."

"Matt moved in next door. That's everything." She had no intention of telling anybody except Paige about him carrying her inside and the way her body had reacted to him touching her neck.

"Everything except the part where you called him a stalker."

Hailey winced. "That was a little crazy, which is why I'm bringing him shepherd's pie."

She glanced toward the oven, feeling a rush of pride at the way the top of the mashed potato layer had formed a perfect buttery brown crust. It would have to cool a bit before she could carry it next door, even with dry oven mitts.

"You should invite him *out* to dinner," Tori said.

"Why would I do that? I want to welcome him to the neighborhood, not date him."

"Because this is the only place to eat, so you'll have to come here and I'll get to watch the two of you together because I bet you *should* date him."

"That's a little weird." She wasn't going to date Matt. She also wasn't going to let him near her neck again, because that made her think about a lot more than dating him. Unless dating was a euphemism for sex.

"I have a feeling about him."

"Then *you* date him."

Tori laughed. "Not that kind of feeling. I think you and Matt the hot game warden would be a good match."

"When you give up designing book covers and waiting tables to become a successful matchmaker, I'll believe you." Hailey paused. "No, I still won't believe you."

"I have a sticky note on my computer reminding me to tell you *I told you so* when the time comes. So, anyway, we need to plan our next adventure."

"Our *next* adventure? You don't think we had enough adventure last time?"

"Are you ever going to let that go?"

"Not until the blisters heal, at least."

Tori's sigh came through her phone's speaker loud and clear. "If we were Thelma and Louise, the movie would have been ten minutes long. Adventures, Hailey. We're supposed to be celebrating being single."

"I can leave my cookies right out on the counter instead of hiding them behind the lightbulbs in the cabinet over the fridge. Isn't that celebration enough?"

"No. You've probably eaten them already, since you're hanging around your house instead of going out and having fun with me."

Tori paused, but there was no way Hailey was admitting she'd thrown away the empty package not ten minutes before her phone rang.

"I have to go change so I can bring this next door and be done with it."

"You're getting dressed up to bring him shepherd's pie?"

She was incorrigible. "No, I spilled coffee on my light peach shirt two hours ago and it looks like I have an abstract brown Ohio on my chest. Then, after I put the dish in the oven, I was dusting my ceiling fans so I'm going to change. Big deal."

"Sure. It has nothing to do with him."

"I have to go. Bye." Hailey hung up on Tori and went upstairs to change her shirt.

She deliberately avoided her makeup basket while she was in the bathroom, but she did take her hair out of the clip and brush it into a sleek ponytail. Not because of Matt, of course. Just because the oven had heated her kitchen and all the escaped wisps were driving her crazy.

Then she swore under her breath and pulled the elastic out. As a shield went, it wouldn't keep a determined man from touching that sweet spot, but at least her neck didn't feel so exposed. And since his determination had been about first aid and not turning her on, she was probably safe.

When she couldn't put it off anymore without risking him already having eaten, she used dry oven mitts to pick up the glass baking dish and went out her back door. She could hear him talking to Bear, and she followed the sound to his backyard.

He was sitting at a small, wrought iron patio set that had gone with the house, while Bear ran around the yard with a knotted length of rope. When the dog saw her coming, he dropped the rope and loped toward her.

She couldn't pet him, but she spoke to him and praised him for not jumping on her before walking the rest of the way to Matt. She set the baking dish on the table and lifted the towel she'd draped over the top.

"I made you shepherd's pie," she said. "Welcome to the neighborhood."

He leaned close enough to smell it. "Thank you. It looks delicious, and I love shepherd's pie."

"Of course you do. It's meat and potatoes." When

he arched an eyebrow at her, she put up her hands. "That wasn't meant to be a dig. I swear there's something about you that makes me say stupid things."

"It happens. It might be the eyelashes." He batted them at her and she laughed.

"I'm not crazy. And I really don't think you're a stalker, which is why I brought you dinner."

"I don't stalk a lot of women, but you're the first to ever reward me with food. I was going to nuke a pizza or make a couple of sandwiches, but this is better. Do you want to join me?"

She looked into those pretty eyes and said yes before she thought it all the way through. Really, it was the neighborly thing to do.

SEVEN

MATT LEFT HAILEY sitting at the patio set and went inside to rummage through the mess that was his half-unpacked kitchen. He grabbed a couple of paper plates, two forks, the salt and pepper, and the butter.

She'd changed her shirt since her dance in her living room. He'd noticed it right away, but wisely decided not to say anything. Her opinion of him wouldn't be improved any by the thought of him watching her. Although it had only been for a minute, because she'd been in his line of vision.

He took everything outside and set it on the table. "I have milk, lemonade and water to drink."

"Lemonade, please. And a spoon for serving if you have one." It only took him a minute to pour two glasses of lemonade and grab a spoon, but she had the table set by the time he returned. "Thanks. I know it's starting to get chilly, but I can't really invite you inside to eat because my dining room table is a folding table and it's currently folded up in the garage. Behind a pile of boxes."

"This is fine. And Bear's enjoying himself."

"If I yell at him, don't be startled. He's learning

the boundary line and he's mostly got it, but he needs some correction now and then."

She picked up the spoon and served them each a steaming helping of the shepherd's pie and the sight of the hamburger, corn and mashed potatoes made him realize he was starving. He loaded it with butter, salt and pepper, then took a bite.

"This is amazing," he said, and he meant it.

"Thank you. It's all in the seasoning."

"It's delicious. My mom makes it, but it's a little more bland." He pointed his fork at her. "Don't ever tell her I said that."

"Now that we're going to be neighbors, I wanted to reboot our relationship, so to speak. I'm actually a nice person. You just seem to catch me at bad moments, I guess."

"I was hoping somebody would bring me a pie. Shepherd's pie definitely counts."

She shrugged. "I don't bake a lot. When you live in this town, you bake in the shadow of Rose Davis and Fran Benoit and the rest of that generation."

"So tell me about yourself." He sipped the lemonade, watching her over the rim of the glass. "You're from here?"

"Born and raised."

"So you have family here?"

She shook her head, swallowing a mouthful of food. "Not anymore. When my younger sister, Tanya, went to UMass, she met my brother-in-law and moved to his hometown when they got married. It's near Springfield, in the western part of the state. He started a business and invited my dad to join him and, since work was scarce here, my parents moved there, too. I'd just gotten the job at the library, so I stayed."

"That's a good hike."

She shrugged. "It's a six-hour drive. I don't make it a lot, but at least twice a year, I try to go down. It's hard because I have to close the library, but I give the town lots of notice and I try to only go when school's in session so they still have a library available. What about you?"

"My family's in and around Augusta. My dad does flooring and my mom's always been at home. My older sister, Deb, is married and has two kids. Georgia's eight and Tommy's six. Her husband's an orthodontist. Deb stays home with her kids, plus she watches my younger sister Brenna's son, Caleb, who's five."

"And you're close with them?"

"Very. They're coming over for a barbecue Saturday after next. My mom can't stand not being able to visualize where I live."

"And the camp you were at? That's yours or a family camp?"

"It's been in my family since my great-grandfather bought it. The amount of land it has, with the cabin right on the river and everything, would cost a fortune now, so I'm glad he did. I probably spend the most time there, but my dad and I try to go together a few times a year. And the family all goes at least once. Sometimes twice."

"That must…" He watched her struggle with a grin. "…smell bad. I'm sorry."

"The key is that if everybody smells, you don't notice." The effort she put into not looking horrified was admirable, but he finally laughed and let her off the hook. "I'm kidding. There's indoor plumbing, installed shortly after my dad took my mother up there for the first time, before they got married. A shower and everything."

Hailey laid her fork on her empty plate and leaned back in her chair. "We went camping once. Only once. Tanya and I were really young, but we had our own tent next to my parents'. It was fun until it got dark. And then it rained and I woke up and our air mattress was floating in water because my dad pitched our little tent in a big dip in the ground. That was the end of camping."

"It's a little different when you have a cabin, although it does get crowded when the whole family's there. Bear!" He pointed at the dog. "Yard!"

"He seems to listen well."

"When he wants to." He took a sip of lemonade and pushed his plate away. "He caught on to the boundaries pretty well. The trees and the bushes help with that. There's none between our yards, though."

"I don't mind if he wanders into my yard. Although if he starts leaving me *gifts,* you'll hear about it."

He laughed. "I'll pick up after him. And he'll probably end up there whether I let him or not because he's going to like you and want to be friends. But he won't go in the road unless he's on a leash and the people at the end of the street have a fence, so I know he can't go far."

"You think he'll like me?"

"He's a black Lab. He likes everybody."

"Gee, you sure know how to make a woman feel special." She smiled at him, then rolled her eyes.

Was he supposed to be making her feel special? Suddenly the casual, spur-of-the-moment dinner didn't seem so casual. He'd taken her desire to apologize and start over as neighbors at face value. Sure, he liked the view when she bent over in the backyard and he liked the way she laughed—and the way she shivered when he touched her neck, which he tried not to think about too much—but they'd be stupid to think about anything more than that.

"I was kidding," she said softly, and he realized that up-against-the-wall feeling might have shown on his face. "I wasn't flirting with you, so don't panic."

"Oh, I know. I was just...I thought of a work thing I forgot, that's all." The lie rolled off his tongue as he stood. "Actually, thanks for the shepherd's pie, which was the best I've ever had, but I need to make a few calls while I'm thinking about it."

"No problem. I made enough so you'd have leftovers." She stood up. "Do you want some help carrying stuff in?"

"Nope, I've got it. Thanks again. Bear, come on, boy."

She looked back when she got halfway to her house and caught him watching her. He waved and she waved back, but she didn't smile this time. It was for the best.

As sexy and funny as she was, he needed to stop focusing on the chemistry crackling between them and start focusing on getting his shit together. He had a house to unpack, a job to do and a town to make home. He didn't have time for a woman who couldn't decide if she liked him or not.

IT TOOK TWO trips with the cart for Hailey to empty the night drop box on Monday morning. And there were also a couple of dollar bills at the bottom, which meant some of the books were overdue and the patrons had tucked fine money into them like bookmarks. Sometimes she had no trouble matching the money with the overdue books, but other times she gave up and pinned the dollars to her board to remind her to ask the patrons later.

When she flipped the sign to open at ten, there wasn't exactly a mad rush to get in, which she'd expected. Mondays were notoriously slow due to all of the residents of Whitford having to survive it being Monday, which meant finding herself busywork. Luckily there wasn't very often a shortage of that. If all else failed, there were always grants to hunt up and apply for.

At eleven, when she was finished checking in books and matching dollars with fines, she picked up the phone and called Fran.

"Whitford General Store. How can I help you?"

"Hi Fran. It's Hailey. Are you busy right now?"

"Nope. What's up?"

"A couple of things. First, I'm hoping you'll sponsor an ice cream party for our summer reading program this year. It'll be in August, shortly before school starts, but I'd love a commitment now so we can both plan accordingly."

"That sounds like a messy party to have at the library."

"If the weather's nice, we'll have it outside. If it's too hot or it rains, we'll push some tables together and try to keep it contained. An ice cream party will be a great incentive to get kids to sign up and participate." When Fran hesitated, Hailey pushed on. "Do I need to read you the statistics about the academic differences between kids who read over summer break and those who don't? I have about three pages of findings right here."

"Hell no, young lady. Life's too short for statistics. I'll sponsor your ice cream party."

"You're the best, Fran. And everybody will know it when they see the big banner thanking the Whitford General Store for supporting the children."

"How big?"

"Big."

"Good. What's the second thing? You said *first,* which implies a second."

"Oh. How come you didn't tell me somebody was renting the Andrews' house? I had no idea until I woke up and there was a moving truck out front."

Fran chuckled. "You mean, why didn't you get a heads up the hunky game warden was going to live mere feet from your door?"

She should have known the woman would enjoy this. "It's more than mere feet. And yes, that's what I mean."

"I didn't know. I was a little under the weather last week, so Butch had to mind the store a couple of times. And *that's* a nightmare, let me tell you. I swear it took me two days to figure out the receipts. But I must have missed talking to anybody who knew he was coming."

"Mmm-hmm."

"As much as it pains me to say this, I don't know everything that goes on in this town, you know."

"Not for a lack of trying." The mail carrier walked in, dumped a pile of mail on the desk and then, after tipping his hat, walked back out. "I have to get back to work, Fran. I really do appreciate you sponsoring the ice cream party. You're the best."

The mail yielded a few bills, several new issues for the periodical shelves, and a packet of photos she'd sent off for developing. When they did events with the older kids, she often scattered disposable cameras around the area, encouraging them to take candid shots of each other. It was an expense she bore, rather than having the library pay, but it was worth it.

She sifted through the photos from the costume party game they'd played two weeks before. The kids dressed up as literary characters and all of the costumes had to be made from things they could scrounge up at home. No store bought costumes. Then the other kids had to guess who they were and then race to find the correct book.

There had been a slight issue when one of the girls showed up with her hair in a braid and her father's compound bow, but during the kids' mad rush to get to the bookshelves, Hailey was able to stow the weapon without incident.

The photos were all fun and she picked a half dozen of the best ones to put on the bulletin board. The rest would go in a basket so everybody could look at them. That reminded her she had pictures on her phone from the OHRV safety class, so she pulled those up.

After printing four of them, she deleted them from her phone. Except for one. The photo she'd taken of Matt to text to Tori, she kept. He did look exceptionally hot in his uniform, she had to admit.

She smiled, remembering the way he'd practically fled into his house when he thought she was flirting with him last night. He'd tried to cover it with a fib about work, but she wasn't stupid. Maybe she should be offended, but she had to admit he hadn't really seen her at her best.

When a patron walked in, she hit the home button on her phone and set it on the desk so quickly she almost dropped it. Then she felt like an idiot. She wasn't a teenage girl to be mooning over a guy's picture on her phone.

But even later, when she was alone again, she didn't delete it.

SHORTLY BEFORE NOON on Tuesday, Matt loaded his ATV into the back of his truck and followed the directions he'd scrawled on the back of an envelope to the Northern Star Lodge.

It was a huge New Englander, with white siding, dark green shutters and a deep farmer's porch that beckoned him to sit and talk for a while. There was a big addition and he shuddered at the thought of how long it must take to clean the place.

At least it was lucrative again, from what he'd heard. The Kowalski family had all thrown in together and turned it around when Josh had broken his leg and finally admitted he needed help. Figuring out a way to bring the ATV business in and turning the Northern Star from a snowmobiling lodge into four-season lodging had been a brilliant idea not only for the family, but for all of Whitford.

And the trails were opening on Saturday, so he was going to go out with Josh and Andy Miller, the police chief's dad, for a tour. They needed to make sure the trails were in good condition and that none of the signs had been stolen by kids with nothing better to do.

He walked up the steps and knocked on the front door, admiring the quality of the woodwork while he waited. It was only a minute before Josh opened the door.

"You found the place okay?"

"Followed the signs for the Northern Star Lodge."

Josh laughed and stepped back to let him in. "I keep forgetting we put those up. Come on in."

Matt followed him into the kitchen, where an older couple was standing at the counter. The guy was trying to reach for cookies on a cooling rack and the woman was slapping his hand.

"We have company," Josh announced, and they both turned. "This is Matt Barnett. We've gotten a lot of support from the warden service but, most importantly, we've got somebody covering this area now. Matt, this is Rose Davis, who'll tell you she's the housekeeper, but she's mostly responsible for raising us. And this is Andy Miller, our trail administrator."

Matt shook hands with Andy, then leaned in to kiss Rose's cheek. "I've heard a lot about you, ma'am."

"I've heard a lot about you, too," she said, and her look made it clear what she'd heard had nothing to do with his new role in town. "And it's Rose or Rosie, not ma'am. I hope you're hungry, because I made lunch."

"I deliberately skipped breakfast this morning."

Her smile was broad and warm. "Oh, you are a charmer. I'm going to like you. Sit."

The problem with the best meat loaf sandwiches he'd ever eaten in his life was that he ate two of them, along with a second helping of macaroni salad, which made him want a nap.

Josh groaned, his hand to his stomach. "I told you we should ride first and then eat, Rosie. Now I don't want to move."

"Nobody made you eat seconds."

"There's not a man born who could have resisted, Rose," Matt said, rubbing his own belly.

She gave him a smile that made him feel like a chosen child. "I can see why certain women in this town want to see you sweep Hailey off her feet."

Luckily, he'd been prepared for this and he smiled. "Hailey seems to like her feet firmly on the ground."

Her eyes narrowed a little, as if he'd issued a challenge. "She's been waiting for the right man to come along."

"Speaking of waiting," he turned to face Josh. "I stopped at the general store to grab some snacks for today's ride and, when I mentioned I was on my way here, the woman—Fran, right?—offered me five dollars off my next purchase of twenty dollars or more if I could get a wedding date out of you."

They all laughed, while Josh shook his head. "That's up to Katie and she can't decide if she wants a summer wedding or a winter wedding. She wants to get married here and then she wants to go to some tropical island and get married on a cruise ship. As soon as she figures out what she wants, I'll have her call you. Wouldn't want you to miss out on five bucks."

"You boys want dessert?" Rose asked, standing to clear plates.

Matt stood, too, and picked up his plate. "If I eat another bite, I'm going to have to rent a room from you and lay down for a while. Maybe until tomorrow."

"It's homemade banana cream pie."

He looked at Josh, and then Andy. "How important is it we hit the trails *today*?"

"Trust me, son, I know how you feel," Andy said. "We'll go do a run now, then have some pie when we get back. How about that?"

"It'll be too close to supper," Rose protested, taking Matt's plate from him.

"I'm so full, a slice of banana cream pie will *be* supper," he told her.

"You stop by here any time you need a good meal." She patted his face as though he were a boy.

"Thank you, Rose. Between you and Hailey, I certainly won't go hungry."

She turned a laser-sharp gaze on him. "Hailey's feeding you?"

He had to get better at this small-town thing. "She made me a shepherd's pie, to welcome me to the neighborhood. It was a huge pan and I've been enjoying the leftovers."

"Hmm." She searched his face, as if looking for any sign a welcome to the neighborhood dish was a euphemism for something a lot more gossip-worthy. "She makes the best shepherd's pie in town. Refuses to give me the recipe."

"I told her it was better than my mother's and she told me it was the seasonings."

"Well, that could mean almost anything. And never, ever admit out loud a woman's cooking is better than your mama's."

"Yes, ma'am. Rose."

"Let's get out of here before I have to put on my wading boots." Josh kissed Rose's cheek. "Thanks for lunch."

Figuring this was a woman whose good graces he

wanted to be in, Matt stepped up and did the same. "It was delicious."

"Ride hard. Burn those sandwiches off so you can have some pie."

He walked back out to his truck while the other two guys went to one of the barns where, he assumed, their machines were stored. He undid his tie-down straps, then dragged out the ramps that were shoved beside the ATV. After fastening the safety straps to the hitch of his truck, he climbed onto the tailgate with a groan. Those meatloaf sandwiches were going to stay with him a while.

After firing up his machine, he backed it down the ramps and parked it off to the side. He didn't bother stowing the ramps, since he'd drive right back up them when they were done and he wasn't blocking any parking spaces.

By the time he'd put the bag of snacks and his water bottle in the cargo box and grabbed his helmet and gloves, the other two guys were ready to go. Josh drove over and handed him a folded map.

"You wanted a copy of this?"

Matt took the map and unfolded it. It was fairly rough, but he didn't have much trouble finding the lodge. He had a couple of permanent markers in his pocket, and he fired up the GPS unit mounted on the handlebar. He not only wanted to get his bearings, but he wanted to see how good a job the Northern Star ATV club had done on their trail map.

He knew they'd had some help from the state in the early stages of making trails and a lot of people had looked over their shoulders in different official capacities to make sure wetlands were avoided, bridges were built where necessary, that trail head parking was available and that all of their road crossings were safe, but this section of the state was his primary responsibility now and he wasn't relying on anybody else's work.

"Thanks. I'm going to want to stop at each intersection, but they'll be quick stops." When Josh didn't say anything, Matt looked up from the map to find him watching him. "What?"

"We've done GPS tracks for this trail system so many times I can probably quote the coordinates in my sleep."

"That's good and makes my job that much easier." He folded the map and tucked it into his tank bag for easy access. "Look. We want the same thing here—people coming to ride these trails while dumping some money into our economy and having a good enough time so they come back and tell all their friends. But there might be times you and I are at odds because you represent the ATV club, your town and your guests, and I represent the state of Maine."

"I don't foresee us having too many problems."

"I just want to get it out there now, while it's just us. I respect what you've done here and I'm going to do everything in my power to make sure both visitors to the trails and the citizens of Whitford are safe and happy while laws are abided. But if I have to give out some tickets and you try to make them go away because your guests are pissed or it's your girlfriend's second cousin's son, we're going to have a problem."

"I've asked around about you and so has Drew Miller. We've heard you're fair, so I don't have a problem with that. Sometimes we get people acting like assholes, running wild, and the landowners get upset and talk about closing their land to four-wheelers. If that happens, all of this work was for nothing, so I don't care if it's my girlfriend's second cousin's son *and* he's staying at the lodge. If he does something wrong, nail him. But if I think you're just throwing your weight around to be big man on the trails, I'll start making phone calls."

Matt nodded and stuck out his hand. "Fair enough."

They shook hands and then strapped on their helmets. Josh led the way around the lodge and into the break in the tree line, with Andy riding behind Matt. The afternoon passed quickly as they covered the miles. At every intersection, Matt checked the map against his GPS and he was impressed. This club knew what they were doing.

They'd done a good job with the trails, too. They were wide enough to account for the bigger side-by-side machines, though there would be places they'd have to squeeze by each other. The terrain was a nice mix. Some easier trails and others a little more rugged. A few were marked on the map as recommended for advanced riders and they had a pretty good time playing on those.

While they didn't cover every trail, Matt felt as if he got a solid feel for the trail system and he could explore on his own both at his leisure and officially. When they got back to the lodge, he drove his ATV up into the bed of his truck, then stowed the ramps and strapped it down.

"I'm impressed," he told Josh and Andy when he was done. "It's a nice system."

"Thanks," Josh said. "We hope to grow it some more over time, but we connect to two other clubs' trails now and we want to make sure this goes smoothly before we invest in too many more miles."

"You think that's impressive," Andy added, "come get a taste of my Rose's banana cream pie."

Mitch groaned and rubbed his stomach. "I think I'm still full. But I bet there's room for pie."

EIGHT

AFTER WORK ON Wednesday, Hailey changed into yard clothes—which consisted of an old T-shirt and older jeans—and pulled her lawn mower out of the storage shed. She had an electric mower, even though the cord was often a nuisance, because it was quieter and easier for her to handle. Less noise pollution and no pollution in the form of gas usage or exhaust appealed to her, and she didn't worry about bothering the neighbors.

She was about halfway through mowing her backyard, when the sound of Bear barking registered above the song being piped through her earbuds. She pulled them out and looked next door just in time to see the dog run up onto the back deck and a big riding lawn mower turn the far corner of Matt's house.

He was shirtless again. That was the first thing she noticed, because his chest was hard to miss. Sometimes the temptation to sneak a picture of him without a shirt to go with the photo of him in uniform saved on her phone was very strong.

Since they'd shared her shepherd's pie, things had been quiet between them. They were both busy and, other than the occasional wave when eye contact was made because it would have been rude not to, they hadn't really interacted. Even though she didn't mind seeing him at a distance, it was probably for the best.

As she watched, he steered the lawn mower around one of the shade trees in his backyard so fast, she was surprised he didn't tip over. Then he proceeded to drag race up and down the yard, making a whole lot of racket to cut not a huge amount of grass.

After a few passes up and down the yard, along with another death-defying spin around a tree, he stopped the lawnmower and shut it off. "What?"

He was talking to her. "Excuse me?"

"You've been glaring at me with your hands on your hips the entire time I've been mowing. I assume I'm doing it wrong?"

She hadn't realized she'd assumed such a damning position while she was watching. "It's your yard."

"But you disapprove."

She laughed, throwing her hands up. "Again, it's your yard."

"I could do yours, too. It'd only take me a few minutes. You did make me shepherd's pie, after all."

"Thank you, but I enjoy mowing my lawn. With my lawnmower that doesn't disturb the entire neighborhood or stink up the yard with exhaust fumes."

"Ah. So it's my big, bad lawnmower that's annoying you."

So much for a quiet, post-shepherd's pie truce between neighbors. "Yes. It is."

"Put your earbuds back in and turn the music up."

She took a deep breath, then tried going about it a different way. "When you drive recklessly like that, I worry about your dog."

"You mean the dog who hasn't left the deck since I drove this around the corner?" Now that he mentioned it, Bear *was* still on the deck. "And I'm not reckless."

"You almost rolled it over going around the tree."

He laughed. "I did not. This thing corners so tight, it's like being on rails."

She had no idea what that meant, but she knew this conversation was pointless. After putting the earbuds back in her ears, she flipped through her playlist for some fun dance music and restarted her lawnmower.

There was no ignoring the big beast devouring the lawn next to hers at a record pace, but she did her best not to look over. She took her time, trying to enjoy an activity that usually relaxed her.

Before she knew it, the noise quit next door and she realized he was already done. She had to admit his way was a lot faster. But on principle, she refused to be jealous and give him the satisfaction of seeing it on her face. It wasn't about speed, it was about taking pride in one's lawn.

During one pass, she saw that Matt had positioned himself on a patio chair with a pitcher of lemonade in such a way he couldn't be doing anything but watching her, with Bear stretched out at his feet. He raised the glass in a cocky salute when she looked over, and she refused to look that way again.

When she was finally done, at least an hour after he finished, she stowed the mower and the cord in the shed and looked out over her lawn. It didn't look any different from his. They were the same length, more or less. Both green. Hers didn't show any sign of having been lovingly mowed in an environmentally friendly way.

"You want some lemonade?" She turned to face Matt, who was still sitting on his deck. He pointed at the pitcher. "I have plenty, and mowing lawns works up a sweat."

"It didn't take you long enough to work up a sweat."

When he grinned, she realized she'd given herself away. "I'd be happy to let you borrow mine if you want to take it for a spin next time."

"Thank you, but I'd probably spin myself right into the trees." She started toward her back door, wanting a tall glass of ice water.

"You sure you don't want some lemonade?"

"No, thank you."

She went inside and closed the door with a bang. Somebody obviously had no sense of boundaries. When people lived so close together, you had to pretend the other had some privacy. Not stare at them while they mowed and then bellow across the yard like a carnival barker hawking lemonade.

Standing at her sink, drinking a glass of water, she tried not to stare at the man playing fetch with his dog in his backyard. She, unlike him, had some sense of boundaries.

But she might have peeked a few times.

ON THURSDAY, MATT rode his quad down the main street of Whitford at the mandated ten miles per hour, getting a feel for the traffic pattern that brought the ATVs out of the woods behind the Trailside Diner and down through town to the Whitford General Store & Service Station, where they could get gas. He'd ridden the trails through the woods with Josh and Andy, but the access to town was vital.

Riders also had access to the municipal parking lot, where they could leave their machines and walk through town to visit other businesses if they were so inclined. The signage was clear, the residents gave him cheerful waves and he hadn't seen any obvious red flags. Again he was impressed by how much thought the Northern Star ATV club had put into building their trail system.

Since he was there, he filled up with gas and then went into the store to pay. Fran Benoit was, as usual, behind the counter. Her thick, gray braid and flannel shirt seemed to be her daily uniform, and she was knitting what looked like a mint green baby blanket.

"Good morning, Fran."

"Matt! It's good to see you again. Are you settling in okay?"

"With a town like Whitford, how could I not? I almost feel like I was born and raised here."

Her cheeks flushed with pleasure, and he thought she might have patted his head if he was close enough. "I knew the first time I met you that you'd fit right in here."

"What are you knitting?"

"A blanket for Liz's baby." She held it up, looking it over with a critical eye. "Have you met Liz? She's Drew Miller's wife."

"I met her at the diner, but I didn't know she was expecting."

"She might be." Fran shrugged. "Or she might not be. But it won't be long. What are you up to today, besides looking handsome in that uniform?"

"I wanted to get a feel for the ATV traffic flow through town, so I'm doing some errands. Once I pay you for the gas, I'll go wander through town a bit. I might stop in to the barber shop. And I need a library card."

The woman lit up as if she'd stuck her knitting needle in a light socket. "Really? If you should happen to hear anything about Liz and Drew, I'd love to know about it. I'd even dig up one of the good chew bones I have out back for that Lab of yours."

"I've been warned about you, Fran."

"I just want an idea of how long I have to knit this blanket," she said with a straight face.

"I'll keep an ear out," he promised as vaguely as possible.

He paid for his gas, then drove the ATV to the municipal lot and parked it. After locking his helmet through the rack, he stuck his ball cap on his head and took a walk.

It was a nice day, and people made a point of waving to him or saying hello. He liked that. Having a good relationship with this community was important professionally, but it was also his home now.

When he got to the barber shop, he stepped inside. It retained that old-fashioned look and smell, and he breathed deeply. This was the way a barber shop was meant to be. A blonde woman with her hair pulled through a Patriots cap looked up from the haircut she was giving when he walked in.

"I'm going to go out on a limb and guess you're Matt Barnett."

"Now what gave it away?" he asked, looking down at his uniform.

"I'm Katie." She set down the trimmer in her hand and grabbed a big brush to clean her customer's neck and ears. "I'll be right with you."

He waited while she took the cape off the older man and made change for him. Matt didn't need a haircut yet, but there was no harm in stopping in.

Not only was she a business owner, but she was the club president's fiancée.

"Josh has told me a lot about you," she said when they were alone, and put out her hand. "It's good to meet you."

He shook her hand. "I've met him a couple of times, and I've met your mom and Andy, so I thought I'd stop in and introduce myself."

"You don't need a haircut right now, but I hope you'll come back when you do." She tilted her head, looking him over. "You did that yourself, didn't you?"

He laughed, feeling self-conscious even with his hat on. "That bad?"

"No, but it's a little crooked where you went around your ear and down to your neck. Hard area to do yourself."

"When it's time for a trim, I'll come in and let you fix it for me."

"Done. So out making the rounds?"

"Yeah. Getting to know people and it's a nice day for a walk. I'll probably go over to the library and get some books while I'm here."

She arched an eyebrow at him. "Really?"

"This town is too much." He shook his head. "There's no ulterior motive behind getting a library card. And Fran at the general store just offered me a chew bone for my dog if I find out if Liz is pregnant yet. Oh, and have you set a wedding date yet?"

That made her laugh. "Is she still offering five dollars off? I swear, that woman. But she's harmless, really. Her and my mom are good friends and if she actually got big news before my mom did, she'd give us all hell."

"Good to know. Be better to save five bucks off my groceries, but I'll live." He stepped toward the door. "It was good to meet you, Katie. I'll see you around."

"I'm sure you will. My mom will want to feed you whenever she gets the chance."

He pushed open the door with one hand, but put the other on his stomach. "Please. I'm still working off her meat loaf sandwiches."

It was a good walk to the library, which was exercise, at least. He was going to have to watch the women in this town, he thought, or he wouldn't fit in his uniforms soon. Hopefully the extra time on the four-wheeler would help keep the pounds at bay.

There were a few cars in the library parking lot, but it was quiet when he stepped inside. There was a low murmur of voices from the children's section and he saw somebody working at a computer.

Hailey was at her desk, putting plastic slipcovers on new hardcovers, but she looked up when the door closed behind him with a muted thump. Her eyes widened when she recognized him, and then narrowed slightly.

"Good morning," she said in a polite voice when he reached the desk.

"I'm doing errands, so I thought I'd get my library card while I was out."

"Wonderful." She gave him a wide smile that was totally fake. "Do you have identification or a utility bill with your name and your Whitford address on it?"

"My identification has my previous address on it and I haven't lived here long enough to get a utility bill yet." Which she damn well knew.

"Our policy is that potential patrons prove they live in Whitford before being issued a library card."

So she was in one of those moods. That was fine with him. "How about if my neighbor swears she watched me move in next door to her. And she did, very closely, judging by how often her curtains moved."

Color tinted her cheeks. "I'm sure it was a draft. She probably couldn't have cared less what you were doing."

"Oh, I doubt it was a draft. It was pretty warm that day. As a matter of fact, it was so warm, I had to take my shirt off because I was sweating."

Her mouth tightened, and he wondered if she was mad or trying not to smile. "Be that as it may, Warden Barnett, our policy requires proof of Whitford residency."

"Is this a big problem you've had? People coming into town and signing up for a library card under false pretenses to steal a book?"

"Our budget's tight. We can't be too careful." She lost the battle to hide her smile, and shook her head. "But, I think, in your case we can make an exception. You being an officer of the law and all."

She pulled a form out of a drawer and started filling it in herself. Of course she knew his name and his address, since she lived next door. Then she looked up at him. "What's your middle name?"

"Is that on the form?"

"No. I'm just nosy."

"Charles. After my dad."

She nodded and slid the form around to him. "You need to write in your phone number and sign the bottom, and I need to see your driver's license."

"My number, huh? Is that really on the form?"

"Yes." She rolled her eyes. Then she looked at his license. "You're only thirty-five?"

"Why? Do I look older than that?"

"No, I just…you're younger than me."

He gave her a thorough looking over, enjoying the way pink spread across her cheeks. "Not by much."

"Five freaking years," she muttered.

"I don't believe it. You should show me *your* license."

She snorted. "Have you ever met a woman our age, or my age anyway, who lied about being forty?"

"It's just a number."

"Says the guy who's only thirty-five."

When he handed her the completed form, she gave him a small card with his name, a number and a bar code on it. "Automated, huh?"

"Partially. I got a grant to put the checkout system on the computer, but we still have the card catalogue in the old wooden drawers."

"I like those, myself."

She smiled and gave him a shrug. "To be honest, I haven't fought too hard to get rid of those, even though purging the drawers twice a year is a pain."

"Be a shame to see it go."

She handed him a small pile of papers, one at a time. "Here are the rules. Books and audiobooks go out for two weeks, videos and periodicals for one. You can call and renew over the phone. The overdue fine schedule is on the bottom. They're doubled for interlibrary loan titles. And here's a list of our clubs and special events. You know, if you like to knit or something."

A woman was approaching the desk with a toddler and an armful of picture books, so it was time for him to go.

"I'm on the quad today, so I won't take any books home, but I'll be back." He skimmed the list of activities. "You've got a lot going on. I could spend *all* my spare time here."

She gave him a *don't even think about it* look, but morphed it into a polite smile as the other patron stepped into line behind him. "Welcome to the Whitford Public Library, Warden Barnett."

"Thank you, Hailey. I'll definitely be back."

He gave a polite nod to the other woman and smiled at her daughter. Then he headed for the exit. But he paused before he pushed open the door because he could see the women reflected in the glass and they were both watching him leave.

It was the uniform, he thought as he stepped out into the sunshine. Almost made the hours of ironing worthwhile.

NINE

HOLIDAY WEEKENDS WERE a special kind of hell. Long weekends meant long hours, drunk people and a whole lot of stupidity, and Memorial Day was a doozie. After a long winter, New Englanders were ready to let loose and live it up.

At two o'clock on Monday morning, Matt leaned against a tree trunk and tried not to fall asleep on his feet. After a full day of chasing four-wheelers, arresting drunks, checking fishing licenses, and responding to a situation at a family barbecue that involved alcohol, a fire, gasoline and fireworks, he'd been about to head home when they got a call about a missing teenage girl.

Five hours of walking through the woods later, they got the call she'd been found. Apparently, she'd gone for a walk with her boyfriend and they had a big fight because somebody said something about somebody else on Facebook, and her boyfriend stormed off. After having a good long cry, she tried to find her way home and missed by a long shot.

It was a happy ending, but Matt was ready to just fall flat on his face and sleep in the dirt for a few hours.

"Bet she's already updating her Facebook status," Pete Winslow said. He was a warden Matt had worked with a lot and they'd become good friends over the years, and he was leaning against the tree next to Matt's. "Probably taking a selfie in the ambulance."

"Too bad she didn't use the phone to, you know, call her parents."

"It was charging when she went for her walk, so she didn't have it. Her mom had it and gave it to her while they were checking her vitals. Probably so she could update her status."

"Where's the dad?"

"He'd had a few and wanted to go after the boyfriend with a load of bird shot, so he's in custody until he sobers up." Pete pushed himself upright with a groan. "Time to head home."

"Easy for you to say. They had me come in from a direction they thought she might go, so my truck's not here at the staging area. And it's in the opposite direction of Whitford."

"I've gotta go within a couple of miles of there anyway, so I can give you a ride. You have a way to get your truck tomorrow?"

"Yeah." No, but he'd find a way. Drew Miller probably wouldn't mind sending an officer to give him a ride. Or he'd pay Butch Benoit to drive him out there in his tow truck. It was the closest thing the town had to a taxi service. "I appreciate it."

Once in the truck, it was tempting to close his eyes for a few minutes, but Pete was as worn out as he was. He kept his eyes open and they both talked about the idiots they'd crossed paths with that day just to stay awake.

When they pulled into Matt's driveway, he shook Pete's hand and opened the door. "You going to be okay? You can crash here if you need to."

"I'll be fine and the wife's going to be asleep on the couch, waiting. I'll put the window down and crank the music up. Sing-a-long time. You know how it is."

Yeah, he did. "Thanks again, Pete. Drive safe."

Matt let himself into his house and spent a couple minutes letting Bear welcome him home. As tempting as it was to simply keel over sideways on the couch and never move again, he had about twenty layers of bug spray on him.

He dragged his ass upstairs and secured his weapon, then left a trail of dirty uniform parts to the bathroom. After a quick, steaming hot shower, he tugged on a pair of sweatpants and fell into bed. He heard Bear settle in the oversized dog bed in the corner, and then he was out.

HAILEY WASN'T SURE what had awakened her when it was barely light outside, but after a few minutes of tossing and turning, she gave up. She had to pee, anyway. She brushed her teeth while she was in there and then went downstairs to start her day earlier than usual.

While the coffee brewed, she glanced out the window and then took a closer look. Matt's truck wasn't in the driveway. Frowning, she went to the living room and looked out that window. It wasn't there. So far, she hadn't seen him park it in the garage, since he had it filled with tools and his ATV and other assorted junk.

As far as she could tell, Matt had left for work the morning before and hadn't been home since.

Worry for him hummed through her as she fixed her coffee and then, a few sips into the cup, she thought of Bear.

He had a doggy door, but what about food and water? If Matt had known he wouldn't be home, she can't imagine he wouldn't have made plans for his dog. Even if he didn't want to get her number from information and call her, he would have called *somebody.* But if something had happened to him or, God forbid, he'd been in an accident, how long would it be before somebody thought of his dog?

Surely if Bear got too hungry, he'd come outside and throw himself on her mercy. Maybe give her those big, sad, puppy dog eyes until she caved and grilled him up a burger for breakfast or something.

By the time she finished her coffee, Hailey knew she had to check on Bear. And not just see him outside, but check on his food and water, which meant going inside. Throwing a hoodie over her tank top, she slipped her feet into her flip-flops and went out her back door.

Halfway across her yard, she hesitated. Bear was a lovable and lazy lump of Lab, but that was when Matt was around. When it came to the neighbor lady breaking into his house, Bear was still a dog.

But he might be a very confused, lonely and hungry dog, and that got her moving again.

Matt had taken the screen door off and stored it in the garage since it blocked the doggy door, so Hailey didn't have to worry about opening that. She twisted the doorknob and muttered a bad word when it didn't turn.

If he'd locked the back door, he'd probably locked the front door, too, but she walked around the house and tried it, anyway. It was also locked. She thought she heard a single bark from Bear when that screen door latched, but nothing after that.

Going back around the house, she resigned herself to the indignity of crawling through the doggy door. Bear was a big dog, so it was a big door and she knew she'd fit. But it was a little ridiculous and she was thankful the only reason she had to do it was because Matt wasn't home. That meant he couldn't witness her latest embarrassing episode.

She got on her hands and knees, then used one hand to push open the swinging door. It wasn't very comfortable and she pushed the flap open all the way so she could focus on *not* kneeling on the door sill because that would seriously hurt.

A chime sounded, followed by a flurry of barking and dog toenails on the wooden floors.

"Bear, it's me," she called, pausing half in and half out of the doggy door as a mountain of black Lab barreled into the kitchen.

DESPITE LESS THAN three hours of sleep, Matt woke in a state of high alert when the dog door chimed. He'd been half-awake for a few minutes already, mumbling at Bear when the dog had let out a woof for no reason. Then the chime sounded and Bear took off at a run.

But if Bear had been in his bed, what had triggered the alarm? Matt usually locked it when they went to bed at night but, in the condition he'd been in, he might have overlooked it last night. Or this morning, rather.

Praying it wasn't a raccoon, which was the risk they ran in exchange for Bear being able to get out, he pulled his service weapon out of the biometric safe on his nightstand and went after Bear. When he got to the kitchen, he hit the light switch, then shook his head.

"You have to be kidding." The top half of his neighbor was through the doggy door and Bear was licking her face, his butt wagging in joy. "Bear, cut it out."

"You're home," she said in a flat voice.

He arched an eyebrow at her, then set his gun on the counter and hit the button to start the coffee brewing. "Is that why you're breaking into my house at six-thirty in the morning? Because you thought I wasn't home?"

She finished crawling all the way into the kitchen and then quickly stood before Bear could get at her face again. "Yes. If I thought you were home, I wouldn't have been crawling through the doggy door."

"Anything in particular you were after?" Maybe she had a drug problem. That would help explain why she ran so hot and cold where he was concerned.

"I wanted to make sure Bear was okay."

He went a little still inside, not sure he'd understood her. "You broke in to check on my dog?"

"I heard your truck leave yesterday morning and I hadn't seen it since. I know he can get in and out, but I didn't know if he'd run out of food and water. And then I thought he'd come get me, but maybe you trained him not to leave the yard at all when you're not home. Or maybe he got scared and scratched at my door, but it didn't wake me up, so he went looking for you and got lost." She stopped, a pink blush spreading over her cheeks. "I wanted to check on him and your doors were locked, so...yeah."

"I guess you've got a Good Samaritan streak, yourself." Maybe she didn't know how to bait a hook, but she'd crawl through a small door in sleep shorts to check on an animal. That said something about her. Something he liked.

"I like your dog."

He nodded, then watched as the dog in question bolted through the dog door. The chime dinged again.

"Doesn't that drive you crazy?"

"Not really. He's a good dog, but I like to know where he is. And I usually lock the dog door at night. I must have forgotten since it was about three when I got in."

Her eyes got big. "Three? Oh, the long weekend, right? It must be busy for you guys."

"Long weekends always are."

He pulled two mugs out of the cabinet, though he wasn't really sure why, and poured them each a mug. "Cream and sugar?"

"I should go, so you can go back to bed. Now I feel even worse."

"Don't feel bad for caring about my dog. And he'll be outside at least twenty minutes. I'm up, so have a coffee with me."

She looked down at herself, as if she'd just realized she hadn't put clothes on before breaking into his house. She was covered, with thin cotton shorts that looked like men's boxers, and a hoodie she'd thrown over her tank top. But, as he looked at her, she zipped the hoodie, covering up the view a little.

He ran his hand over his naked chest. "I guess it's a good thing I put sweatpants on before I fell into bed."

The corner of her mouth quirked upward. "I guess that depends on your point of view."

"Are you flirting with me?" Even as early as it was, being ogled by a pretty woman wasn't a bad way to start the day.

"I can be a bit shameless when it comes to coffee. Sorry."

He gestured to one of the stools at the island. "Have a seat. So, cream and sugar?"

"Yes, please."

He got the half and half out of the fridge. "For future reference, Bear's food is in that blue bin over there. It's just a lift-top lid. He stays out of it as a rule, but if he gets hungry enough, he can get into it. And he's got that big tank of water there that feeds into his dish but, as gross as it sounds, I always make sure the toilet lid's up. Just in case."

"I feel better knowing that."

"If something happens to me that's bad enough so they call my parents, somebody will come get Bear. But if you're willing to break into my house, are you also willing to give me your number so I can call you if I can't get home? Just because he won't starve doesn't mean I like him being alone overnight. And I'll give you the extra key so you don't have to crawl through the doggy door."

"Funny, but yes. We should have each other's numbers anyway. Being neighbors and all."

"Speaking of being neighborly," he said, setting her coffee in front of her and grinning, "any chance I can sweet talk you into giving me a ride to my truck later? If not, I can try Drew Miller."

"Your chances of sweet talking Drew are pretty slim." She smiled, then took a sip of her coffee.

"I bet you're not too susceptible to sweet talk, either."

"Not usually, but when a guy with no shirt on makes me coffee, it softens me up."

He put the cream back in the fridge and then went to the back door to check on Bear. As expected, the dog was sniffing every blade of grass to make sure nothing had changed during the night.

On his way back to the island, he watched Hailey lower her head to drink her coffee and his body tightened. Her hair was pulled to one side, exposing her neck, and he remembered her shivering when he touched her there and how she fought so hard to hide it.

He shouldn't touch her. He knew it. Not while he was overtired and feeling soft toward her because she tried to take care of his dog. Not while she was wearing barely anything. But as he crossed the kitchen, he couldn't help himself.

"That bug bite healed nicely," he said, and he ran his fingertip lightly down the line of her neck.

TEN

HAILEY SUCKED IN a breath and she knew there was no way she could hide the hot flush that felt as though it was covering every inch of her body.

"You are the master of mixed signals," she said, deciding if she couldn't hide her reaction, she might as well face it head on.

He walked back around the island, which in a way was worse because now he could see the blush on her cheeks. "What do you mean?"

"The night I brought you shepherd's pie, you thought I was flirting with you and you practically ran into the house. But then you go and do that."

"First aid is part of my job description. Just doing my duty, ma'am."

She laughed at him. "You're so full of crap."

"Maybe." He gave her a sheepish grin. "You're not exactly consistent with the signals, either, you know."

He might have a point there, so she kept her mouth shut and drank her coffee until a way to change the subject popped into her head. "What made you become a game warden? I'm guessing it wasn't the promise of nine to five."

"Nine to five. That's funny." He took a sip of his

coffee, then shrugged. "I love being outside and always spent every minute I could in the woods. I love animals. I always wanted to be a police officer. It sounds trite, but I think I was born to be a game warden."

"It must be hard, sometimes. The hours and not knowing what's going to happen each day. I mean, barring something huge happening, I can tell you what my schedule will be three years from now. And usually a broken binding or a paperback that reeks of cigarette smoke or—God help me—cat pee is my biggest emergency."

He wrinkled his nose. "Cat pee should be a chemical weapon."

"Tell me about it. And the book was in the night drop." She laughed at the face he made. "Yeah, it was like that. But we're talking about you, not me."

"The hours don't really bother me unless they affect Bear. Obviously you know that's occasionally a problem, but I've always had a good support system. It's been hard on relationships in the past, though."

"A friend of mine from college is married to a police officer in Boston. It's hard on her, but she believes in what he does and tries to support him."

He nodded. "One of the hardest things is the wildlife sometimes. Caring about them sometimes means putting them down and that sucks. My first week out we had to track down a deer that had been hit by a truck and, when we found her, there was no saving her. Even when done in mercy, putting an animal down hits me pretty hard."

She reached across the island and squeezed his hand. "They're lucky to have people who care out there watching out for them and advocating for them. It matters."

He smiled and squeezed her fingers. "Except when they're hurt, dealing with animals is a more enjoyable part of the job than dealing with drunks, idiots and walking around in the woods looking for marijuana plants, I can tell you that."

"Pot? Really?"

"You'd be surprised. It's a thriving backyard industry." When he laughed, she guessed her expression was disbelieving. "It is. I haven't found Whitford's yet, but there's a grow somewhere. I can almost guarantee it."

"No way. In Whitford?" She shook her head. "The police would have found it. We're not good at secrets."

"No disrespect to the Whitford PD, but town cops tend to stick to the roads unless they have cause to do otherwise. If I spend enough time out in the woods, I'll find one eventually."

"I hope it's not Fran or Butch. Or anybody at the diner."

He arched an eyebrow. "Any reason you mention them in particular?"

"No!" She jerked her hand back, hoping she hadn't

gotten anybody in trouble. "But that's our only grocery store, our only gas pumps and our only restaurant. It would really suck if one of them went to prison."

He laughed. "I don't think Fran, Butch or anybody at the diner will be going to prison. The food and gas supply in Whitford is safe for now."

Bear pushed his way back into the kitchen and fell upon his food bowl as though he hadn't eaten in days, even though Hailey knew there had still been food in the dish when she came in.

"He always eats like that in the morning," Matt said. "I guess he really works up an appetite sleeping all night."

Since her cup was empty, Hailey stood. "I should go and let you either take a nap or get dressed. And, obviously, I need to get dressed, too. What time do you want to get your truck?"

"Any time. Like I said, I'm up now. Later on today, I'll probably put on a game or the news channel and take a nap, but I won't be able to go back to sleep now."

"You shouldn't have had that coffee."

He smiled at her over the rim of his cup. "It was worth it."

There he went again, sending her *interested* signals when they both knew he wasn't. Or shouldn't be, anyway. "I'm going to shower and get dressed, so give me an hour and then any time you want to go, just come over."

"Sounds like a plan."

She unlocked the back door so she could exit properly instead of going through the doggy door again, and went back to her own house.

Sometimes she could be such an idiot. Breaking into a man's house through a damn dog door had to be one of the more ridiculous things she'd ever done. Of course Bear would have access to food and water. The guy worked weird hours quite often and obviously loved his dog. He wouldn't let him starve.

It was as if something about the man short-circuited her brain and made her act like an idiot. He'd been very gracious about it, she had to admit. He'd even thanked her for breaking into his house at six-thirty in the morning when he'd only been asleep for three and a half hours.

She tried to not to think about the way he'd touched her neck. It wasn't a *first aid is part of my job description* touch. It was a touch that let her know without a doubt that he knew how to wind her up. It was deliberate, but she didn't know if it was just to mess with her or if he liked the idea of turning her on for a different reason.

After showering, she threw on some jeans and a summer-weight sweater. Instead of pulling her hair into a ponytail, she took the time to blow it out so it was soft and full around her face. Not because of Matt, of course. She was sure she'd read somewhere that it wasn't good for hair to be in a ponytail all the time.

By the time Matt knocked on her door, Hailey had regained her equilibrium. He had undoubtedly touched her neck in an effort to be funny, probably as payback for her breaking in. It meant nothing and therefore there was no need to feel awkward about it.

After grabbing her wallet and keys, she opened the door to find him trying to convince Bear to go back in the house. But the Lab had apparently decided to forget that command.

"He's welcome to go along," she said. "Unless there's a reason you don't want him to."

"Are you sure? He'll shed on your seat."

"We have these awesome inventions called vacuums now. And, yes, I'm sure. He missed you. You can't turn around and leave already."

"Thanks. He loves going for rides." He opened the back door of her car and, when he waved him in, Bear hopped up onto the seat.

When she tried to back out of the driveway, Hailey looked in the rearview mirror and saw nothing but happy black Lab. "I think he's grinning at me."

"I can't remember the last time he rode in the backseat of a car. He probably thinks you're his new chauffeur."

"I had worse jobs in college."

"Tell me about them."

She sighed. "Well, I can tell you I might make a mean shepherd's pie, but I suck at making pizzas. I was so bad, they decided to have me do the deliveries, instead. You might not know this about me, but I don't have a keen sense of direction."

"No." He laughed, and they swapped funny college stories while Bear used copious amounts of slobber to lick her back windows clean.

MATT WAS SURPRISED Bear rode back with him in the truck. The dog was so infatuated with Hailey, he half expected him to stay in her car and refuse to get out. But when it came time to leave the lot where he'd left his truck, Bear remembered who his best friend was.

"I don't blame you, though," he told the dog. "She's really pretty. She always smells good. And she's funny, too. I like her."

Bear cocked his head, as if confused by what his man was saying. Matt didn't blame him. He was confused by what he was saying, too. Of all the women in the world he could be attracted to, the blonde from the woods was not the one he would have picked.

When they got home, he waved his thanks to Hailey, who pulled into her driveway just a minute after he pulled into his. "Let's go have some lunch and then we'll see about a nap."

Bear ran to the backyard first, so Matt went inside and poked through his fridge for sandwich fixings. He had ham and cheese, but no mustard, which sucked. There was good old peanut butter and jelly, but he wasn't in the mood for that.

Bear barked once and it sounded like he was at the back door, which was odd. Obviously the doggy door wasn't locked, since it had been used that morning. A second later there was a knock on the door. "Come in."

Instead of using the doggy door, Bear entered with Hailey. He was obviously happy to have his two favorite people back in the same place and was wagging his tail so hard his butt was in on it, too.

"I found this in my car when I dragged the vacuum out," she said, holding up the pocketknife his dad had given him when he turned thirteen.

"Thanks. I had it in my pocket, but it must have slipped out. I don't usually carry it, but I found it in a box I was unpacking and I meant to put it in my drawer." He pulled a loaf of bread out of the bread box. "You want a peanut butter and jelly sandwich?"

"No thanks. I should get back to what I was doing."

"You're vacuuming the car already? The dog hair's been there how long?"

She rolled her eyes. "I had planned to vacuum the car today anyway, for your information."

"Right." When she reached for the door handle, he felt an urge to stop her. "You should go on a date with me. My kind of date."

That definitely stopped her. She turned back to him, frowning. "Why should I do that?"

"Because it would be fun."

"We have nothing in common." But she stepped closer to lean against the island.

"We both like to have fun."

"But I think we have very different ideas of fun. And your kind of date is probably not my kind of date."

There was one activity he was sure they'd both find fun, but he tried to stay focused. "You don't think you'd have a good time with me?"

"I…I haven't really thought about it."

"I think maybe you have." He took a step closer to her. "I can tell by the way your face flushes when I get too close to you."

"Personal space issues."

"Really?" He reached out and ran his fingertip down the side of her neck. "Is that why, when I touch you, you shiver?"

She didn't break eye contact, so he saw the humor lurking there along with the heat. "That's the story I'm going with."

Wondering what she'd do if he kissed her, he smiled and shifted his gaze to her mouth. "Why do you need a story?"

"I've already told you you're not my type."

"And, again, we've already established you're not mine. I generally like my women to be more sturdy."

"Sturdy?" She stepped back and he realized he'd made a critical mistake. "What the hell kind of word is that? We're not furniture."

Maybe sturdy wasn't the best word, but he couldn't think of a better one. "You know, women who like being outdoors and don't worry about breaking a nail."

She rolled her eyes. "Sorry to be wicker in your rock maple fantasy world."

He leaned against the counter, one eyebrow arched. "How come it's perfectly okay for you to tell me I'm not the kind of man you'd date, but when I say it about you, you get offended?"

"It's a character flaw. I have a lot of them, so you don't want to be around me."

"I don't, huh?"

"You don't. And you should stop touching my neck, too."

"I see." And he did. "You want me to go away because you don't trust yourself to resist me."

"I can almost feel your ego sucking the air out of the room."

"Let me ask you a question. If the first time you ever met me was the day I did the safety class, would that have changed things?" When she hesitated, he smiled. "Be honest."

"Okay, yes. If that was the first time I ever met you, I probably would have already gotten you to ask me out while making you think it was your idea." She held up her hand to signal she wasn't finished. "*But*, I can't forget the version of you I met in the woods."

"You do realize that was the tail end of a two-week vacation, right? Just me, my dog and my dad in a cabin in the woods?"

"I get that. It's not so much the appearance that's the issue. It's the fact you obviously love being outside and doing all that outdoorsy stuff. Hunting and fishing and playing in the mud and all that."

He laughed. "Playing in the mud?"

"You know what I mean. The four-wheeling and all that."

"I love being outside, yes. I didn't become a game warden accidentally. As a matter of fact, I really don't like being inside at all. The only good reason to be in a house is indoor plumbing, heat and not having mosquitoes attacking your ass while you're having sex."

"You couldn't pay me to have sex outside." She paused, then cleared her throat. "Of course, you can't pay me to have sex anywhere because I'm not a hooker. It would be awkward if I was since you're a law enforcement officer. Trust me, the new game warden citing the town librarian for prostitution would probably be the biggest scandal in Whitford history."

"I love the way you babble when you're nervous. It's cute."

"Cute?" She made a sour face. "If I agree, can this conversation be over?"

"Yup."

"Fine. I'll go on a date with you. *Your* kind of date."

Oh, the sweet thrill of victory. "Awesome. Be ready to go about four-thirty."

"That's a little early for supper, isn't it? And the library's open until five."

"In the morning. Tomorrow morning. Four-thirty a.m." The way her eyes widened made him chuckle. He knew she was going to balk, but he was counting on her pride to keep her from backing out entirely.

"I have to work."

"I have tomorrow off and you'll be back in plenty of time to get ready, especially since you don't have to work until ten. Which must be nice, by the way."

She laughed on her way out the door. "You're probably going to want to take that nap if you're getting up before four-thirty."

"I'll be ready. Don't be late."

When she was gone, he looked down at Bear. "Don't look at me like that. It's just one date."

ELEVEN

THE LAST TIME Hailey remembered being awake—deliberately and fully clothed—at four-thirty in the morning, she'd been in college. And it had been a case of still up rather than got up.

It wasn't her best time, that was for sure. And Matt hadn't given her any clues as to where they were going, so she'd spent ten minutes glaring at her closet over the rim of her coffee mug. They probably weren't going dancing or to a movie before dawn. Knowing Matt, it involved being outside, so she settled for jeans.

Bundled into a fleece pullover, hat and gloves to ward off the early morning chill, she stood at her counter and drank coffee until she heard Matt's truck start. Then, because the idea of hanging her naked ass over a log to pee was nothing short of ludicrous, she went to the bathroom again.

He was just pulling up to the curb in front when Hailey walked out of her house. She wiggled the handle to make sure the door was locked, and then walked toward Matt's truck. She liked that he got out and walked around to open her door for her. And he'd either cleaned his truck last night or he was the neatest guy she'd ever ridden shotgun with. There was more tech equipment than she'd seen in other trucks, but not so much as a gas receipt in the console.

"No travel mug?" he asked once he was in the driver's seat.

"I figure there's a good chance there's no indoor plumbing where we're going."

"And yet you're here anyway."

"I said I would."

He grinned and put the truck in gear. "It'll be worth it. I promise. Well, as long as we don't get stood up."

"Whoa. Stood up? I'm willing to put up with *you* at freaking dark o'clock, but this isn't exactly social hour for me."

"Trust me."

It was a good thing she did trust him because it wasn't long before he'd steered down a network of dirt back roads she'd never find her way out of alone. But when he pulled over in what was little more than a wide spot in a glorified cow path, she gave him a skeptical look.

"We have to go the rest of the way on foot," he said.

"It's still pretty dark out there. I mean, I'm not afraid of the dark or anything, but I think we know I'm not exactly at my best in the wilderness."

"This is hardly the wilderness."

He didn't laugh at her, but she could hear the

amusement in his voice and it got her back up a little. Maybe she wasn't going to win a Miss Rugged Outdoors pageant any time soon, but she wasn't some hothouse flower, either.

She was already out by the time he walked around the truck, and she plastered what she hoped was an optimistic smile on her face. It was early, though, so she couldn't be sure.

He had a backpack slung over his arm and, after locking the truck, he held out his other hand. "Ready?"

She slid her hand into his, thankful the glove would act as a buffer between her skin and his. It was one thing to acknowledge to herself they had sexual chemistry, but holding hands seemed so… intimate. Romantic.

"How come you didn't bring Bear? It seems like a walk in the woods would be right up his alley, no matter what ungodly hour it is."

"He's a great dog—probably the best I'll ever be blessed with—but he's still a dog. You'll see."

It was eerie, walking through the woods while it was still too dark to see into the trees around them, but Matt's fingers laced through hers gave her comfort. He walked the barely there path with confidence, occasionally pulling on her hand to guide her around a hole or rock, or warn her of an exposed root.

But when the path came to a dead end at a rock

face, she decided she'd let him steer the ship long enough.

"Nice walk, but I guess you took a wrong turn somewhere. If we head back now, we can call dibs on the first pot of coffee at the diner."

He pointed up toward the top. "I didn't take a wrong turn. Up you go."

"I draw the line at scaling cliff faces before breakfast."

Raising his arm over his head, Matt set the backpack on top of the rock. "Cliff face? Really?"

"Fine. A very small cliff."

"Put your foot there." He pointed to a crack in the boulder. "Grab the lip of the rock and then swing your leg up and over."

"Maybe it's not Mt. Katahdin, but I'm not as tall as you."

"I'll give you a boost if you need one."

Hailey put her hands on her hips. "Did you drag me out here at the butt crack of dawn just to get your hands on my ass?"

The innocent wide-eyed look was ruined by the tilting corners of his mouth. "Pretty drastic measures, don't you think?"

A little, since they both knew if he put his hands on her ass on any given day, she wouldn't push him away. Not hard, anyway. "You go first."

"No, ma'am. Trust me, you'd rather have me give

you a boost from below than drag you up over the edge by your wrists."

"There's no way around it?"

"No, and daylight's coming."

With a melodramatic sigh, Hailey lifted her leg to shove the toe of her sneaker into the crack. After a couple of big hops, she was able to grab the edge of the boulder, and then she tried to figure out how to get her other leg up there.

She'd never been so self-conscious about her ass in all her life. It was right there, just waiting for Matt to give it a boost, and she had no doubt he was checking it out.

"Need that boost now?"

"No." She stretched her leg out and up, trying to catch her heel on the rock. What she was going to do then, she had no idea, but she hoped she'd figure it out.

"How about now?"

She had no choice. "Fine."

To her surprise, he didn't take advantage of the opportunity to grab her butt. Instead, he put his hands at her waist and lifted. A panicked scramble that almost included an accidental kick to his head later, Hailey was on top of the boulder. After an embarrassingly few seconds, Matt joined her without even breaking a sweat.

Hailey handed him his backpack, but her attention was on the view in front of her. In the dim, early light, she could make out a marshy pond surrounded by tall grasses and scrubby trees.

"Move over a sec."

She shifted to the edge of the rock and watched Matt pull a thick fleece blanket from his bag. He spread it over the rock, then patted it. Once she was comfortable, he pulled out a Thermos and poured coffee into the steel cup.

She took a sip and almost moaned. There were gallons of coffee in her near future. Just as soon as she was someplace with a bathroom.

"Look," Matt whispered, pointing off into the distance.

She tried to focus on where his finger was pointing and, when she saw them, she let out a hushed gasp. A moose wandered to the edge of the water and lowered her head to drink. Behind her, two lanky calves wandered, plucking at the brush.

"Are they twins?" She kept her voice low so she wouldn't spook them.

"Yeah. There are a lot of twins this year. That means food is plentiful and the overall health of the herd is good."

Hailey watched the mother and her babies, awed by how strangely beautiful they were. They were goofy looking animals, but here in the early morning light, they looked almost majestic.

She'd seen moose before, of course. Their part of the state boasted a dense moose population and attracted tourists hoping to catch a glimpse of one. She'd dodged a few over the course of her driving years, and sometimes one would stand in a clearing, causing cars to line the sides of the roads so families could take pictures.

But she'd never been moved by them before. Here in their world, they felt safe and secure, and looked totally at ease. They didn't rush, but lingered for a long time, foraging and drinking.

Without thinking, she slid her hand into Matt's and squeezed. "I never thought I'd say this, but they're beautiful."

"They are." He squeezed back. "It's already getting warm, so they'll head back into the woods soon. And the bugs will be looking for breakfast."

"Just a few more minutes," she whispered.

Maybe walking through the woods to a remote marsh would have landed somewhere in the bottom two percent of dates she'd like to go on, but she wasn't ready for it to be over yet.

MATT SIPPED THE coffee Hailey had handed back to him, watching the cow and her twins forage. He'd been out here a few times over the last couple of weeks and he was thankful mama moose hadn't chosen today to change their routine.

He'd banked on Hailey not laughing at him outright when he brought her to the rock or, even worse, storming back to the truck, but he was pleasantly surprised by her willingness to sit quietly and watch the small family roam. Sitting on the fleece-covered rock and holding her hand was one of the best mornings he'd had in a long time.

"I think they're leaving," she whispered.

"They're going to go back into the woods a bit, though they won't actually go too far, I don't imagine. This is a sweet spot." He offered her more coffee and, when she shook her head, he screwed the cup back on the Thermos and tucked it in the bag.

"I'll get down first," he told her. Not that he thought she'd jump, but he didn't want to take any chances with her.

Once he was back on the ground, she turned and sat with her legs dangling over the edge. She looked down at the ground and then back at him. "This might hurt."

"I'm not going to let you fall."

Reaching up as high as he could, he urged her to move forward until he caught her around the waist. With her hands on his shoulders, he had to take a step back to brace himself, but he could take her weight.

He lowered her slowly, so her body slid down his until they were eye to eye. "I told you I wouldn't let you fall."

When some of the strain lifted, he knew her feet were on the ground, but she stayed on her tiptoes with her hands still on his shoulders. "If I thought you would, I'd still be sitting up there, trying to figure out how to get down."

His fingers tightened on her waist, and he could tell by the way she looked into his eyes that she knew he was going to kiss her. He paused, his mouth not an inch from her lips, to see if she'd pull back.

She didn't, so he closed the space between them. Her lips were soft and he kissed her tentatively, testing her reaction. When her hands slid from his shoulders to the back of his neck, holding him to her, he deepened the kiss. Their breath mingled as he caught her bottom lip between his teeth for a second, and then he slid his tongue over hers.

He sucked in a breath when she turned the tables, nipping at his lip while her fingernails bit into his neck. He wanted to back her against the boulder, her legs wrapped around his waist, or lay her down on the mossy forest floor, but he restrained himself. He savored the feel of her mouth against his and her hands on his body.

Before his self-control totally left him, he broke off the kiss. His hands slid up her back and he smiled at her slightly dazed expression. He probably looked about the same because it had been some kiss.

"This is the best date I've ever been on at four-thirty in the morning," she said, the corners of her mouth quirking upward.

"Me, too." He pulled the blanket off the rock and shoved it back into the backpack. After slinging it over his arm, he took her hand and they walked slowly back to the truck.

Once they were in, he started the engine, but the last thing he wanted to do was take her home. "Want to go get some breakfast?"

"When you say *get* instead of *have,* do you mean somewhere other than your kitchen?"

"We may not get dibs on the first pot, but the diner does a good breakfast."

"Oh." She hesitated, avoiding eye contact as if she had something to say he wouldn't like hearing.

He put the truck in gear. "Hey, if you don't want to go to breakfast in public with Jeremiah Johnson, just say so."

"I'm sorry about that." Her grin disarmed him. "You have to admit you were looking pretty rough that day."

"I'd been working my way through the storage shed that everybody in the family throws stuff into, but never takes back out. It was pretty gross, I admit. Now, you admit why you don't want to have breakfast with me."

"You've only lived here a couple of weeks, so you might not get how the town works yet. If you and I go to the diner for breakfast together, we'll instantly be a couple."

Even though he tried to keep the defensiveness stamped down, her words hit a nerve. "So you don't want people to know we were on a date?"

"That's not what I'm saying." She gave him a look that clearly broadcast her opinion he was being an idiot. "You're going out of your way to be offended by things I'm not actually saying. Stop it."

Maybe she was right. It took a few tight turns to get the truck facing the right direction and he drove slowly back to the main road. "Okay. Assuming I'm okay with the good people of Whitford jumping to conclusions, would you like to have breakfast at the diner with me?"

"I'd love to have breakfast with you."

OF COURSE THE Trailside Diner had to be busy when Hailey and Matt walked in. It was probably her imagination, but it sure seemed like everybody paused for a fraction of a second, noting the fact they'd come in together early in the morning.

She'd be getting a few phone calls later in the day, and it wouldn't surprise her at all if Tori ended up at the library.

"There's a booth over there," Matt said, pointing toward the back corner. His hand rested at the small of her back and she saw that people were noticing the gesture.

But if he didn't care, neither would she. She went to the booth and slid onto one bench while he sat across from her. Liz acted the professional when she brought menus and the coffeepot, but she managed to give Hailey a *what is going on* look when Matt wasn't looking. Hailey ignored it.

She went for a couple of scrambled eggs and toast, but she wasn't surprised when Matt ordered the steak and eggs. They fixed their coffees, then chatted about the moose for a while. He was not only knowledgeable about them, but she could hear affection in his voice, which made her smile.

Forcing herself to remain oblivious to the sideways glances and whispers happening around her, she focused only on Matt. And Matt's mouth. The memory of the kiss in the woods was almost as sweet as the kiss itself, and she savored it. His mouth had been gentle at first, but it wasn't long before he was taking her breath away.

Thankfully it hadn't gone any further than that. She wasn't sure what she would have done if he hadn't ended it when he did. Sex in the great outdoors had never been on her list of things she ever wanted to do, but at that moment she might have considered it.

If they had been inside, though, all bets would have been off after that kiss. When a simple touching of lips felt that way, it was hard not to imagine how good sex with the man would feel. A sense of inevitability and anticipation washed over her. She had no doubt it was going to happen. A short, enjoyable detour on the road to her true destination.

"Am I dribbling coffee?"

Jerked away from those very pleasant thoughts, she frowned. "What?"

"You're staring at my mouth."

"Sorry. Just lost in thought."

That delicious mouth curved into a suggestive smile. "Nice thoughts?"

She was saved from having to respond to that by Liz's arrival with their plates. Whether it was the fresh air or the calories her body was burning through being all revved up for the man across from her, Hailey was starving. She dumped ketchup on her scrambled eggs, ignoring Matt's grimace, and dug in.

After a few bites of his breakfast, he took a sip of his coffee and then smiled at her. "The food in this town totally makes up for having a crazy neighbor."

She laughed. "Hey, not every woman will crawl through a doggy door in her pajamas. You're lucky to live next door to me."

"It has its moments." He winked, then cut into his steak. "So tell me how you came to be a librarian."

"When I was a kid, I loved books, but I always wished our library was more fun. I should be embarrassed to admit it, but I spent a lot of time daydreaming about how I'd run the library if it was mine."

"My sisters practically lived at the library when we were young. My dad wasn't as big on reading as an activity for boys, so I used to sneak their library books into my room and read them."

She held up her hand. "Don't even get me started on gender bias and reading. I could rant for hours."

"Since you obviously went away to college, how did you end up back at the Whitford library?"

Between bites, Hailey told him about college and how getting her degree had coincided with the previous librarian's retirement. "Not only was I finally going to be a librarian, but it was *my* library. Basically, it was a dream come true. Except for the paperwork."

"They never warn you about the paperwork."

They lingered over breakfast and coffee for so long, Hailey was surprised when Liz asked her if the library was closed. "You only have a half hour, you know."

"That's not enough time to go home and come back, is it?" Matt gave her a sheepish look. "I'm sorry. Do you have your keys? I can just drop you off unless you need something at home. Otherwise, I think the town will survive you being a few minutes late."

Hailey thought about it for a moment. Her keys were in her pocket and there was no reason she couldn't wear what she had on. Since it was only her, the dress code at the library tended to be rather casual, anyway. "I could go right to the library. And I can find somebody to give me a ride home."

"I'll pick you up. Five, right?"

"Yeah. You don't have to, though. I can find a ride."

"I want to." He pulled cash out of his wallet to cover the bill and tip, then waved away the money she pulled from her back pocket.

When they pulled into the library parking lot, he left the truck running, but he still got out to open her door. "I'll be back at five to get you."

"I had a good time. It'll be a long day, but I'm glad you asked me to go."

"Me, too." He kissed her goodbye, keeping it quick. "I'll see you later."

They gave her five minutes to get settled, and then a text message from Tori popped over a caller ID screen telling her Paige was calling. She closed the text from Tori and answered Paige's call. "Was I even out the door before Liz called you this time?"

"I doubt it. Tell me."

"I'm busy right now."

"No, you're not. Did you spend the night with him? I mean, why else would you be out having breakfast with him, right?"

"I did not spend the night with him. At four-thirty we went out in the woods to watch a moose and her twin calves at a marsh."

Paige laughed. "Sure, I believe that."

"It's true. And after we left the woods, we went to breakfast and then he dropped me off at the library."

"That's it?" Her friend sounded deflated. "You were moose watching?"

"Well, and kissing."

"I knew it. Good kissing?"

"Very good kissing." Kissing she'd be thinking about all day now.

"When are you going to see him again?" Paige asked, and then she made quiet shushing sounds Hailey assumed were intended for Sarah, who she could hear starting to fuss in the background.

"Well, aside from the fact I live next door to him and will probably see him every day for the foreseeable future, he has to pick me up after work because he dropped me off."

Sarah was working up to a full screech now. "Damn. Poor thing doesn't feel so hot today and she won't let me put her down. But I'm going to call you tomorrow and I want to hear everything."

"Okay. I can have him drop me off at your house if you need a break, you know."

"Thank you, but Rose just pulled in the driveway and Mitch will be home later tonight. You have fun, if you know what I mean."

"Funny. Try to get some rest."

After the phone call, she pulled up the text from Tori. *I told you so.*

Hailey rolled her eyes. *You told me I'd have breakfast with Matt?*

The door opened and a few older women walked

in. They were forming a crocheting club and intended to make granny square blankets to raise money for the town's Santa Fund. They'd asked to meet at the library, where there were no husbands or chores demanding their attention, and she'd welcomed them. One of the women had even renewed her library card, which had expired in 1976.

Her phone buzzed, but she waited until she had the ladies settled before she gave it her attention.

Smart-ass. Did you spend the night?

No. Early morning date. Breakfast.

Who has early morning dates?

It was a valid question. *Game wardens, I guess. We watched moose.*

There was a long pause before Tori's reply came back. *Is this a prank?*

Nope.

Put a sign on the door you're closing for lunch one day this week.

She'd known that was coming. Tori worked at home, but she claimed she worked best on a second shift schedule. So she didn't mind working mornings and she could do lunch dates, but she was usually unavailable from early afternoon until hours most of them considered past their bedtimes.

Maybe. I'll let you know.

With Paige and Tori satisfied, Hailey turned her attention to work and willed the clock to move. It did, but slowly, until finally she could turn off the lights and close the door.

His truck was in the parking lot, just as he'd said it would be. Once she'd secured the library doors and unlocked the night drop box, he got out of the truck and opened the passenger door for her.

"How'd it go?"

"Slow day today." She climbed up onto the seat. "Except the rush to get details about our breakfast together. But that died out fairly early. They probably got bored and made up their own stories."

He shook his head and closed her door. Once he was buckled in his own seat, he put the truck in reverse. "Does it bother you that everybody's talking about you today?"

She laughed. "Not particularly. I've lived here my entire life. This isn't the first time I've been the subject of conversation. What did you do today?"

"Maintenance stuff. Cleaned my weapons. Changed the oil in my quad and stuff like that. Laundry, which is my least favorite thing to do."

Once they were parked in his driveway, he turned to face her. "I've got chicken and gravy in the slow cooker. If you want to come in for dinner, I can cook up some white rice to put it on."

Hailey suspected if she went inside with Matt, they were going to do more than eat dinner. The kiss had been the end of denying there was serious chemistry between them, and if she didn't put distance back between them, they were going to end up in bed together.

But, remembering back to the unfortunate horny monkey analogy, there was no reason she couldn't climb this tree, and then climb down and find another.

"Hailey?"

"Sounds good. I'd love to."

TWELVE

HAILEY HAD BEEN in Matt's kitchen, of course, but she hadn't seen the rest of the house. Because they went in through the front door, she found herself in the living room. It was sparsely decorated, not counting the shelving unit bearing what looked like the entire electronics section of a department store and a huge television.

A large brown leather couch dominated the room, with one end obviously belonging to Bear. The leather was pretty beat up and scratched, and the cushion had an indentation that would match a curled up black Lab.

There were still boxes here and there, so obviously he wasn't done unpacking. Hopefully some of the stuff in the boxes was meant to be hung on the walls because they were totally bare. She didn't like a lot of clutter, but his house was still lacking some personal touches.

They said hello to Bear, of course. Even though Matt had been home most of the day, he was greeted as if it had been days since the dog last saw him. Then it was Hailey's turn to get the same treatment before he took off into the backyard.

Matt stepped up behind her, his arms wrapping around her waist. "I've been thinking about you all day."

"I stamped the wrong return date in about a dozen books because my mind was on our date and I forgot to change it."

"I liked kissing you." His breath was hot against the back of her neck and Hailey knew he was doing it deliberately. "I want to kiss you again."

He did, pressing his lips to the sweet spot his breath had warmed. She shuddered, her hands sliding over his forearms. With her back to him, there was nothing she could do but surrender to the sensation of his light kisses over her skin.

When he ran his tongue from the base of her neck up almost to her hairline, she moaned and leaned backward so her body was pressed against his. She could feel his erection through their jeans and she rocked back against it.

"Pretty frisky for a first date," she murmured.

"Mmm. Technically, this might be our second date. And if you count our walk in the woods and the OHRV safety class, this could be our fourth date." He pulled back a little. "I feel like I've wanted you for a long time, but we can slow down."

She gripped his arms, preventing him from backing up too far. Being rescued in the wilderness probably didn't count as a date, but he was right about one thing. This thing between them had been building since they met. "I think fourth dates are a good time for frisky."

The chime sounded, and Bear wandered into the living room. While it didn't kill the mood, he was definitely a distraction.

"Come upstairs with me," he murmured against her neck.

She nodded, and he took her hand to lead her toward the stairs. Nerves danced in her stomach, but there was no way she was backing out now. She wanted this man—had wanted him for a while if she was honest with herself—and she was going to have him.

"Stay," Matt told Bear, who jumped up on the couch and lay down.

He guided her into his room and kicked the door closed behind him. His mouth came down on hers hard, all the hunger that had been building between them evident in his kiss. She raked her fingernails over his back before grabbing the hem of his T-shirt and lifting it.

He broke off the kiss long enough for her to pull the shirt over his head, and then his lips were on hers. His tongue slid over hers and he backed her up against the door. The kiss grew more demanding as her hands ran over his abs and up his back.

"I have wanted you so badly," he said against her mouth.

Her top went next and he pulled down the cups of

her bra to expose her breasts to his gaze and to his touch. Bending his head, he ran his tongue over her nipples before sucking hard enough so she gasped. The door was hard against her back and she had nowhere to go as he lavished attention on her neck and breasts.

When her knees went weak, he went back to kissing her mouth and turned her toward the bed. She undid the button and zipper of her jeans, then did the same for his. Her sneakers, she kicked off, and then he was pushing her backward onto his bed.

His hand slid between her legs, the heel pressing against her through denim, and she arched her hips. He increased the pressure while leaning forward to kiss his way from her stomach to her mouth, stopping to swirl his tongue around her nipples.

She wanted more so she shoved the waist of her jeans down, urging him to take them off.

Matt stood and did just that, peeling her jeans and underwear off and tossing them aside, followed by her socks. She felt slightly self-conscious as he stared at her, his gaze roving over her body, but there was so much heat in his eyes, it passed quickly.

He dropped his jeans and boxer briefs, stepping out of them, and then he reached down to pull off his socks. When he joined her on the bed, his naked body sliding over hers, she sighed and wrapped her arms around him.

There were more kisses and she lost herself in

the way his mouth claimed hers—possessive and demanding without being punishing or aggressive. She'd never experienced kisses like them before and she couldn't get enough.

He explored all of her, his hands and mouth roving over her as if looking for more places as sensitive as the back of her neck. The hollow at the base of her throat. The palm of her hand. Behind her knees. When he found a spot that made her squirm, he was merciless. Licking and gentle bites drove her almost out of her mind, until she reached down and pulled him back up.

He grinned at her, his hand sliding over her stomach and dipping between her legs. "What's the matter?"

She barely had enough breath to answer him. "You're killing me."

"I can't help it. You're delicious and I want to make it last."

"You can have seconds. I just…"

He stroked her clit with his thumb as he slid a finger inside of her. "You just what?"

A growl of frustration escaped her as she lifted her hips against his hand. "Matt, please."

There was a crinkle of a condom wrapper and then he leaned onto his forearms, one hand on each side of her head. Looking into her eyes, he reached between their bodies and guided his shaft into her.

She was ready for him, and she sighed as he filled

her with slow, steady strokes. When he was completely buried in her, he paused. He trembled under her touch, and she trailed her fingertips down his back.

He kissed her, his teeth closing over her bottom lip, and then started moving again.

"You feel so good," he murmured against her mouth.

She put her hands on his ass, pulling him into her. "Faster."

He lifted himself off her and hooked his arms behind her knees. His pace quickened and she reached up to brace her hands against the wall, resisting so each thrust drove harder into her.

The orgasm took her breath away and she arched her back. Matt pounded into her as she came, and then his body jerked. He groaned as his orgasm wracked his body, and then released her legs as it subsided to tremors. She wrapped her legs around his waist and held him close as she tried to catch her breath.

After a few minutes, he rolled off her and leaned over the edge of the bed to the trash can. Then he collapsed on his back next to her and laced his fingers through hers. He lay there for a long time, until she started to wonder if he'd fallen asleep. She didn't have the energy to lift her head to check, though, so she squeezed his hand.

He squeezed back. "I think we do have something in common."

"I think you're right."

Matt rolled so he was facing her. "Go out for a ride with me."

"Now?"

"No. Not now. Maybe tomorrow after work. I'm talking about four-wheeling, by the way. I think you'd like it."

She wasn't so sure. "I rode once with a boyfriend in high school. He hit a bump and I fell off the back. If I'd been sober, it probably would have hurt."

He rolled his eyes. "I'm sure you've outgrown being stupid. And it would be fun. Andy Miller has a two-up machine I bet I could borrow."

"Two-up?"

"It's designed for two people. It has a passenger seat with its own handholds and footrests. I bet if I tell Rose Davis I want to take you out in the woods but I'm not supposed to have you on my government-issued quad, she'd give me the keys to Andy's so fast he wouldn't even know what happened."

She slapped his chest. "You wouldn't dare."

"Dare what? To borrow his quad?"

"Get Rose involved. It's bad enough the entire town thinks we're sleeping together because we had breakfast at the diner."

"Which is a fairly ironic thing to say when we're naked in bed."

She grinned. "Their speculation was premature."

"Mmm." He nuzzled her neck and slid his hand

up her stomach to cup her breast. "I'm glad that was the only thing that was premature."

"Didn't you promise me supper?"

"Ten more minutes."

MATT SET TWO dishes of chicken and gravy over white rice on the table and then sat down across from Hailey. She had the look of a very well-satisfied woman and he'd be lying if he said that didn't boost his ego a little.

"Why are you staring at me?"

"I didn't mean to. You just look especially pretty right now."

She blushed, shaking her head. "Thank you. But I'm starving and this smells delicious, so what comes next might not be as pretty to watch."

Since he'd worked up an appetite himself, he didn't mind at all. They ate in silence for a few minutes, or almost silence, since Bear was eating, too. The dog's manners as he worked his way through his bowl left a little something to be desired.

"So you up to a ride tomorrow?" he asked.

She paused, fork halfway to her mouth. "You were serious about that?"

"Of course."

"Oh." She took the bite of chicken and chewed slowly, probably trying to buy herself time to think. "Seeing the twin moose was very cool, but you seem to be forgetting I'm not really an outside kind of girl."

"It's fun. And four-wheelers are becoming a big

thing for Whitford. Don't you think you should at least see the trails?"

"I don't think the librarian having firsthand knowledge of the trail system is going to make or break Whitford, but nice try."

"How about I just want you to go out riding with me?"

She looked at him, her head tilted slightly as if she was trying to figure him out. "Like another date?"

"Sure." Whether that would be a plus or a minus in her eyes, he couldn't guess. "I honestly think you'll have fun or I wouldn't have asked you."

"Why tomorrow after work? Why not on the weekend?"

"I have court tomorrow, which almost guarantees I'll be home on time, if not a little early."

She frowned. "Court?"

"I'm not in trouble. I have to testify on a couple of cases. It's not my favorite part of the job, but it means I'm not available for calls."

When she started moving rice around on her plate without eating it, he got the feeling her mood had taken a turn for the serious, but he wasn't sure why. He didn't want things to turn serious. The morning had been fun. The sex had been *really* fun. He'd like to see it go on the same way.

"This dating thing…it's just about having fun, right?" She wouldn't meet his eyes. "Nothing too serious?"

Because he wasn't the kind of guy she was looking to get serious with. It was a small blow, but not too painful because he wasn't looking to do serious, either. He'd known the sexual chemistry between them was too strong to be ignored and, after their kiss that morning, he'd known—or at least desperately hoped—sex was in their near future. But in the long term future, they were both looking for something different.

"I like having fun," he said. "You like having fun. No reason we can't have fun together for a while. Dating's just a convenient word, I guess."

"Okay. In that case, I *guess* it wouldn't hurt me to go four-wheeling with you. At least I hope it won't hurt, anyway."

He leaned back in his chair and pushed his empty plate away. "You won't get hurt. I'll call the lodge in the morning and see if I can borrow the two-up from Andy."

About the time she took her last bite of the chicken and rice, Matt realized there was some awkwardness dead ahead. Was she expecting to spend the night with him, or was she going to go home? Since they'd just agreed they weren't really dating, but were just having fun together, he guessed she wouldn't stay, but he couldn't be sure.

"That was delicious," she said. "I hate to eat and run because it's rude, but I need to get home. I will never go on a four-thirty in the morning date again."

He laughed and got up to dump their plates in the sink. "Duly noted."

"So…thanks, I guess."

"I feel like I should walk you home."

She laughed and shook her head. "I think I can make it next door without getting lost."

"That's not what I meant. It's the gentlemanly thing to do, you know."

"It's dumb for you to put on your shoes and get Bear all excited to go for a walk when you could hit my house with a rock." She walked over and looped her arms around his neck.

Kissing her made him rethink her going home, but she was right. A four-thirty date followed by an evening of great sex made for a long day and his alarm would go off early. "I'm going to watch until I'm sure you're inside. Just so you know."

She smiled and then put her sneakers on without bothering to tie them. Then she kissed him again, rubbed Bear's head and went out the back door. He followed her as far as the deck, then watched her walk across their yards.

He laughed when she flashed her outside light twice, then waited for Bear to do his business.

It would have been nice to have her in his bed when he slid between the sheets, but at least he knew where they stood. Nothing too serious, but the potential for a whole lot of fun. It didn't sound like a bad deal, even if it meant sleeping alone.

THIRTEEN

MATT LEANED AGAINST the Kowalskis' barn, arms folded across his chest, and watched Hailey put her helmet on for what had to be the seventh or eighth time. At the rate they were going, he'd be too old to drive a quad by the time she was ready to hit the trail.

"You know what the worst part is?" Andy Miller asked. He was also holding up the barn wall, watching the show. "About the time she gets that helmet just right, she's going to have to pee again."

Matt sighed. "I wouldn't bet against it."

Apparently, her hair was the problem. She started with it in a high ponytail, but that made a lump that was uncomfortable under her helmet. She tried a lower ponytail, but that had the same problem. She took the elastic out, but her hair plastered around her face when she put the helmet on and she didn't like that. Then came gathering her hair at the base of her neck with the elastic, but when she pulled on the helmet, it pulled her hair at the crown.

Finally, Rose had come outside, sat her down on the porch and done some kind of fancy braid that held all of her hair while remaining flat. Now it seemed like they might be on the right track. When she had it settled on her head and gave him a thumbs up, he walked over to her and did the buckle under her chin.

"You finally ready?"

She nodded, then held up a finger. "I'm going to go pee one more time."

"Do *not* take that helmet off," he called after her.

Andy was shaking his head. "What do you think the chances are that girl knows how to pee over a log?"

"My plan is to give her enough water to keep her hydrated, but not enough to make her have to go." He was mostly kidding. "Thanks again for letting me borrow your machine. I have a sneaking suspicion we won't have it very long."

"It's not a problem. Rosie doesn't ride with me very often, but I like having the option. Half the time I go out, I take one of the boys' machines because they have the tool racks and cargo boxes on them, anyway."

"You guys have done one hell of a job here."

Andy beamed. "I think it was Mitch who first suggested trying to get the four-wheeler traffic to the lodge so they could be open year round instead of just during the snow. All of the kids were behind it, but once Josh wrapped his head around it, he was all in."

Matt saw Hailey come out of the house, thankfully with her helmet still on. "I guess she might be ready. Finally."

Once she was settled on the seat behind him, Matt waved to Andy and then headed toward the trail. He kept it slow enough so Hailey wouldn't get bounced around too much, but he wanted to go fast enough to make it fun, too.

He heard her laugh a couple of times, which he took as a good sign. Then, in a particularly rocky section, she dug her fingernails into his back so hard he was pretty sure there would be holes in his shirt. If not blood.

"Use your handholds," he yelled. Not that he was mad, but with the engine sound and both of them in helmets, it was the only way to be heard.

"Sorry!"

The first time he stopped was in a clearing next to a brook and he had her keep her helmet on. He just wanted her to relax her muscles a little because the trail he was going to take was a little more rugged and it took some effort to not get bounced off the back of a quad.

She did great, though. Every once in a while she'd try holding on to him instead of the handholds, but she didn't try to puncture him again. The hill they had to climb made her nervous. He could tell by the way her knees gripped his thighs, as if she was on a horse she thought might buck her off.

The clearing he pulled into this time had a decent view, and the club had put in a picnic table. He helped her unbuckle the helmet and kept a very straight face when she pulled it off and all of the loose wisps that were escaping the braid stood out around her face.

He didn't think she'd appreciate knowing that was going on, even if bad hair went hand in hand with women and helmets.

"It's very quiet here," she said, probably trying to fill the silence.

"Do you want some water?" He pulled the storage compartment under the passenger seat.

"Just a sip." She took the bottle, grimacing at her hands. "Is my face as dirty as my hands? I feel really dirty."

"You're four-wheeling. You're supposed to get dirty."

"You're four-wheeling. I'm just sightseeing." She grinned and took a long sip of the water.

He thought she looked sexy as hell with a couple of smudges of dirt on her face and her hair all mussed up. He stepped close to her, sliding his hand over her hip. "You know, one of my favorite things about being out in the woods is the privacy. There's nobody around for miles."

"Oh, no you don't. I am not having sex with you in the woods." She put her hand on his chest and pushed. "There is zero chance of that happening."

"Yeah, I didn't think you would."

"Is that disappointment I hear?" She put her hands on her hips. "Did you actually think there was a chance I'd get naked out here in the dirt? With leaves and bugs and sticks and…dirt?"

"You don't have to get totally naked. Or touch the dirt at all." Her skeptical look made him chuckle. "I could demonstrate if you want."

"I'm not having sex with you outside."

"Sex with you inside was pretty damn good, so I suppose I'll live."

She smiled at him. "The four-wheeling part isn't as bad as I expected, if that makes you feel any better."

"It does make me feel better knowing the time you spend with me doesn't *totally* suck." It wasn't a glowing endorsement, but he'd take it. "Do you want to drive?"

"No." She laughed. "I'm fine riding on the back, thank you. But I have to pee."

"Any chance at all you'll pee in the woods?"

She shook her head, not even considering the idea. "No."

"I didn't think so." He chuckled and handed over her helmet. "We'll head back now. We're not too far out."

"Okay. And if you could not hit any bumps, that would be great."

THE FOLLOWING DAY, it didn't take a lot of coaxing on their part to talk Hailey into closing the library for lunch and heading to the diner to see Tori and Liz.

On the off chance she would come, Hailey sent a text to Paige, too, telling her the plan. Surely four women could handle one baby in public, even if one of them was supposed to be working.

When she arrived at the Trailside Diner, Liz and Paige were already in a booth in the back, with Sarah's baby seat on the bench beside her mother. Hailey slid in next to Liz and waved at Tori.

"I'm starving," she said, reaching for a menu, but changing her mind. She knew everything on the menu already.

"Great sex will do that to a woman," Liz said.

Tori set four empty coffee mugs on the table with a thump. "So will skipping breakfast."

"Yeah, but she's smiling and you're slamming cups around. Hailey's having sex."

"If this is the only reason you talked me into coming, I'm going back to work," Hailey said, though she wasn't sure she'd follow through on the threat since she now had a cup of coffee sitting in front of her.

Tori poured decaf for Paige and then fixed the fourth mug for herself. "I'm going to leave this on the edge of the table and drink it as I can. I might also eat off your plates. You've been warned."

They ordered food and then sat back to catch up. It quickly became obvious they were a lot more interested in what Hailey was up to than sharing what was going on in their own lives.

"Not pregnant," Liz said.

Tori shrugged. "Work. More work."

"I have an almost two-month-old daughter," Paige said. "She is pretty much the sum total of my life at the moment. Although I did take a shower without Rosie being there. Progress."

Then they all focused on Hailey, who tried to play dumb. "Fran's agreed to sponsor the ice cream party for the summer reading program."

"That's funny," Liz said. "How are things between you and Matt? Really?"

She shrugged. "Well, as you said, I'm a smiling, starving woman. Other than that, nothing's really changed."

Liz shook her head. "Sex changes things, whether you think so right off or not."

"He's fun. He's hot." Hailey stirred her coffee. "Is he Mr. Right for me? Still no."

"I heard you and Matt went out four-wheeling yesterday," Paige said. "Be honest. Did you have sex in the woods?"

"No! Really? In the woods would be like the last place I'd want to have sex."

"Public bathroom," Tori said.

"Supply closet," Liz suggested.

Paige added, "Walk-in freezer."

"Fine. It could be worse, but it's on my personal bottom five places. I think this is the Saturday his parents are coming to visit."

They all leaned toward her, disbelief on their

faces, but it was Paige who spoke. "His parents are coming to meet you?"

"No. His parents are coming to see his new house and have a barbecue. It has nothing to do with me."

"But you'll meet them?" Tori asked.

"I doubt it. I'm just his next-door neighbor, and I may or may not even be around on Saturday."

"I have to go take care of my customers," Tori said. "You're boring me."

They laughed as she walked away, but they knew she'd be back. They had her coffee.

"Is she always this cranky?" Paige asked, and Hailey remembered that, while she simply viewed Paige and Tori as her friends, Paige was Tori's boss.

"No, she's not. And she's only being like this because it's us. If you watch her, you'll see that she's nice to everybody else."

"It's true," Liz agreed. "Everybody loves Tori. You have nothing to worry about."

"Okay. I'll stop worrying then. Now, back to Hailey." Hailey groaned, wishing their food would come so she could shove it in her mouth and not have to talk. "Why aren't you going to meet his family? You're his girlfriend, so—"

"No. I'm not his girlfriend."

"It sounds more polite than describing yourself as the neighbor lady he's banging," Liz said.

"Which is the reason I probably won't meet them. And the word girlfriend doesn't apply here. Girlfriend implies a journey. Girlfriend to fiancée to wife."

"To ex-wife." Tori was back.

"You're too young to be so cynical," Paige said.

"You haven't met my parents."

When she disappeared again, Hailey hoped it was to get their food. She'd had a toaster pastry for breakfast and she was pretty sure she'd burned that off just walking to her car. She desperately needed to take the time to make a trip to the big grocery store and stock up. Maybe Saturday, so there would be no chance of awkward introductions to Matt's family.

Tori delivered their lunches and, since it wasn't very busy and everybody was happy, Liz and Hailey scooted close so Tori could perch on the end of the bench and pick from their plates. Sarah made a couple of squawking noises, as if she had a baby radar that told her Mom was going to try to eat, but then she quieted again.

"So back to Matt," Paige said. "You're dating him and having sex with him, but we're not using the word girlfriend?"

"It's more like hanging out than dating."

Liz pointed a fry at her. "You went moose watching, which I still have a hard time believing. And you went riding on the four-wheeler."

"Exactly." Hailey wasn't sure she could make them understand. "Seeing the moose and the twins was cool, and the four-wheeling wasn't as bad as I thought it would be, but they weren't really *dates*. Not my kind of date, anyway."

"Go into the city. Dinner and a movie or something," Liz said.

"But then I'd be more like...his girlfriend." There was silence for a few seconds and she caught them making *what is she talking about* faces at each other. "Look, the fact that we're totally wrong for each other doesn't matter as much if I'm just the neighbor lady he's banging, as Liz put it. We're just burning through the sexual tension."

"Um." Paige gave her a pointed look and nodded her head toward the sleeping baby. "So were Mitch and I."

"You guys are perfect for each other, though."

"We didn't think so in the beginning."

"You should give it a chance," Liz said. "Go out on some real dates."

Hailey wasn't sure if she wasn't explaining the stumbling blocks well enough or if her friends didn't want to see them, but she didn't see any point in dragging the conversation out. She was afraid, to Matt, those *were* real dates and that was a problem for her. The other women might be convinced they had a shot, but Hailey knew when the sparks settled, they'd just be two people with nothing in common anymore.

MATT PULLED A grocery cart free from the line and pushed it toward Hailey, and then he got one for himself. "Want to race?"

"My list is longer than yours. And there are more fruits and vegetables on my list, which take longer to pick out."

"Got your excuses all ready to go, huh?"

She gave him a look and pulled her list out of her back pocket, along with a pen. "I don't need excuses because I'm not racing with you."

With a shrug to indicate it was her loss, he went into the store to see how fast he could conquer his two-page list. He not only needed staples, but he needed stuff for the barbecue the day after tomorrow. His mother and sisters would bring side dishes and probably at least one dessert, but he needed meat to throw on the grill.

After work, he'd been using bungee cords to secure empty coolers in the bed of his truck when Hailey pulled in her driveway, so he'd asked her if she needed anything at the grocery store. When she grimaced and admitted she'd been putting it off for so long she needed a *lot* of things, he'd suggested they go together and save gas. He'd also thought it would make the shopping more fun, but since she didn't want to make it interesting with a race, that remained to be seen.

She paused when they were inside. "Which end do you start on?"

"The first thing on my list is mustard."

"Really?" She leaned over to look at his list. "What kind of order is that?"

"It's the order that things popped into my head."

"You're going to do a big shopping and the first thing you think of is mustard?"

He pulled his list away so she couldn't see it anymore. "Mustard is important. Let me guess, your grocery list magically comes to you in alphabetical order?"

"I have an app on my phone for groceries. I took the time to arrange the aisles the way they are in the store, so now as I add things, they're in the order I'll find them on the shelves. I still print it out, though, because I hate when I have to keep unlocking my phone over and over while I shop. But it's all in order."

"You sound very smug about that."

She grinned. "Maybe I should agree to that race, after all."

"Ready, set, go."

"I'm not really racing," she called after him, but he didn't look back.

Only three aisles in, he made a mental note to ask her which app she was using for her grocery list. He spent more time scanning his list to see if any of the items matched the aisle he was in than he did putting things in his cart. And he'd already backtracked twice in three aisles, so it was probably a good thing they weren't racing.

He ran into her in the pasta and rice aisle. She was

looking at boxes of flavored rice, and he leaned over her shoulder. "I like the chicken flavored."

After tossing two boxes of pilaf into her cart, she gave him a sweet smile and looked at his cart. "If we *were* racing, which we're not, you'd be losing."

He snorted and kept going. By the time he'd loaded up on boxes of macaroni and cheese, because a guy couldn't have too many of those, she was gone again. He grabbed spaghetti fixings, then what looked like a lifetime supply of egg noodles. It was easy to throw meat in the Crock-Pot, then dump it over noodles at the end of a long day.

When Matt turned the corner into the canned vegetables and baked beans aisle, he saw Hailey again. She was talking to a guy who was seriously over-dressed for a trip to the grocery store. Looking at his suit and tie, with the leather shoes and perfectly styled hair, Matt knew this was the kind of guy Hailey had been waiting for.

She laughed at something the man said, and Matt's fingers clenched around the cart. Then he turned and went back the way he'd come. He could get baked beans once Hailey was finished trying to pick up Mr. Perfect in the grocery store.

His mood soured, he went about checking off everything on his list as fast as he could. He ran into Hailey a few more times and managed to give her a wave and a smart-ass comment each time, but he couldn't shake the image of how she'd been smiling at the guy in the suit.

A guy in the woods with a beard and flannel shirt must be a serial killer, but put on a suit and hit the grocery store and you were Mr. Wonderful.

Hailey must have gotten held up thumping melons or whatever in the produce aisle, because he had three-quarters of his bags in the back of the truck before she wheeled her cart out of the store.

"I guess you would have won if we'd been racing," she said.

"Yup. Since I'm already up here, just hand your bags up to me. And there's room in this cooler for your milk and the meats."

She handed the bags up to him a few at a time. Since he was standing in the bed of the truck, he had a perfect view when she paused to wave goodbye to the man in the suit, who was pushing his cart a few aisles over.

"Did you get his number?"

She handed him the last few bags, frowning. "What?"

He hopped down off the tailgate and slammed it closed. "I saw you laughing with him in the canned goods aisle, and he looks like your type. With a suit like that, he must be a great guy."

"He *is* a great guy. He's been married to one of my best friends from school since the summer after we graduated and I was laughing because she has a cold and sent him to get some groceries after work, but he doesn't know where anything is."

"Oh."

She gave him a look that clearly broadcast her feelings about him being ridiculous, then walked away to return her cart to the corral. Cursing himself for an idiot, he got in the truck and fired it up.

The awkwardness faded as they argued over which fast food drive-through to hit. It was late enough so neither of them would want to cook by the time they got home and unloaded all the groceries. She won, of course, and he ate his burger as they drove back to Whitford.

"This is the weekend your parents are coming to visit, right? And the reason for the big shopping?" she asked, once all the wrappers were crumpled up and shoved in the bag.

"Yeah. Drew's going to make sure somebody's out on the department ATV to cover for me, which was what I was hoping would happen when I told Mom we'd barbecue."

"That'll be fun. Are they all coming?"

"Yeah. I'm fielding a little guilt over moving so far away. What about you? Is the library open?"

"No, it's my Saturday off. I was planning to go to the grocery store, but now I'll find something else to do." She paused to take a sip of her soda. "I'll probably visit Paige or see what Tori's up to."

Too late, he realized there had been an opening

to invite her over for the barbecue and he'd missed it. Had she been fishing for one? He could casually throw an invitation out there, but how would he introduce her to his family? As his neighbor? He wasn't sure how Hailey would take that, seeing as how they were sleeping together, but if he used the word girlfriend, his mother was going to be all over that like frosting on a cupcake. He didn't think Hailey would take kindly to the kind of speculative glances and probing questions his mom and sisters would start pestering her with.

Then Hailey changed the subject, asking him about the ATV club and how things were going, and he shoved thoughts of introducing her to his family to the back of his mind. Work was something he had no trouble talking about, and they discussed it until he pulled into her driveway.

"I'll help you carry yours in, then I'll do mine." He got out of the truck and tussled with Bear for a minute while Hailey unlocked her house and propped open her screen door.

After two trips he came up with a brilliant plan to ensure he got to see her again once their groceries were put away. He liked her company, but they'd already eaten and he was having a hard time just straight out asking if she wanted to spend the evening with him. So, as he loaded up for another trip in, he snuck a box of toothpaste out of her bag and dropped it into one of his.

"Why are you stealing my toothpaste?"

Busted. He hadn't realized she was back already. "I forgot to buy some and you bought two."

"Even if you weren't lying, and I saw toothpaste in your cart, that doesn't mean you can steal mine."

He pondered which was more embarrassing—being thought a thief or behaving like a teenager. "Having your toothpaste in my bag gave me an excuse to knock on your door later. You know, to give it back."

"Really?" He waited for her to laugh or at least make some mocking comment. Instead, she blushed. "My garlic powder might have already jumped into one of your bags. I was planning to come over later and ask if you found it."

It took a few seconds for her admission to sink in, and then he chuckled. "Did the garlic powder jump before or after I acted like an idiot?"

"After." She shrugged. "We all have our moments. I'll come over when I'm done and we can watch TV… or something. And give me my toothpaste back."

FOURTEEN

ON THE DAY his entire family was showing up for a barbecue, Matt's phone rang at eight-thirty. When he saw the Northern Star Lodge on his caller ID screen, he knew there was a good chance he'd be going to work.

It was Andy. "Hate to bother you, but we've got a couple of idiots we need to catch. I know my boy was patrolling today because you've got a family thing, but I don't think it'll take long."

"People are tearing the place up already? They couldn't have had breakfast first?"

"You know how it is when they travel a long distance. They hit the trail early to cover every mile they can. These guys came in from the east and, from what I understand, they've already done some damage on the neighboring trail system. Went off trail and were verbally abusive to a woman—a landowner, no less—who gave them hell for trespassing. By tracking complaint calls, we know they're coming into Whitford."

"Do you know what trail they're on?"

"No. We haven't heard anything since the main junction, so we don't know which way they went. I'd just wait for them at the gas station, but if they're carrying cans, they might not risk coming into town. Josh headed out from here and Drew went in behind his property. If you can get into town and head in from the trail to the diner, one of you is bound to run into them."

"On my way."

He always had a uniform ready to go, so in less than ten minutes he was headed into town. Calling his dad from the road, he told him what was up. He'd left the door unlocked for them and he'd be home as soon as he could. They knew the drill. Deciding Paige wouldn't care, he parked in the diner's parking lot instead of the designated municipal parking to unload the quad and hit the trails.

Knowing the two riders he was after were riding recklessly, with no regard for laws or common sense, he had to be careful in the corners, but Matt kept a good pace. He was glad the trails wouldn't see too much use until later in the day because if the riders ran into Drew first and tried to outrun him, somebody could get hurt.

When he came to a junction, he stopped and shut his machine off so he could listen. He thought he could hear a machine coming from the east, so he backed into the trees a little and waited. Best case scenario was him witnessing the breaking of laws with his own eyes.

But the machine that slid to a stop at the intersection was the police department's and Drew Miller spotted him right away. "They must have come through here. You didn't see them?"

"I drove the ATV route through town in my truck and then I rode in from the diner, so they didn't get by me. They must have passed through here already, which means they're between us and Josh."

"Shit." The police chief shook his head. "All he can do is yell at them."

They hauled ass then, with Drew in the lead since he knew the trails a little better. This being the main trail, it was a little wider and they slid through the corners, steering with the throttle.

Matt kept his body loose, leaning when he needed to and jumping the water bars. It felt good, even if they were out there hunting for a couple of jerks who thought they were special and could ruin it for everybody.

Suddenly Drew's machine was sliding as he braked hard and Matt followed suit, coming to a stop alongside the police chief. Josh Kowalski's quad was broadside across the trail ahead and he was reading the riot act to the two riders. They were all off their machines, helmets off, and one of the guys took a swing at Josh.

Josh dodged it but his buddy jumped in and caught him with a left. Josh staggered back one step, then put the guy on the ground with one hit. He started to get back up, urging his friend to hit him, but Drew yelled to get their attention. The guys turned around and Matt saw all the fight go out of them when they saw the uniforms. They were busted and they knew it.

The assault was enough for handcuffs, so Drew read them their rights. They probably wouldn't be charged for the machine mayhem, but if the damage was substantial, they'd pay some hefty fines and be banned from riding the trails in the future. Since most of the reports that would accompany those incidents technically happened outside of Drew's jurisdiction, Matt would get to do those honors. Which also meant Matt would get to do the paperwork.

While Drew called for a cruiser which, luckily, could get within an eighth of a mile from their location by road, Matt started the process of questioning the pair about their activities of the morning. They admitted to the things Josh and Drew knew about and Matt had no doubt more complaints would be waiting when they got back.

The most important thing, of course, was that Josh and the other club's president would be able to assure the landowners that the rogue riders who'd disrespected their property had been caught and wouldn't be back. Land closures meant trail closures and nobody wanted that.

"Since I'm taking them in for assault and the rest of it's pretty much paperwork, why don't you go ahead and take off," Drew said. "We've got to get these idiots back to the station. Josh and Andy are going to take care of towing their machines out and we'll hand them over to Butch for impound. The paperwork can wait and you've got family coming."

"Normally I wouldn't, but it's a two-hour drive for them. I owe you one, though."

By the time he rode back to the diner and loaded up, then drove home, another hour and a half had passed, so he wasn't surprised to see vehicles in his driveway. Instead of going through the house, he walked around the outside, then stopped at the sight of Hailey sitting with his family on the deck, laughing with them.

He watched them for a minute, trying to sort out how he felt about her being there and looking so at home, until Bear spotted him.

HAILEY HADN'T BEEN sure what to do when Matt's family pulled into his driveway. She assumed he'd called them to let them know what was going, but it still felt awkward to be out in the yard and not say anything to them. Especially when Bear ran over, all excited to show off his company, and they all looked at her.

"Hi," she said, walking over to the group. "I'm Hailey, Matt's neighbor."

She had no idea what, if anything, he'd told his family about her, so that's all the information she intended to give them.

Then she had to keep up while they introduced each other. His parents, Charlie and Connie. His older sister, Deb. Her husband Jeff, who Hailey thought she recognized from moving day. Their kids, Georgia and Tommy. And Matt's younger sister, Brenna, and her son, Caleb. The Barnett family resemblance was strong, and she probably could have picked them out of a lineup as being related to him.

"Matt called while we were on the road," Connie told her. "He had to work, but he'll be along shortly."

"I saw him leave in uniform. Hopefully it's nothing serious." She was uncertain as to what to do next.

It would be awkward for her to invite Matt's family into his house and offer them refreshments. She should probably go home and finish cleaning her coffeemaker, since it was sitting on the counter full of hot vinegar. But she was curious about his family, too.

"Where's Uncle Matt's bathroom?" Georgia asked her.

"He has a bathroom downstairs next to the kitchen," Hailey told her, but when the little girl hesitated, her decision was made for her. "I'll show you."

The entire family went inside and she got caught up in helping to carry in the coolers of food they'd brought with them and pack it in the fridge. By the time they were done, Connie had already poured her a lemonade and she ended up sitting on the deck with them.

The kids ran around the yard, playing ball with Bear. He was quite possibly the happiest dog Hailey had ever seen at that moment, and she enjoyed watching him with Matt's niece and nephews.

"They love that dog," Deb said, following her gaze. "We're trying to plan a family trip to camp around the last week of July. We try to do it at least once a year, and I don't know who's more tired at the end, Bear or the kids."

"I met Matt near your camp. My friend and I were separated from our tour group and he found us and made sure we got back to our car." It was as if a light-bulb went off over the entire group and she shook her head. "He told you about us, didn't he?"

When Jeff opened his mouth to say something, Deb elbowed him and spoke instead. "He mentioned coming across two lost women in the woods."

"Did he mention I called him Jeremiah Johnson?"

Her grin was almost identical to her brother's. "He might have mentioned that. And the boots."

"And the makeup," Brenna added.

"I'm not really the outdoors type," Hailey admitted.

"We got that impression," Connie said. "So you're the librarian, right?"

"The one and only. It's not a big library, but it has a lot of support from the community."

They talked about books for a while. They were all big readers, and she and Brenna had similar tastes in books. Then, somehow, the talk turned back to their cabin and the guys started telling stories.

Hailey's glass was empty and she was waiting for a lull in the conversation to excuse herself, but Charlie was a funny guy and she kept getting caught up. Right after the next story, she told herself.

Then, just as she was going to stand and tell them goodbye, Bear took off running toward the corner of the house and she saw Matt. The kids shouted his name and took off after the dog, and it became a pig pile of man, dog and kids.

He laughed and hugged the kids, ruffling their hair and talking to each of them. It was obvious he adored them and they felt the same way about him. Bear showed a little jealousy, trying to shove his way between Matt and the kids, which made them all laugh.

He finally extricated himself from the kids to say hello to the rest of the family. He hugged his parents first, then his sisters and shook his brother-in-law's hand. Hailey felt a pang of longing for her own family and made a mental note to call her mother for a nice long catch-up session. Facebook kept them in touch almost daily, but there was no substitute for hearing her mother's voice.

"I should go," Hailey said, seeing her opportunity to escape. "I was halfway through cleaning my coffeemaker, so I'll be a sad puppy in the morning if I don't finish it."

Matt was giving her a questioning look, but she couldn't exactly let him know in front of everybody that she hadn't told them their relationship had been more than neighborly. In addition to the fact it wasn't her place, she had no idea how to define it.

"Matt, invite your neighbor to stay and eat," Connie said. "She helped us carry all the food in and we've been enjoying her company."

His gaze flicked to Hailey's and she was glad that question had been answered. Neighbor. Not girlfriend or any other term she might have used. Now he knew how she'd introduced herself.

"Hey, neighbor," he said. "You should stay and eat."

She couldn't resist the chance to spend more time with him and his family. Not only was he very different from her, but they were very different from her family. Not in the love and how close they were, but the outdoors thing. All of their stories had taken place outside and centered around canoes, fishing, jumping off docks or riding ATVs and snowmobiles.

Her father had soft hands, didn't fish and drove a Cadillac instead of a pickup. They went to Old Orchard Beach and walked on the boardwalk instead of going out in the woods. As far she knew, her dad had never owned a camouflage item in his entire life, and her mother had been just like him. It stood to reason their daughters wouldn't be any different.

But she liked the Barnetts, so she nodded. "Thank you for the invitation, neighbor. I think I will."

IT WASN'T UNTIL they'd eaten and had the Jell-O salad Brenna brought for dessert that Matt finally had a chance to be alone with Hailey. She'd gone inside to put some things away and he followed her in with a load of condiments.

She was at his sink with her back to him, and he stepped up behind her. Sliding his arms around her waist, he planted a kiss at the base of her neck.

"I hope it's you, Matt, or this barbecue just got really awkward."

He chuckled, but didn't move. "I was happy to see you over here when I got home. I wasn't sure if you'd be around."

"I happened to be outside when they arrived and Bear made sure I went over and said hi. They probably thought I got lost in my backyard."

"Ouch." He kissed her neck again. "It was a funny story. I had to tell it."

"But they like me anyway. And I like them."

"They can be pretty rowdy at times, but I think they're nice people. I'm a bit biased, of course."

"They make me miss my family. And the kids are adorable. Neither my sister nor I have had any yet, much to my mother's dismay." She leaned back against his chest. "You can't get enough of your niece and your nephews. How come you haven't gotten married and had kids of your own?"

The question was asked in a light tone, but it weighed heavily on Matt's shoulders. He didn't want to go in to how hard it was to have a relationship with his hours and how women liked to reel him in and then try to polish him up to their liking. "I haven't found a woman yet who likes my lucky fishing hat."

"I shudder to meet the woman who does."

"So now you. How come you're not married with a bunch of little ones?"

She shrugged. "Waiting for the guy who doesn't think Bach is what a chicken says."

He knew there was truth under her attempt at humor, but they were in his kitchen with his family on the other side of the door. It wasn't the time for a heart to heart conversation about their life goals and dreams even if they'd been at that point in their relationship. Or whatever it was.

"I really do need to finish my coffeemaker," she told him. "I had a whole list of things I needed to do today and sitting on your back deck all day wasn't on there."

"When you get home, add it to the list and then cross it off. You'll feel like you accomplished something."

"You're bad." She turned in his arms and gave him a quick kiss. "I'm going to go now. Sit and relax with your family."

Reluctantly, he moved out of her way. And just in time, too, because his mother came through the door a moment later. "Matthew, I haven't even seen your house yet. You need to give me a tour."

"I'm heading home," Hailey told her. "It was wonderful to meet you."

"I'm so glad you stayed to visit. You should come up to camp sometime. I think you'd enjoy it."

Matt actually laughed out loud, and Hailey crossed her arms, glaring at him until he stopped. "I'm sorry, Hailey, but that's funny."

"Your mother thinks I'd enjoy it."

"My mother hasn't been in the woods with you."

Hailey smiled at Connie. "Thank you for the invitation. I might take you up on it sometime just to annoy your son."

"Honey, I'm married to his father. I totally understand."

Hailey gave him a sweet wave and went outside, presumably to say goodbye to the rest of the family. Rather than move to the window to watch her, he turned his attention to his mom. "Time to show you my house."

He gave her the grand tour, thankful he was good at picking up after himself. Between work and Hailey, he wouldn't have had a lot of time for pre-maternal visit binge cleaning.

"I like Hailey," his mom said when they'd peeked into his bedroom, and Matt frowned, wondering if she'd left some article of clothing behind. An article of clothing with her name on it, even. But it seemed to be merely a coincidence she'd mentioned his neighbor while touring his bedroom.

Once she'd assured herself her son wasn't sleeping in squalor, his mom continued down the hall and he followed along. "She liked you, too."

"How long before you show up on her doorstop dripping with mud and smelling like bear poop and skunk spray?"

"It was one time, Mom."

"It was one time you ran off a very nice girl because of what Ciara did to you." She turned and gave him a stern look. "You're not going to find a woman who won't complain about having that in her washing machine."

"Well, I don't have to bother showing up on Hailey's doorstep like that. I already know she wouldn't open the door."

Her brows furrowed. "So you two aren't an item?"

"An item?" Boy, he hated to lie to his mother, but if she got it in her head he and Hailey might have a real relationship, she'd never leave it alone. "She's my neighbor. She hates being outside."

Neither of those statements was a lie, which made him feel better. They didn't answer the question, of course, but his mother was free to infer what she pleased from them.

"That's too bad. She's pretty and you'd have pretty babies."

When she turned her back on him to go back downstairs, he rolled his eyes. Three grandchildren already and she was still hung up on him giving her more. And that always seemed to be the quality she prized most in his potential girlfriends. They'd make pretty babies.

He just wanted a woman who'd enjoy spending time with him doing what he loved to do. It should have been easy, especially in Maine, but he was thirty-five years old and hadn't met her yet.

FIFTEEN

HAILEY CLOSED HER book and tossed it onto Matt's coffee table. She'd finished it, then read the excerpts for other books at the end, and the baseball game on the television was showing no sign of ending.

Chalk up another thing they didn't have in common, she thought. She'd never gotten into sports, and baseball seemed to be something Matt was passionate about if the cheering, cursing and other sound effects were anything to go by.

"How much longer is this on?"

"What?" He tore his attention away from the TV for a second. "Three more innings."

"Can you translate that into minutes for me?"

"A lot. Did you finish your book?"

"Yeah." She could run next door for another, but she was restless.

He hit mute on the remote and shifted his body toward her. "You sound bored."

"Just a little." When he lifted his arm, she snuggled against his side. She'd been thinking about something since the weekend, so she decided to ask him. "What would your family have done if you hadn't come home when you did on Saturday?"

"What do you mean?"

"You weren't supposed to work, but you got called in. What if the call had taken a lot longer? Would they have turned around and gone home?"

She felt his shrug, since his arm was around her. "I'd given them a rough estimate, so they knew I was coming. And it happens."

"But still. It's four hours of driving, round trip, and there was the risk they wouldn't even see you."

He was quiet for a moment and, since she was paying attention, she noted he started talking right after one of the guys on TV caught the ball. "They're used to it."

"You may as well turn the sound back on. You're still watching it, but now you just can't hear it."

"I'm fine. And my family knows I might get called out at any time. It's a huge state with a lot of rural roads that take time to drive. If there's an emergency, you call in the guy who's closest."

"I don't think I could get used to that. Forget special occasions or barbecues. How would you even plan supper? You rarely come home at the same time every day."

Maybe it was her imagination, but his body seemed to tense up a bit. "I use the slow cooker a lot. Quick meals on the grill."

"I guess. My mother put dinner on the table at five-thirty every single night when I was growing up."

"And that's what you want?"

She thought about it. "Not five-thirty exactly, but there's something to be said for routine. Both home at five, make dinner together, then sit and eat while talking about the workday."

"A lot of women feel the same way, I guess. At least the ones I've dated in the past."

Something about his tone made her sit up straight so she could see his face. "I wasn't trying to be a drag. I was just curious about how your family would have handled it if you hadn't shown up."

"They would have been disappointed, but they understand my work's important. It's not like I'm calculating taxes and can punch out at four-thirty on the dot. Maybe they would have camped out on my floor. I don't know. But the hours are hell on relationships and eventually women get sick of waiting or being stood up."

"I'm pretty sure there are a lot of happily married game wardens."

"Yeah. They're the lucky ones, I guess."

His voice was tight, and Hailey guessed some woman had done a job on him in the past. It was tempting to pry a little, but it wasn't really her business. And they'd established they were just hanging out and having fun. Poking at the skeletons in his past relationship closet was deeper than that.

"That guy just hit the ball into the audience. That's a good thing, right?"

Matt laughed and pulled her close again. "The audience? As if I needed further proof you're not a sports fan. And, no it's not a good thing. We're rooting for the guys with Boston on their shirts."

"Oh. That makes sense."

He hit the power button and tossed the remote onto the table next to her book. "So is that what you're looking for? A guy who'll walk through the door in his business suit every day at quarter after five?"

"It's how I've always imagined my life." Why she didn't just say yes, that's what she was looking for was beyond her. It sounded a little *Stepford Wives* when he said it.

He snorted. "That sounds boring."

"Or stable. I guess it's all in how you look at it."

He ran his hand up her back until it was cupping the back of her neck. "While you're waiting for this paragon of promptness, how about we see if I can do any better than Boston at getting to second base."

"I could really start liking this sports thing."

FRIDAY WAS A quiet day for Matt. He spent most of it in the woods around Whitford since he was still getting to know the trail system. Next week, school would be ending for summer break and there would be a sharp increase in the amount of out-of-town ATV riders with kids along.

He ran into a few riders, though, and checked to

make sure their machines were registered. When the trails skirted homes, he stopped in and introduced himself if people were home. He wanted to have a good relationship with landowners and assure them he was out there keeping an eye on their property.

Riding through the woods, with nothing but the drone of his engine to keep him company, gave him time to think and today his thoughts kept circling around to Hailey.

He couldn't forget her questions about his family and what they would have done if he'd been called out for a more serious issue. It was hard to explain to somebody who hadn't lived with it, as his family had, but flexibility and learning to roll with it just became normal, the way eating at five-thirty every night had been normal for her family.

But she'd made her thoughts on that pretty clear. *I don't think I could get used to that.* He knew a lot of guys whose wives and kids had learned to cope with their demanding hours, but he wasn't sure how they'd managed that. It hadn't been covered in warden school, that's for sure. He seemed destined to be attracted to women who wanted reliability and routine, and that wasn't something he could offer. Sometimes he'd work regular shifts for days on end, then suddenly end up in an operation—often a search and rescue—that meant days on the job with little or no sleep.

It wasn't easy on the families, even when they

went into it willingly, thinking it would be okay. Admitting up front she wasn't sure she could ever get used to it was a big warning sign where Hailey was concerned.

And, since he was thinking about warning signs, he decided to take a ride up to the picnic area. He'd found signs of an illegal campfire, along with empty beer cans, up there after his ride with Hailey. The club had put up a sign specifically banning open fires and spelling out the consequences, so Matt wanted to check and see if there'd been any more problems. Fire, alcohol and the forest didn't mix.

When he got to the top of the hill, he saw there was already a machine parked there and recognized it as Josh's. He parked next to it and, by the time he got his gloves and helmet off, Josh had emerged from the woods.

"Good to see you," Josh said. "Any problems today?"

"No, it's been quiet. I've seen some people, but no issues. Thought I'd check out the area up here and see if fire's still an issue."

"Yeah, that's why I'm up here. I found a few more beer cans, but no signs of fire. I'm hoping it was teenagers and the sign scared them."

Matt was doubtful a sign would deter teenagers. "If it's a problem again, I'll put up a camera and see what we come up with."

"Sounds like a plan. The club voted down buying one at the last meeting. One, they don't want to spend the money. But they're also afraid if we put one camera up, any landowners who have problems will demand cameras, too, and we'll have to have video of the whole damn trail system."

"It's a possibility, but it's getting hot and we're a little shy on rainfall. Anybody building illegal fires in the woods is going to get nailed."

"Understood." Josh leaned against the cargo box on his machine. "You watch baseball?"

When he wasn't rounding the bases with Hailey, he thought, fighting not to chuckle at the memory. "Yeah. When I get the chance."

"We get together at Max Crawford's house when we can to watch whatever sport's on. Katie and I are going over Saturday afternoon to watch the Indians game. You should join us. Max's is the closest thing we have to a sports bar in Whitford."

"Max Crawford." Matt mentally sifted through all the towns folk he'd run into. "I don't think I've met him."

"Yeah, Max doesn't get out much. Good guy, though. We all bring food or a snack or whatever, then park it in front of his TV."

A fleeting thought to ask Hailey if she minded brought Matt up short, but he shook it off. Even if they were looking for something serious, which they weren't, they were still well short of him asking her if he could watch a ball game with the guys. "Sounds good. I've been watching them alone since my dad and brother-in-law don't live close enough anymore."

"What about Hailey?"

"She's not really a sports fan."

"I've got the opposite problem. Katie loves sports and she tends to get pretty wound up. It doesn't even matter what sport it is."

"I've already been warned to cheer for the home teams if I'm in her barber shop chair."

Josh laughed. "I'd like to assure you you'd be safe, but to be honest, I couldn't vouch for your haircut if you pissed her off."

"It's about time for a trim, so I'll keep that in mind." He put his helmet back on and buckled the strap. "Since you've already checked the area, I guess I'll head back out."

"I'm heading back to the lodge. We've got guests arriving tonight, so Rose has been baking all day, if you should feel like stopping by."

Oh, hell yes, he thought. "I'm willing to bet between here and there, I can come up with an official reason to need to talk to the trail administrator."

Josh grinned and pulled on his helmet. "I like the way you think."

"You know what she's baking?"

"No, but there are usually brownies. First one back gets the soft ones from the middle of the pan."

Matt yanked on his gloves and fired the engine. "I have a flashing blue light."

"Unlike you, the only power I need to abuse is sheer horsepower."

Matt hit the throttle hard and yanked the bars, throwing the ATV into a doughnut so he was pointing back the way he came. He heard Josh's machine as he did the same, and then they were off. He had to yield to the other guy when they came to a narrow spot in the trail, but then he took him on an inside corner.

Those brownies were as good as won.

SIXTEEN

A WEEK AFTER the barbecue, Hailey squeezed her car in next to the others filling Fran's driveway and killed the engine. After skipping last month's movie night to go on her ill-fated adventure trip with Tori, she hadn't dared skip this one.

It had been tempting. She'd rather be curled up on Matt's couch with him, watching movies and making out than stuck in a room full of women who were going to ask her about him, but the first Saturday of the month was movie night. Period.

She'd brought homemade pizza rolls, which she was a lot better at making than actual pizzas, and she carried the foil-covered baking dish up the walk to Fran's front door. The old farmhouse-style building was set back behind the general store and gas station, with a line of trees to separate their home from their business, and it had the same white siding with cranberry trim. The rooms inside were on the small side, which meant movie nights at Fran's were cozy and loud, but everybody got a turn hosting.

As soon as she opened the door, she was hit by a wave of sound. Everybody was talking at once, and she waded through them to get to the kitchen. After adding the pizza rolls to the bounty, she grabbed a plate and started filling it with a little bit of everything.

Fran and Rose were in the corner talking, but as soon as they saw Hailey, they descended upon her. And since she was in the middle of trying to make room for buffalo chicken dip on her plate, Hailey couldn't retreat.

"You made it!" That was Fran, whose excitement seemed a bit much considering Hailey rarely missed move night.

"We weren't sure you'd come," Rose added. "I think if I…lived next door to a man like Matt Barnett, I'd find an excuse not to hang out with a bunch of women."

Hailey's gaze bounced back and forth between them, trying to figure out just how suggestive Rose's pause was meant to be. She trusted Tori, Paige and Liz implicitly, which meant the two women were fishing.

"Watching him through the window might be a pretty picture," she said, "but there's no dialogue."

Both of them looked a little crestfallen, but Rose recovered first. "It's only been…how long?"

"It's been a month since I met him."

Fran raised her eyebrows. "That was quick. Keeping track are you?"

"Really, Fran?" Sometimes she had no patience for the mind games. "Since I met him the day Tori and I skipped movie night—which is once a month—to go on an adventure tour and I'm here for movie night, I went out on a limb and guessed a month."

She turned and went back to the living room with her plate. Guilt poked at her because her tone had bordered on disrespectful and they were an older generation, but sometimes it was ridiculous. Hell, the town had never forgotten Hailey and Mitch Kowalski had gotten busy in the back of her dad's Cadillac when they were teenagers and had still brought it up whenever the opportunity presented itself, until Paige and Mitch started dating. That had been the end of it, thank goodness. And Paige had never had a problem with the fact her best friend and her husband had shared one night of drunken stupidity a *very* long time ago.

Hailey saw Tori sitting on the heavy oak chest that housed a fraction of Fran's knitting supplies and headed straight for her. "Make some room."

It wasn't very wide, but it had a cushion and Hailey didn't mind bumping elbows with her. "Fran's being about as subtle as a jackhammer tonight."

"You knew that would happen when you went to the diner with him."

"Right now, if there was another store in Whitford, I would totally shop there."

Fran and Rose were the last ones into the living room. They didn't have to worry about seats, since they got the two matching recliners by right of age.

Jilly Crenshaw, Tori's aunt, was there, sitting on the couch with Liz and Nola, who worked at the town hall. Katie was sitting cross-legged on the floor in front of them. Hailey waved to them all, then gave her attention to Fran, who was clearing her throat over by the television.

"Tonight, for the June movie night, we're watching…" Fran paused dramatically, then held up the movie case. *"Deliverance!"*

Hailey groaned. "Real funny, Fran."

"It kind of is," Katie said, grinning.

"We're not really watching that, are we?"

"We didn't all get to live it, honey." Fran said. "Just you."

Tori looked at Hailey with a horrified expression. "How much did you embellish that story?"

"I didn't!" Not much, anyway.

"I think this is a horror-type version, though," Fran continued. "Who thinks Hailey's working on a romance version?"

Unanimous agreement. Big surprise there. Hailey dragged a tortilla chip through buffalo chicken dip and popped it into her mouth to keep from saying anything rude.

Tori leaned close enough to whisper. "She thinks she's being funny, but you know she loves you. Just let it go."

"Stop being the voice of reason on my shoulder," she mumbled around a mouthful of very hot dip.

"I guess we have the wrong version," Fran announced. Then she slid the picture of the *Deliverance* movie poster out of the plastic slipcover to reveal the cover of *Thor*. "I thought we'd mix it up a little and watch an action movie because look at this guy. He's got a very impressive...hammer."

There was applause from the ladies, and Hailey was relieved when everybody's attention shifted away from her.

"I should have stayed home and had sex with the hot game warden," she murmured to Tori.

Tori stole a pizza roll from her plate. "We're supposed to be celebrating being single."

"Oh, I'm celebrating. Trust me."

"You know, I could start hating you very easily. And you probably won't be single much longer, which means I'll have nobody to go on adventures with."

"What's that supposed to mean?"

Tori arched her eyebrows. "Come on. You keep saying there's nothing there, but you're still pretty hot and heavy for a couple who's not a couple."

"We're not a couple." When her friend rolled her eyes, she sighed. "Okay, we're kind of a couple. But it's temporary."

"Mmm-hmm."

Hailey would have said more, but the movie started and anybody still talking got a stern shushing from Fran. And she wasn't sure there was anything to say, anyway. She was falling into couple-hood with Matt and, no matter how much she denied it to her friends, she couldn't deny it to herself.

MATT WANDERED INTO the library about mid-morning on Tuesday, hoping to catch Hailey during a lull.

Boy, had he misjudged. There were small children everywhere and he realized he'd stumbled across some kind of story hour. Whether they were all arriving or leaving, he couldn't tell right away, but he could see Hailey was in her usual spot at her desk. She smiled when she spotted him and waved him over.

"I didn't think you'd be busy," he said. "I was wrong."

"It's story hour, but I have a volunteer helping me today. Are you here in an official capacity, Warden Barnett?"

He smiled and leaned on the desk. "I could be. I do want to talk to you at some point about doing another OHRV safety course this winter, in preparation for snowmobile season. But I really came by to get some books."

"Anything in particular you're looking for?" She stood and stepped out from behind the desk. "I happen to be very good at recommendations, but I don't know your reading tastes since you haven't unpacked that box of books in your garage yet."

"I like true crime stuff. Thrillers. Biographies.

Science Fiction. Westerns." He paused, trying to remember what he'd read recently that he enjoyed. "Are
you aware it's freezing in here?"

She gave him a look that told him everything he
needed to know about her feelings regarding their
HVAC system. "I have a call in, but having too much
air-conditioning is apparently less of a priority than
not having it at all. I should be wearing flannel today.
It's June."

He kept pace with her as she walked around the
bookshelves, and took a careful look around to make
sure there was nobody within earshot. "I may have
fantasized about you in flannel."

"You're kidding"

"Nope. You in my button-down flannel shirt…
and nothing else. I'd tell you more, but this isn't a
good place to talk about it."

"But we will talk about it later." Her cheeks were
flushed as she looked over the shelves, pulling out
a few books. "Try these. Though your tastes are
broad enough so I could give you almost anything
and you'd probably like it."

"Sorry. I'll try to be more narrow in my reading
choices next time."

"Oh, hush. It wasn't a complaint."

He took the books from her and followed her back
toward the desk. "Being hushed by you is kind of
sexy, too."

"Stern librarian in flannel fetish? I don't think I've heard that one before."

"I'm unique." He fished his library card out of his wallet and waited while she checked out his books. "You're sure that's the right return date?"

She blushed at the reminder she'd forgotten the day he'd taken her out in the woods and kissed her. "I'm sure. How late are you working tonight?"

"Barring any emergency calls, probably by six. You stopping by?"

Handing him his books, she shrugged. "I might."

"I hope you do."

When he finally walked through his front door at ten after seven, he knew something was up because Bear just lay on the couch and looked at him. Matt gave him a pat, wondering if the dog wasn't feeling well, but then he realized Bear was looking at something behind him.

He turned and saw Hailey at the bottom of the stairs. She was wearing his red plaid flannel shirt.

And nothing else.

The shirt hit her at mid-thigh, making her legs go on forever. And she'd left enough of the top buttons undone to give him a tantalizing glimpse of her cleavage. He was instantly, almost painfully aroused, and he told the dog to stay.

"You're late."

They were words he'd had thrown at him in the

past, and they took the edge off the need that had flared at the sight of her. "I had a call. It happens."

He waited for her to complain. To tell him she had better things to do than hang around waiting for him to decide to come home.

"I guess we'll have to make up for lost time, then," was all she said, and then she crooked her finger at him in a come-hither gesture that re-fired his engines in a big way.

Just as he got to her, Hailey turned and went up the stairs. With each step, he was gifted with a teasing flash of skin and, by the time they got to the top, he had his shirt and T-shirt off.

When she reached his room, Hailey turned to face him, though she kept walking slowly backward. She fiddled with the top button of the shirt, drawing his gaze there. Undoing his pants to relieve some of the pressure, he watched her unbutton two of the buttons.

"Shit, it takes me forever to get these boots off," he said, wanting desperately to be naked.

"Don't worry about the boots. Just sit in the chair." He sat on the straight-back chair in the corner like she told him.

Hailey slowly unfastened every button on the flannel shirt, but she didn't let it fall to the floor. It hung open, giving him access to everything he wanted to touch if she'd just come a little bit closer.

"You're the most beautiful woman I've ever seen."

She smiled, moving almost close enough to touch.

"Enjoy this look because there's a good chance you'll never see me in plaid flannel again."

"I'll see it every time I close my eyes for a good long time."

A flush of pleasure crept across her chest and he reached for her, practically begging her to come closer. When she straddled his lap, he groaned in anticipation and prayed like hell the chair would hold their weight.

He slid his hands under the flannel, cupping her breasts. She lowered her head and kissed him, her mouth sweetly insistent against his. It took some maneuvering, but he managed to get his pants down enough to free his cock without making her move.

When she reached down and closed her hand over him, he almost exploded. It felt so good, and the way her nipples played peekaboo from behind the shifting red flannel inflamed him. He caught one in his mouth, sucking hard to make her feel the same sweet agony of anticipation he was suffering.

Finally, she pulled a condom from the shirt's pocket and shifted herself backward while he put it on. Then she put her hands on his shoulders and very slowly lowered herself onto his shaft.

His breath left him in a ragged hiss as she rocked, taking him deeper inside of her with each stroke. Her warmth enveloped him and he knew this wasn't going to last long. With his hands on her ass, he urged her to ride him faster and she did.

She arched her back and the flannel slid away, exposing all of her body to him. He licked her nipples, then her neck, and felt her shudder. Circling her hips, she ground against him and he dug his fingers into her waist.

He felt her orgasm, her body squeezing his as she rocked and moaned. He lifted her slightly, then brought her down hard again and again until he came with a guttural groan.

When the shudders passed, she collapsed against his chest. They were both breathing hard, and he ran his hands over her flannel-clad back. "This is my favorite shirt now."

He felt her body jerk when she made a breathless sound of amusement. "Does that mean you're never going to wash it again?"

"Smart-ass." He slapped her ass, making her jump. "Remind me to tell you about my fantasies more often."

"They don't all involve flannel, do they?"

He pretended to think about it for a moment. "Yeah, they mostly do."

She groaned and kissed his neck. "That explains the L.L.Bean catalog in your bathroom."

THE FOLLOWING DAY, after work, Hailey got comfortable in a mound of throw pillows, with a glass of water within reach, and pulled up her mom on speed dial. "Hello?"

"Hi, Mom. You busy right now?" She hoped not because she needed to talk to somebody who wasn't tapped into the local grapevine.

"No. I was working in the garden a little, but I'm never too busy to talk to you. How's life in Whitford?"

"Whitford is the same as it's always been."

"Hmm." Water was running in the background, so Hailey pictured her mom with the phone trapped by her cheek while washing the garden dirt from her hands. "Is that a good thing or a bad thing?"

"Mostly good. But you know how the gossip gets."

"I was born and raised there, too, honey. I guess if it's annoying you, they're talking about you?"

"I'm kind of seeing somebody. I guess."

"You guess?"

"My neighbor and I have been spending a lot of time together." And having sex, but she assumed her mother would be able to read between those lines all by herself.

"Your neighbor?"

"He moved in over a month ago. He's a game warden and they're stepping up their presence in the area because of the new ATV trails."

"A game warden?" Her mom laughed. "I have a hard time picturing you dating a game warden, honey. They're very…outdoorsy."

"Tell me about it. He's the most outdoorsy man

I've ever met. You know that lumberjack guy in the paper towel commercials? More outdoorsy than that."

"No wonder the town's talking about you. I always thought you'd marry a doctor."

"We don't have a doctor."

"That does complicate things. So you met this game warden when he moved in next door?"

Hailey sighed. "Not exactly."

She told the story—again—about being left behind in the woods. She told her everything, from the ineffective bug spray to the unflattering mountain man comparisons. "It was pretty bad, Mom."

"I should have made you play outside in the yard when you were younger. You were always reading. You especially loved those glitzy soap opera romances from the eighties, but I should have taken them away and told you to go out in the yard."

"Sometimes I sat in the tree and read."

"That's true. So not my fault, after all. Back to your neighbor. So, after all that, he likes you, anyway?"

"Well, he seems to like certain aspects of our relationship." Maybe she should have told her mom about the weather instead.

"Let's pretend you're talking about your cooking. Are you cooking for him exclusively?"

Hailey rolled her eyes, picturing her house as a fast food drive-through. "Yes. And I believe he's only eating what I cook for him."

"Oh, well that's good, then."

"But I think we have different tastes in seasonings and our flavors aren't compatible in the long run."

There was a long pause on the other end of the line. "Oh, for God's sake, I'm so confused. You're having sex with your neighbor, but you don't think you're compatible long term?"

Hailey laughed. "Yes, Mom. Exactly that."

"Then enjoy the short term. Eventually a doctor will move to Whitford, I'm sure." Sometimes Hailey had a hard time telling whether or not her mother was being sarcastic. "Just make sure, if you don't think this man is a keeper, that you don't end up with a bun in your oven."

"I won't." Leave it to her mother to be practical.

"Why aren't you compatible long term?"

"You're not the only one who thought I'd marry a doctor. Or a lawyer. Or any guy who dressed nice and worked somewhat regular hours. And believed mowing the lawn and planting a few flowers was ample outside time."

"So you think, once the bloom is off the sex rose, you won't have enough in common to make a relationship work?"

"I don't just think it, Mom," she said. "It's pretty much a fact."

"As much as I'd love to see you settled, sex isn't enough."

Hailey knew that, but it was hard to imagine going

back to a just-neighbors status with Matt. "I like him, though. He's fun and we enjoy each other's company. Usually. I don't know if I'll ever like four-wheeling."

"And now you're arguing the other side of the coin."

"I know." Hailey sighed. "I do it to myself every day."

"Stop overthinking it and enjoy today. Tomorrow will sort itself out."

Hailey felt as if she'd reached the age where she needed to get her tomorrows sorted out ASAP if she was going to have the family she wanted, but she knew her mother wouldn't have much more to add to the topic. "Enough about me. How's Tanya?"

"She's not nearly as interesting as you at the moment." Her mother laughed. "I'm kidding. She's doing fine. They're finally looking at adoption now, so I might get to be a grandmother soon."

"That's wonderful! And how's Dad?"

Once her mother got rolling on what was happening in Massachusetts, Hailey was free to sip her lemonade and mostly listen for a while. She'd have to look at her calendar and try to schedule a trip to visit them soon. Or at least see if they'd meet her halfway for a weekend somewhere.

Too soon, it was time for her mother to head out for a hair appointment, but first she circled back to the topic of Matt. "You should put a picture of him on Facebook so I can see him."

"We're trying to fly under the grapevine's radar, Mom. I'm not putting a photo of him on Facebook."

"I'm going to Google him. But right now I really have to run."

Since she was pretty sure she hadn't given her mom Matt's name, Hailey felt fairly safe ending the call without admonishing her mom about the internet, privacy and accidentally posting something on Facebook for everybody to see.

"I'll talk to you soon. Love you."

Hailey dropped her phone and lay back against her throw pillows. Her house was clean. Matt was at work and so was Tori. She knew Mitch was home, so she didn't want to bother Paige.

With a sigh, she picked up her phone again and went surfing the ebookstore she liked. Maybe some of those glamorous eighties novels were available in digital now. She could use a dose of glitz in her life.

SEVENTEEN

On Saturday afternoon, Matt pulled up at the address Josh had given him and parked in a line of pickup trucks that had arrived before him. He grabbed the Crock-Pot off the passenger seat and made his way to the front door.

His knock was answered by a tall, blond guy who matched the description he'd been given. "Hi. You must be Max Crawford. I'm Matt Barnett."

"Barnett. Oh, you're the game warden who moved in next door to the librarian. Harley? Hailey? I swear, I can never remember her name."

"Hailey. And yeah, that's me. Josh said you wouldn't mind if I came over and watched some baseball with you guys."

"Of course not." He stepped out of the way, but then held up a hand. "Wait. You're not an Indians fan, right?"

Matt laughed. "Born and raised a Red Sox fan, my friend."

"Okay. I invited an associate to watch a football game with us once because he was passing through, but I didn't know he was a Jets fan. The other guys wouldn't let him eat their food, so it was rather awk-ward."

"I can see how it would be." Matt set the slow cooker on the counter. "You mind if I plug this in?"

"Feel free. What's in it?"

"Swedish meatballs. I wasn't sure what to bring, but they go with anything."

Max lifted the lid and sniffed at the steam roll-ing out. "I'm glad Josh invited you. The others are in the living room. The game starts in about five minutes, I think."

He went in the direction his host pointed and was glad to see he knew everybody in the room. Josh and Katie were there. Butch Benoit, Fran's husband and owner of the town's only wrecker service and gas station. Luckily for all of them, the Benoits were good people because having all the food and gas was a golden opportunity for price gouging. And he recognized Gavin Crenshaw, even though he'd only ever see the cook through the kitchen window at the diner. Since he tried to pay attention to things like connections, he also knew the young man was Tori's cousin.

"Small crowd today," Josh told him, shaking Matt's hand. "A lot of honey-do lists were handed out this morning and not all the guys finished their chores in time to come."

"You didn't bring Hailey with you?" Butch asked,

his voice booming in the room. Or maybe that was just in Matt's mind.

"No, sir." He didn't elaborate. It was none of their business, and he wasn't sure if Hailey had been confirming the stories that had to be circulating, or ignoring them. She hadn't outed their relationship to his family, so he wouldn't out it to the town. They could suspect, but he wouldn't confirm.

"Did you get some food, Matt?" That was Katie, who gave Butch a stern look.

"Not yet. I thought I'd say hello first. I also contributed a Crock-Pot of Swedish meatballs."

"Dibs!" Josh headed for the kitchen.

Butch scowled at him. "You have a Crock-Pot? Aren't you single?"

Matt wasn't sure what to say to that. Working the hours he did, the slow cooker saved him from eating nothing but microwave pizzas or cans of beef stew all winter when it was too cold to throw a frozen slab of meat on the grill. But apparently, to a certain generation, Crock-Pots were for women.

"You're looking a little ragged, Butch," Katie said, and Matt was grateful for the change in subject. "You need to get into the shop before you can't see past your hair to drive the tow truck."

The older guy looked over his shoulder toward the kitchen. "I bet Max has a decent pair of scissors around here. You could give me a little trim while we watch the game."

She snorted. "Sure, and I bet you've got your tools in your truck. You can go change the oil in my Jeep during the seventh inning stretch."

"Oh, you're a hard one, Katie Davis."

"And you're a cheap one, Butch Benoit." She turned to Matt. "Go fix yourself a plate before the game starts."

He did as he was told, loading up a paper plate with a variety of snack foods that weren't good for him, as well as a few meatballs. Max was doing the same and, when the silence became awkward, Matt felt compelled to talk.

"So you're single, too, huh?"

"Yes." That was all the guy said for a long moment, but then he scowled. "Aren't you dating the librarian? I think somebody said that."

"People in Whitford seem to say a lot of things. Some of it's true. Some of it's not." And he didn't say which it was in this case.

"Are you looking for a wife?"

That was a weird question. "I haven't put out any personal ads, but I'd like to have a wife someday. It'd be nice to have somebody to come home to at the end of the workday."

Max nodded, pausing in the act of scooping meatballs out of the slow cooker. "I work in my basement, but it would be nice to have somebody to come upstairs to. I've been thinking about finding a wife."

Matt wanted to crack a joke about ordering one

online, but he wasn't sure Max would get it. That was probably enough wife talk. "Your basement, huh? What do you do for work?"

"According to the gossip network in this town, I kill people." Matt must have looked shocked, because Max put up his hand immediately. "It's not true, though. I paint brass rolling stock. Uh, model railroading stuff. Though I'd appreciate you not spreading that around."

The guy was a little odd, but Matt found himself liking him nonetheless. "Don't want people thinking you're not a killer?"

"It's more about the value of what's in my basement, most of which is very limited edition and belongs to other people. But the speculation does amuse me, yes."

"I won't tell a soul." Matt grabbed some plastic cutlery and a napkin, then juggled those so he could take a soda from the ice bucket on the end of the counter. "Sounds like they're gearing up for the first pitch."

Matt thoroughly enjoyed the afternoon, watching the Red Sox play the Indians with his new friends. He'd liked Whitford from the start but, now that he was becoming a part of the community, it was starting to really feel like home.

It would have been nice to have Hailey there with him, but she said she'd rather get together with Tori and catch up over coffee and pie at the diner since sports weren't really her thing. Wednesday night, when he put the Sox and Orioles game on, she'd curled up against him with a book and read while he watched it.

It had gotten a little rough when a bad call pissed him off and she whacked him with the book in the middle of his rant because she only had one chapter left, but all in all, it wasn't a bad way to share their time.

She liked to read a lot. And reading books could be done anywhere. At a cabin in the woods. On a fishing boat. In a tree stand. Of course, there wasn't a comfy leather sofa at the cabin, on their boat or up the tree, but it was a start.

Something happened on the TV and the crowd in the room went wild, but Matt had missed it because he was thinking about Hailey. More importantly, because he'd been thinking of ways he could make his life more palatable for her.

He really needed to stop doing that.

SLEEPING IN ON a Sunday morning was a wonderful thing, Hailey mused as she burrowed deeper under the blankets, but it wasn't very conducive to getting chores done. Neither was spending more time at one's neighbor's house than in one's own, which was why she'd made a point of sleeping in her own bed last night.

Matt had stopped by yesterday after the baseball

game and they'd fooled around on the couch for a while. But he'd needed to get home because he'd been doing laundry earlier in the day and the longer his uniforms sat in the dryer, the harder they were to iron. She'd declined to join him. Not only because she had no intention of being charmed into helping him iron, but because going back and forth between their houses was starting to feel a little ridiculous.

Stretching, she rolled over to look at her clock. She really needed to get up, get dressed, and clean her house. And she'd taken a roast out of the freezer, so she needed to cook it before it had to be tossed. Maybe that's what she'd do today. She'd make a roast dinner with herbed potatoes and have Matt over for supper.

After she showered and dressed, she spent the morning doing some much needed cleaning. Then she paid a few bills and dumped the stack of junk mail that seemed to be multiplying on her counter into the recycling bin in her garage. Only once she'd accomplished the bare minimum she had to get done for the day did she text Matt.

Do you have supper plans?

I plan to have supper. That's all the plan I have.

Roast at my house?

Hell yes.

She smiled and started going through the prep list in her head. Baking wasn't her thing, but she was a good cook and she was looking forward to showing that off a little. Maybe she'd even break out some candles to make it a little more special.

It was probably as close to a nice, romantic dinner date as she was going to get.

That thought lingered as she dug through her pantry for the seasonings she'd need, festering until she couldn't keep it shoved to the back of her mind anymore and had to acknowledge it.

She wanted to go on a real date with Matt. A date that didn't involve bug spray. She didn't expect him to take her to an opera, but somewhere she could wear sexy shoes would be nice.

When she heard Matt's lawnmower spring to life, she shoved the resentful thoughts back into the recesses of her mind where they belonged. Matt was who he was, and he hadn't pretended otherwise. If she wanted to go someplace nice, it was going to be on her to get them there.

Looking out the window, she saw Bear lying on the deck, pouting. He wasn't allowed off the deck while Matt was mowing and he made no secret of the fact he resented every minute of it.

Since it would be a while yet before she had to put the roast in the oven, Hailey walked next door and sat on the top step of the deck next to Bear. He nuzzled closer until his head was in her lap and they watched Matt do laps on the riding lawnmower. He'd started doing hers, too, since the last incident, and she hadn't bothered complaining about the big riding mower again.

When he was done, he joined them on the deck. He yanked his T-shirt up and mopped the sweat off his forehead with the hem of it. "It's getting humid today."

"All you do is sit on it and steer. How do you get so gross?"

"Gross?" He actually looked offended. "It's sweat. It's something people do when they work in the yard in the summer."

"Fine. Not gross. All you're doing is steering the mower. How do you get so covered in manly sweat?"

"That's better. And when you're going that fast, it takes some effort to steer it."

"I won't bother to point out you could slow down."

"Then it would take longer. Why are you cooking a roast tonight?"

She shrugged. "I had it in the freezer and I thought it would be nice to have a roast with herbed potatoes. Maybe some steamed carrots if I have any."

"Sounds like the kind of meal I'll need to take a shower for."

She wrinkled her nose. "Right now a granola bar is the kind of meal you'd need to take a shower for."

"Oh, is that right?" He stood and grabbed her hand, hauling her to her feet. "I've missed you today, Hailey. Let me hold you."

She yanked her hand away and backed up. "Don't you dare."

"I thought women liked sweaty men."

"We like *looking* at sweaty, shirtless men. Not touching them."

He advanced toward her. "One hug."

She fled down the deck. "I'll text you what time supper is when I put the roast in."

Fortunately, the cooking time on the roast gave him plenty of time to shower and shave, so when he walked into her kitchen at the time she'd given him, he wasn't gross at all.

"That's better," she said, putting her hands behind his neck and kissing him.

"There's almost no limit to what I'll do for roast and potatoes."

"I'll keep that in mind for the future. Where's Bear?"

"Napping in front of the television. Sometimes having Bear is like living with a two year old and other times it's like living with a really old man. Can I do anything to help?"

"Should I bother with salads?"

He grinned. "I vote no."

"That's what I thought. Everything's ready to go on the table, so all you have to do is sit and eat it."

"You lit candles."

"I do that sometimes." She didn't consider it a big deal, but he was looking at them as if they were going to fall over and burn her house down. "Do you not like candles?"

"What? Oh, candles are fine. Just fancy, that's all."

Now that she looked at the table, it probably looked like a romantic dinner for two. But apparently it was only a romantic dinner in her mind. In reality, it was just supper with added candles.

She had just set the serving platter in the center of the table when Matt's cell phone rang. For a split second, she hoped he'd hit mute and ignore it, but he couldn't do that. The conversation was mostly one-sided, with Matt doing more listening than talking, but she got the gist of it.

The look he gave her when he hung up was heavy with apology. "I have to go. There's an aggressive animal in a residential neighborhood and they haven't identified it with certainty, but it went after a kid and I'm closest. I'm sorry."

"Okay." There wasn't anything else she could say. A roast wasn't more important than children being terrorized by a possibly wild animal.

"I don't know when I'll be home." He gave her a quick kiss and was gone.

Hailey stood for a minute, looking at the beautiful dinner she'd prepared for them. It was damn near perfect.

So much work for nothing. How the hell was a person supposed to plan things when he had to run off like Batman every time somebody waved the signal around? He'd almost missed his own barbecue after his family drove two hours, and then she'd hung out in his stupid flannel shirt for over an hour, waiting for him. And now this. She wanted to pick up the platter and bounce it off the wall.

Instead she grabbed a loaf of bread from the box and the mayo out of the fridge. She sliced the roast as fast as she dared without cutting herself, then slapped some mayonnaise on the bread. A little salt and pepper, then she wrapped the sandwiches in a paper towel.

She was almost across the yard when he rushed out of his house in uniform. He unlocked his truck and was about to climb in when she called his name.

"I turned the roast into sandwiches so you can eat while you drive." She handed him the paper towel bundle. "But carefully."

He looked at the sandwiches in his hand and back at her. Then he slid his other hand behind her neck and gave her a long, firm kiss. "Thank you."

Bear wandered over to sit next to Hailey's feet, and she rubbed the top of his head with one hand while waving goodbye to Matt with the other.

Once the truck was out of sight, she looked down at the dog and sighed. "I guess it's just you and me, boy. Let's have some roast."

IT WAS STRANGE how often wild, possibly rabid beasts turned out to be hungry stray dogs. And when faced with a firm voice, a steady look and a uniform, the child who'd run from the dog admitted he'd thrown

rocks at it. Matt had seen it more times than he cared
to count, but he'd also seen the calls be legitimate,
so he never stopped taking them seriously.

Figuring out they weren't dealing with a wolf,
bear, mountain lion or any of the other scary preda-
tors reported by the panicked members of the community had been the easy part. The fact it was a dog
and it had been provoked didn't change the fact Matt
couldn't leave it there.

Once the dog had been located and identified,
it had taken over an hour to coax the poor guy out
and, even then, he hadn't been easy to catch. But
with patience, a soft voice and some dog treats, Matt
had finally won what little trust the dog was willing to give. Now he was safely in a shelter, being
given food, medical attention and some tender loving care. Hopefully he'd go on to find a home with
people who'd treat him right.

He assumed Hailey would be in bed by the time
he pulled into his driveway, so he sat in the dark for
a few minutes after he turned off the ignition.

Something had shifted inside him when she
handed him the sandwiches. He knew how much
work and thought she'd put into making them dinner,
and he could tell by the small touches she'd wanted
it to be romantic. Yet, when he'd been called away,
she not only hadn't complained, but her first concern
had been making sure he ate.

It was a simple gesture. It should have been no

big deal, but when he'd driven away with the warm sandwiches in his center console and Hailey petting his dog in his rearview mirror, he'd felt a sweet ache in his chest.

He was falling for her. Somehow this woman who didn't like being outside and who drove him crazy half the time was turning out to be his type, after all.

It scared him a little. And he kept trying to rein in the feelings that slipped their leash when she handed him the sandwiches. Sure, she'd been great about it. But this wouldn't be the last time it happened, and how would she react when it happened again? Or when she'd made plans and he didn't even show up because things went to shit at work and he lost track of time? His job tended to wear on relationships after a while and it was only a matter of time before she remembered he wasn't what she was looking for in a man.

He realized suddenly that Hailey was standing in his living room window, watching him. Shaking off the melancholy, he got out of the truck and greeted Bear, who came rushing out when she opened the front door. Then he walked up the steps and kissed her hello.

"Was it bad?" she asked while he sat on the bench he used for taking off his boots. Lacing and unlacing the damn things was a pain in the ass.

"No, it wasn't too bad. Turned out to be a stray dog who'd been on his own for a while. I got him to the shelter and they'll take care of him."

"Oh, that's good then. You looked like you were trying to shake off a bad night," she said. "When you were sitting in the truck."

"No, I was just thinking about some stuff I need to do. You didn't have to stay here and wait up with Bear, you know. It's kind of late."

"After I cleaned the kitchen, we came back here so he could have his dinner, and then we were cuddling on the couch, watching a movie. He's a good date and I lost track of time."

Matt chuckled and rubbed Bear's head. "How much roast did you give him?"

"Just enough to make him love me forever."

"One bite should have done it. It was that good."

She beamed and, because he was still unsettled by his train of thought in the truck, he looked down at Bear. The dog was sniffing his pants with an intensity that made him smile.

"It was only the one dog, Bear, and he didn't mean anything. I swear."

Once he'd satisfied himself that the dog he smelled on his owner's pants wasn't hidden in his pockets or his crotch, Bear lost interest and flopped in front of the television with a big sigh.

"I guess I should get home and let you get to bed."

He snagged her hand as she walked by. "Or you could stay."

She looked into his eyes and smiled. "Or I could stay."

EIGHTEEN

HAILEY RAN HER finger down Matt's naked chest, from the base of his throat down to the point where the sheet was barely protecting his modesty. Or it would be if he had any. The sheet was mostly about her modesty, not his.

"I've been thinking…" She trailed her fingertips back up his stomach.

"This can't end well for me."

"There's this bistro in the city I've heard about. Rumor has it they have a scampi dish to die for."

"Bistro? What the hell is a bistro? I bet you could make a good scampi dish."

She was prepared for a little resistance, and she wasn't going to give up easily. "Everything tastes better if somebody else cooks it."

"You want me to drive an hour there and an hour back for scampi?"

"They also have steak. And burgers."

"I bet you could talk Gavin into making scampi at the diner. Kid's a helluva cook."

She propped herself up on her elbow so she could see his face. "I watched the moose. At four-thirty in the morning, I might add. And I rode on the ATV. I think it's my turn to pick a date, don't you?"

He sighed. He couldn't argue with that. "I have Bear to consider."

"Bear is fine when you're working. He'll be fine when you take me out for a nice dinner."

"A *nice dinner* is code word for dressing up and spending too much on a glass of wine."

"I'll pay, cheapskate." She didn't say anything about not dressing up because she intended to. And he was going to, as well. As dressed up as she could get him, anyway.

"That's not the point."

She slid her hand under the sheet, teasing the skin that was as low as she could go on his stomach without brushing against what was no doubt a quickly developing erection. "What's the point?"

"What?" He shifted slightly, subtly trying to steer her hand. "Oh, my point. What were we talking about?"

"We're talking about you taking me out for a nice dinner."

"Oh, yeah. Maybe. Sometime." He lifted his hips and his hot, hard flesh brushed against her palm.

She closed her fingers around him and he moaned. "When?"

"Soon."

With one long, slow stroke, she had his hips lifting off the bed. "Not good enough."

"*Very* soon."

She released her grip and ran a single fingertip lightly down his shaft with a regretful sigh. "Too bad. It would be so fun to dress up. I have a little red dress and sexy black heels I bought last year and haven't had a chance to wear yet."

Matt reached down and closed his hand over hers, effectively closing her hand over his erection. "I'll take you there whenever you want. Wear the shoes."

She resisted when he tried to slide their hands up his shaft. "I want to go Thursday night. You mentioned having court that day, so there's a better chance you won't work late."

"Fine. We'll go Thursday night. Just…please…"

Stroking him with a grip held firm by his fist staying closed over hers, she lowered her head and nipped at his nipple. He liked when her hair tickled his chest and she knew by his breathing he was close.

She began kissing her way down his stomach and he uttered a guttural groan that may have been her name. His free hand fisted in her hair, though he didn't force her head lower.

When her mouth closed over the head of his shaft, she pulled her hand free. He stroked himself and she followed his fist with her mouth, his knuckles bumping against her lips.

He came in a hot stream and she swallowed, not releasing him until his grip slackened and he stopped jerking against her mouth. His hands fell limp to his sides and she rested her head on his stomach as his breath came in rough gasps.

When he lifted his head to look at her, she smiled up at him. "Holy hell, what just happened?"

"You promised to buy me a convertible sports car."

His head flopped back onto the pillow. "Okay. Red?"

MATT GLARED AT his reflection in the mirror, wondering how the hell he'd gotten himself into this situation.

Well, he knew how. Hailey had soft hands and a warm mouth and somehow he'd promised her a nice dinner date. Now he was in khaki pants, a button-down shirt and the dress shoes he'd had to polish that morning. He was thankful he didn't have to wear a suit and tie, but he preferred to relax and enjoy his meals in jeans and T-shirts. He had enough of button shirts, belts and neatly ironed pants when he put on a uniform every day.

To make matters worse, they were taking her car. She'd informed him the night before that she had no intention of climbing in and out of his truck in a dress, and that had been that.

They were even going on a work night, which he thought was ridiculous, but she knew he was more likely to work late or be called back out on a weekend, so she'd insisted. Since she didn't work until ten, it wasn't a big deal for her. For his sake, they were leaving earlier than they might usually have gone out.

Taking a deep breath, he forced himself to relax. It was dinner. His shirt had buttons and a collar. So what? She'd put up with his erratic hours and attempts to drag her outside. The least he could do was drive into the city and give her the romantic dinner he'd ruined on Sunday.

He knew where the nerves came from. Fancy meals at bistros weren't really his thing and he was afraid she was going to look at him across the table and remember he wasn't her type. The last thing he wanted was for her to look at him the way Ciara had.

After making sure Bear had everything he needed, including cartoons on the television, he told him he'd be back in a few hours and went out the front door. Hailey was in the process of locking her door and one look at her went a long way toward killing the cranky mood he'd been trying to fight off.

A red dress hugged the top of her and then flared out a little at the bottom. She was wearing one of the black half-sweater things over it, with black high-heeled shoes he might have talked her into wearing to bed if he'd known about them. Her hair was down, framing her face, which she'd done up to accentuate her eyes. She looked beautiful and he suddenly felt underdressed in his best outfit, not counting his dress uniform or wedding-slash-funeral suit.

Her face lit up when she saw him, and he met her at her car. "You look gorgeous."

She did a little twirl, showing off her swirly skirt and legs that didn't quit. "Thank you."

When she handed him her keys, he realized she wanted him to drive, which was nice. Driving his truck would have been nicer, but he could see how getting in and out would be an issue in those shoes.

She talked most of the way there, telling him about her day and about the preschool story hour. The summer reading program would be starting soon and she was still trying to finalize the details for that. He liked when she talked about her work and found himself relaxing.

Until they pulled into the parking lot. It was obviously more upscale than the Trailside Diner, and he liked the diner. But he went around the car and helped Hailey out, like a gentleman. She took his arm to walk to the front door, which he held for her.

The romantic atmosphere set him on edge, as did the number of glasses and forks on the table where they were seated. While none of the women were as beautiful as Hailey, most of the men around them were wearing suits, or at least ties, and he felt conspicuous.

She leaned across the table, her eyes sparkling in the dim light accented by a flickering candle. "Isn't this place gorgeous?"

"Mmm." When she frowned at his noncommittal answer, he mustered up a smile. He owed her a good time. "It is."

Then he was handed a wine list that amounted to a bunch of words that meant nothing to him. He scanned it and his first instinct was to just pick one, but he wasn't sure how to pronounce anything on the list.

"I'd really prefer coffee," he told the waiter. Then he handed the list to Hailey. "You can pick one for yourself, if you want."

"I'll have coffee, too. And water." When the waiter left, she grinned at him. "I guess you don't speak French?"

He knew she was teasing, but he was feeling a little out of his element and it threw him off. "Just a few words I picked up during a trip to Montreal my junior year of college. Probably nothing you'd want me to say in here."

"Probably not. What are you going to eat?" She was looking at the menu, so he did the same.

"I'm guessing shepherd's pie isn't an option."

She laughed. "Even if it was, it wouldn't be as good as mine."

"Since I like simple, home-cooked meals, I'm betting nothing on this menu will be as good."

He heard her sigh even over the classical music being piped in through well-hidden speakers. He was disappointing her already. "They have steak, Matt. I *know* you like steak."

Of course it wasn't as simple as ordering a steak. They didn't have mashed potatoes and he didn't catch half of what the guy said, so he ended up going with a baked potato. And the vegetables couldn't be plain. There were a number of options, none of which he was familiar with. He just said *that one* when he got bored.

Once the annoying guy with the snotty attitude went away, he tried to focus on Hailey. She looked so pretty, especially in the romantic lighting, and he tried to relax. It was a restaurant. With food. Who cared if he wasn't wearing a tie?

"The music's a little loud," she said. "I feel like I need to yell at you across the table."

"Could use a little more country and a little less of this, too. Whatever this is."

"I think this particular one is Rachmaninoff." She smiled at him. "Definitely not something I could dance to in my kitchen."

Or in her living room. He'd gladly watch her dance to almost anything, he thought. "Happily, I don't see a dance floor."

"We can go dancing another time."

And so it began. Dinner. Dancing. Before he knew it, she'd be dragging him to fancy functions and making apologies for him in embarrassed whispers. "We'll see."

The waiter brought a salad for each of them, along with a decanter of some oily substance that didn't remotely resemble ranch dressing. And how many different kinds of lettuce could they find for one plate?

"Thanks," he said brusquely when the man appeared to be waiting for a response from him.

"Your entrees should be out shortly."

Hailey was watching him as he dumped some of the oily stuff on his bowl of lettuces, and her mouth quirked up in a grin. "I thought he was waiting to see if you knew which fork to use."

Because everybody knew he wasn't good enough to eat in a place like this. "Maybe I'll exceed everybody's expectations and eat with my hands."

She set her fork down. "You know, this whole *laughing with you, not at you* thing would work better if you actually laughed."

"I laugh when something's funny."

The look she gave him should have incinerated him on the spot, and it only went downhill from there.

He didn't want to be there and she knew it. And the harder he tried to shake it off and the more guilty he felt, the worse he got. By the time they were done with their *entrees,* she wasn't really speaking to him, and she didn't even consider dessert.

Maybe, subconsciously, he'd been a jerk and taken offense to torpedo the evening deliberately. Her walking away from him now would suck, but maybe it wouldn't be as painful as ending things with Ciara. But when he looked across the table after pay-

ing the bill, he didn't see disapproval or embarrass-
ment in Hailey's eyes. He saw hurt.

He'd never been so happy to finish a meal in his
entire life, but an hour was a long time to drive with
a cold shoulder riding shotgun.

BY THE TIME Matt parked the car in her driveway and
turned it off, Hailey had had just about enough of
his attitude. When he pulled the keys out of the ignition, she held out her hand, saying nothing, until
he dropped them into her palm. Then she pulled her
clutch bag out of the door pocket.

"Thanks. It was ever so fun." She opened her door
and started to get out, but he grabbed her arm.

"Hailey, let's talk about this."

"Oh, now you want to talk to me? Really? You've
been a jerk all night."

"We could have just gone to the diner." She
jerked her arm away and got out of the car. He did
the same, then faced off with her over the roof of the
car. "You're the one who pushed to go to a bistro."

"I got up at the ass crack of dawn to watch the
moose. I went four-wheeling with you. I'm sorry you
weren't willing to sit through *one* dinner in a nice
restaurant for me."

"It was dumb to get all dressed up and drive two
hours for a meal."

"I've met your family, so I know you weren't
raised by wolves." Anger burned through her, fur-

ther ruining what should have been a lovely night. "You're perfectly capable of being an adult, including compromising like grown-ups do for each other."

He pointed a finger at her, which made her want to break it. "I dated a woman just like you, once."

"Excuse me?"

"I was good enough to sleep with and she loved how all of her friends told her how hot I was, but when things started to get real, she wanted a spiffed-up version of me. I embarrassed her."

"I wasn't *embarrassed* by you tonight, Matt. I was hurt. And I'm not carrying the baggage some other woman saddled you with." He stared at her, his jaw clenched, but he didn't say anything. She tried not to think about how that woman must have made him feel. It had nothing to do with her. "Is that what's happening here? Things are starting to get real?"

It took him forever to answer, every second feeling like a lifetime. "You've told me all along I'm not your type. Maybe I should have listened."

"Don't turn this all around on me. You've made it clear all along I'm not *your* type, either. And yet here we are."

"Yeah. Here we are. With you pissed off because I didn't like your fancy date."

"No, I'm not pissed off that you didn't like it. I'm pissed off that you couldn't just enjoy being with *me* and let *me* enjoy a night out on the town, even if it wasn't your favorite thing to do." She backed away from the car, shaking her head. "I was right from the beginning. You're definitely not the man for me."

"No, I'm not. You've been waiting for some fairy tale prince in a fancy suit to come waltzing into Whitford and take you dancing in glass slippers. I'm no prince."

"You're not Prince *Charming,* that's for damn sure." She slammed her car door. "Prince Asshole, maybe."

She started walking toward her house and, when she heard the driver's door close, she hit the button to lock the car, but she didn't look back.

"Hailey, wait."

"Good night, Matt. Call me if you need me to take care of Bear. Other than that, you stay in your yard and I'll stay in mine."

She slammed her house door, too, just because she could. When her heels were kicked off, she walked through her house and up the stairs without turning on a light. Then she curled up in the middle of her bed, still too angry to cry.

Since the very first minute she'd laid eyes on Matt, she'd told herself he was all wrong for her. She'd known it then, and she should have listened to herself. And she definitely should have ignored her friends. And ignored *him,* with his big heart and sexy body and ability to touch her the way she'd craved being touched.

Her clutch was still in her hand and she pulled

her phone out to pull up Tori's number. *No, I told YOU so.*

A couple of minutes passed before she got a response. *What happened? Do you want me to come over?*

No. I'm going to bed. Just wanted you to know I was right.

I'm sorry.

She'd get over it—over him. It's not as if she'd had big dreams of a wedding and babies and rocking chairs. They were having fun and she'd known eventually they'd stop having fun. She just hadn't expected it to be so soon, or so painful.

The first tears filled her eyes as the anger dulled from a flare to a smoldering ember. She knew she should get up and start getting ready for bed, but the tears spilled over and kept on coming.

The daylight streaming through her window woke her up the next morning, which was good since she hadn't turned on her alarm.

Wincing, she rolled onto her back and squinted at the ceiling. Crying herself to sleep in her makeup and a dress had been a bad idea. Almost as bad as talking Matt into taking her on a real date.

She pushed herself to her feet and stripped off her clothes from the night before. A very long, insanely hot shower was what she needed. And makeup remover. Very deliberately not looking out her window, she went into her bathroom and tried not to look in the mirror, either.

An hour later, she was ready for work, though it was seriously tempting to take a sick day. All she had to do was call the police station and ask them to post a sign on the door. She didn't do it often, but with only one librarian it had happened a few times over the years.

But she wasn't going to hide. Staying in her house, licking her emotional wounds and feeling sorry for herself wasn't her style. If she was going to have to live next door to Matt for the foreseeable future, she needed to set the tone now.

It was fun, but now it's not, so how about those Red Sox?

When she walked out to her car, she was relieved to see his truck was already gone. It was one thing to have a plan for returning to a state of neighbors-only, but she was still a little raw to put it into play.

Bear came barreling toward her, and she stopped to play with him for a few minutes, as she always did. He was so sweet, and she hoped Matt wouldn't be a jerk and not let the dog come visit. She wouldn't have guessed he'd act like that, but she hadn't guessed last night would happen, either.

When she couldn't put it off any longer, she gave Bear a belly rub and then told him to go in the house. Once he was gone, she got in her car and started it. She had to adjust the seat because Matt had been driving and just that small reminder made her mad all over again.

It wasn't a good day at work. Very few patrons stopped in, which became a problem for about a month between the weather being too nice to be inside and being so hot they wanted the air-conditioning, which meant time crawled by. She deflected texts from Tori and then from Liz. Then Tori again. Even Katie texted her.

Finally she started a group text to get it over with. *I'm trying to work. Matt & I are over. End of story.*

It wouldn't be the end of the story, of course. They'd want all the details. But she wasn't ready to talk about it quite yet.

She wasn't even sure what there was to say. She'd changed her expectations. He hadn't. That's all there was. It didn't make for a great story.

It made for one hell of a heartache, though.

NINETEEN

MATT FOLLOWED PETE up the old logging road, the ATV engine roaring between his legs. They'd been trying to catch a couple of punks who were trespassing and riding wetlands for a while and now they were at it again.

Because they'd spread the word through the surrounding community, the residents were watching and an older woman had called in a tip. Based on her information, they knew the riders had to have gone through wetlands and across posted property to get where they were and they had a good idea where they'd come out of the woods. Matt and Pete intended to be waiting for them when they did.

They were cranking up the dirt road, with about two miles left to go. Matt calculated, based on when their caller had seen the suspects, that they'd arrive at the point where they'd cross paths with only a few minutes to spare.

It felt good to be out on the quads, blowing off some steam. God knew, he had plenty to blow off.

He'd overreacted to Hailey. In the back of his mind, he'd been aware of it even as it was happening, but he couldn't help himself. And now, in the light of a new day, he knew he'd been an asshole. Or Prince Asshole, as she'd called him. He'd always thought he had a good sense of humor, and hers was one of the things he liked most about Hailey, but he hadn't been able to laugh off what he knew she'd meant to be funny. She'd pushed his hot button without knowing and, rather than explain, he'd pretty much killed any chance she'd get close enough to push it again.

Now the question was whether he should apologize to her and try to explain, or if they were both better off the way it was.

He heard the pitch of the machine Pete was riding change and had to let off his throttle a bit to leave space between them. Pete was definitely slowing down and Matt pulled toward the center of the road a little, intending to speed up and pull along side him. If they didn't haul ass, they were going to miss bagging the rogue ATV riders.

Then Pete hunched forward, his right arm coming up toward his chest. His machine slowed drastically without his thumb on the throttle, but his body jerked, yanking the left side of the handlebars toward his body.

He still had enough speed so the machine turned to the left, too sharply. His tire caught and the machine lifted.

"Pete!"

If he'd had control of the bars, he might have been

able to throw his body sideways and pull the machine into line, but Pete let go totally to clutch his chest. As the machine rolled, he was thrown and Matt shouted as he hit the tree line.

Matt tore off his helmet and was calling for help even as he ran toward his friend. They'd already called for backup and a truck was en route, but he had to call it in as a medical emergency now.

Pete wasn't moving and Matt felt the cold sweat of fear break out over his body. He didn't think Pete had actually hit a tree, but it was hard to tell. He shouldn't move him, but he knew from the events leading up to it that it wasn't the crash that was going to kill him.

From the angle, he guessed Pete's arm was broken. Maybe his leg, too. It wasn't obvious but, judging by the way he'd landed, his right side was probably busted up. But, worse than any broken bone, Matt didn't think he was breathing.

Yelling at the phone he'd put on speaker and dropped next to his knee, trying to update them on the urgency of the situation, he moved Pete as carefully as he could to his back. After undoing his vest and parting it as best as he could, he checked his breathing and hunted for a pulse.

"I need help!" He took off his own vest, needing it out of the way and leaned over his friend. "Don't you dare die, Pete."

He started CPR, his world narrowing to nothing

but breathing for Pete and listening to the woman on the other end of the phone assuring him help was coming.

HAILEY LOCKED UP the library and drove to the General Store because she needed a few groceries. If it had only been milk for her coffee, she might have stopped by the diner and begged some from them rather than face Fran, but she needed a few other things, too. Including comfort food.

She was going to drown her feelings in a bag of salt and vinegar potato chips. Maybe she'd fry up a hot dog to go with them, or maybe she'd just eat the entire bag for dinner. Sure, she'd be sorry tomorrow, but no more sorry than she already was for getting involved with Matt Barnett.

If she could go back in time, she would never have brought him the shepherd's pie. They both would have been better off if he'd kept on thinking of her as the crazy lady who lived next door and couldn't be trusted in the woods.

The bell rang over the door when she stepped into the general store. Fran looked up and frowned. "Did you hear the news?"

Hailey realized Fran wasn't sitting in her usual knitting chair. She was on a stool near the scanner she usually kept down to a volume just loud enough to be annoying. "I just left work. Did I hear what news?"

"A game warden was in an ATV accident."

Hailey froze. "Where?"

"I'm not sure."

"There are a lot of game wardens. I mean, I hope whoever it is is okay, but there's no reason to believe it's *our* game warden." She wasn't sure if she was trying to convince Fran or herself. "What happened?"

"I don't know a lot. I just heard it on the radio. They were calling in a LifeFlight helicopter to take a game warden to the Central Maine Medical Center in Lewiston. I'm almost sure I heard Matt's name, but I missed the context."

Hailey's entire body went cold and for a long moment, she wasn't sure she could even move. Or breathe. "You don't know if he was the warden hurt or if they were reporting he was the warden on scene?"

"I don't. I'm sorry, honey. The radio chatters all the time and, by the time I realized what was going on, I'd missed some of it."

"I have to go."

She ran to her car and drove home, her fingers tight on the steering wheel. Once she was in her driveway, she took a breath and tried to call Matt's cell phone. It rang and rang, and then went to voice mail.

"Dammit." She went inside, indecision making her mind whirl.

It might not be him. Whoever was talking might have been letting the other person know Matt was on the scene. He could have been a witness. Or the investigating officer. She had no evidence he was the one hurt.

But she couldn't stand not knowing and, in the pit of her stomach, she had a bad feeling. Her hands were shaking and her stomach was churning and there was no way she could go about the rest of her day pretending there wasn't a chance Matt was fighting for his life.

She pulled out her phone again and dialed Drew Miller's cell. He answered on the second ring. "Drew, do you know anything?"

"There's a lot of confusion on the scene and nobody has time to talk to me. I know two game wardens went on the helicopter and one of them was Matt, but I'm told only one of them was hurt."

"I'm going."

"Hailey, it's a two-hour drive. By the time you get there, I'll probably already know what happened."

"Even if he's not the one hurt, he'll need somebody. He won't have a vehicle. He left here on his ATV and his truck's still in the driveway."

She heard him sigh. "Do *not* speed, Hailey Genest. You wrapping yourself around a tree won't help anybody."

"I'll be careful. Call me if you hear anything."

She hung up and made a quick trip to the bathroom. Then she called the Northern Star Lodge and got Rose. "Hailey, how are you?"

"I have to go to Lewiston. Can I drop off Bear with you guys?"

"Wait. Bear…that's Matt Barnett's dog, right?"

"There was an accident. I don't know if he's the one hurt, but I know he was on the helicopter to Central Maine Med. I'm going, but I don't want to leave Bear, just in case."

Just in case of what, she didn't want to think about. She knew he'd said if his family got a phone call with bad news, they'd get Bear, but how high on their priority list would he be?

"You go ahead and go. I'll send Josh to get Bear because he knows him. And I know Fran started carrying his brand of dog food, so he'll stop and grab a bag. You just go ahead and leave."

"Thanks, Rosie. I'll leave his back door unlocked. Ask Josh to leave a note on the counter with the lodge's number in case somebody from his family shows up, and to lock up when he leaves. I'll let you know if I find out anything."

After hitting the bathroom, she grabbed a sweatshirt and a water. She hated leaving Bear next door, but she knew he was used to Matt being late sometimes. And, even if Josh turned out to be busy, somebody from the Northern Star would come and get him. And it would already be almost eight before she got there.

She ate up the miles without hearing anything from Whitford. Stopping for gas and coffee at the three-quarter mark, she tried to get through to Drew but, whether it was her phone or his, the call didn't go through.

When she finally arrived, she parked in the emergency room parking lot and went through the sliding doors. She wasn't sure where they'd be or if anybody would tell her anything, but she was going to try. She wasn't being turned away until she knew what had happened to Matt.

Then she saw him.

He was leaned up against the wall at the end of the hallway, his head tipped back and his eyes closed. With his arms hanging limply at his sides, he looked like a man who was beaten and exhausted and praying for good news. But he wasn't hurt.

"Matt."

He lifted his head and it seemed to take a few seconds for his eyes to focus on her. "Hailey?"

She started toward him and he met her halfway, pulling her into his arms. She wrapped her arms around him and held him tight. It wasn't him. That meant somebody he worked with, maybe even a friend, was on the other side of the big, double doors, but it wasn't Matt.

"Fran heard on the radio that two game wardens got on a flight here, that one was hurt, and she heard your name. That's all anybody knew."

"You didn't have to drive all the way here." But he didn't let her go.

"I had to know."

"It's Pete. My friend Pete. He had a heart attack, I guess, and wrecked his quad. It was…" His words died off and he shuddered in her arms.

"Do you know anything yet?"

"I know he's alive." He took a deep breath and let her go.

She looked into his face and gave him what she hoped was a reassuring smile. "That's good, then. Are you alone here?"

"A couple guys came, but there's a kid—a young one—missing near a lake, so they had to go."

"Do you want some food? Some coffee? Anything?"

He shook his head, his gaze never leaving hers. "I can't believe you drove all the way here."

"Your phone went to voice mail."

"I broke it. At some point I crushed it somehow and my satellite phone's in the cargo box on my four-wheeler."

She nodded, knowing calling her would have been way down on his list of priorities anyway, if there at all. "I called the lodge and Josh is going to get Bear. I hope that's okay."

A small smile broke through the weariness on his face. "You don't mess around in an emergency, do you?"

She felt ridiculous now that she'd seen he was okay. He could have been on his way home already and she'd be running around the hospital looking for him and his dog would be at the Northern Star. "It was stupid. I overreacted, I guess. I should have stayed home with Bear and waited for you to call."

He grabbed her hand. "No. It means a lot to me that you came. I feel bad that it was for nothing, though. I should have called you."

"It wasn't for nothing." She tried to keep the emotion from showing, but the relief was still making her shaky. She'd known her feelings for him had grown despite her resistance, enough so walking away from him had been one of the hardest things she'd ever done, but she hadn't realized until now they were strong enough to knock the wind out of her.

He looked like he was going to say something else, but the double doors opened and a doctor emerged. "Warden Barnett?"

Matt released her hand and turned to face the doctor. "How's Pete?"

"He's going to pull through. You can come on back now and I'll talk to you about his condition. I've spoken to Mrs. Winslow, who's still almost an hour out, and she said I could update you. He's not awake right now, but you can sit with him."

Matt looked at Hailey, and she could see his desire to get through those doors in his eyes. "Go. I'm glad he's going to be okay. Just go."

"Thank you for coming, Hailey." He didn't look back again as he followed the doctor through the doors.

ONCE PETE'S WIFE and daughter arrived and the doctor had given them the good news Pete would be in the hospital for a few days, but would make a full recovery, there wasn't much reason in Matt sticking around any longer.

There would be reports to write and so much paperwork he'd feel trapped in red tape hell, but that was for tomorrow. Or maybe, if he was very lucky, the next day. For now, he felt as if he'd been dragged for miles by a runaway horse, so he kissed Pete's wife on the cheek and made his escape.

He felt a pang of regret when he thought of Hailey. It was a four-hour round trip for her and he'd given her maybe five minutes before he disappeared. He'd gone out into the hall at one point, but he hadn't seen her and she hadn't been in the waiting room. He didn't blame her for leaving. He'd run off and left her with barely a goodbye and that was after he'd been a total asshole the night before.

Even though he'd acted like a jerk, she'd taken care of his dog and then driven two hours to make sure he was okay. He wasn't sure what to make of that, but he'd be giving it a lot of thought when he wasn't halfway to being a zombie.

He could either scrounge around for a ride back to

Whitford, or he could dig deep and summon enough charm to sweet talk the ER nurses into giving him a bed or a cot to crash on for the night. He was leaning toward the latter, but he wanted to get some fresh air first.

As he passed the waiting room, he happened to glance in and saw Hailey curled up on the sofa, reading a magazine. He stepped inside and she glanced up.

"You're still here," he said.

The wave of unexpected feeling almost staggered him. He hadn't realized until he saw her face how much he didn't want to be alone right now. Staying with Pete's wife and daughter had seemed intrusive, and so did calling his family, but he wasn't ready for silence after the day he'd had.

But Hailey had waited for him and he could see the concern in her eyes just as clearly as he'd seen the relief when she spotted him earlier and realized it wasn't him who'd been hurt. She cared. And so did he. More than he'd wanted to admit to himself. He'd known he was falling, but he hadn't realized just how far.

She tossed the magazine onto the side table and stood. "You came on the helicopter with your friend, so I wasn't sure how you'd get home."

"Somebody would have given me a ride." He kept his words tight, not trusting the emotions he felt to stay put so he could analyze them rather than them pouring out of his mouth. "A local officer, maybe."

"Oh. Well, no sense in anybody going out of their way. You live next door to me, so it's not out of my way. Maybe a *little,* since I have to drive by my house to get to yours and then backtrack, but it's only fifty feet or so. And you'd probably be a decent guy and offer to walk that far."

He smiled. "You're babbling."

Her expression grew serious and she shrugged one shoulder in an embarrassed kind of gesture. "I couldn't leave you here all alone."

Those words hit him in the gut and he wasn't sure what to say.

"I know there's nothing I could do," she continued, "but I couldn't just turn around and drive home, either, you know?"

"I was going to crash on a cot somewhere here. I'd rather go home."

"Do you need to talk to anybody first? Or get anything? Do you have stuff somewhere?"

She asked the questions in a take-charge kind of way, and Matt felt his muscles ease a little. He could relax with Hailey and she'd make sure he got home okay. "I've already said goodbye to Pete's wife and talked to his nurse. I have everything, I guess. I took off my vest before I started CPR. I tossed it somewhere, so somebody grabbed it, I'm sure. And my helmet was there, too. I'm ready."

"I moved my car to the visitor's lot," she said, and he realized she'd probably been doing that when he'd looked for her. He felt like such an idiot. "I wasn't sure how long you'd be and I didn't want to take up an ER space. Do you want me to go get it and pull it around?"

He smiled and shook his head. "I can walk that far."

She stayed at his side as they walked out into the night, and he filled his lungs with fresh, cool air. The only thing worse than being inside was being inside a hospital, but there had been no way he would let Pete make that flight alone. Now that he could leave, he felt almost guilty about the relief he felt.

Once they were buckled up, Hailey started her car and steered it toward the hospital's exit. "Do you want me to find a coffee shop or some fast food or anything?"

"If you want something then go ahead, but I'm good."

"I singlehandedly depleted the hospital vending machines of anything with caffeine or chocolate, so we'll head for home. I called Rose while I was moving my car, and Bear's fine. And she'll let everybody know you're okay."

"Thanks," he said. It seemed like a weak word when he was more grateful to her than he could say, but it was all he could manage.

There were two hours ahead of them and he felt

himself getting drowsier with every passing mile. A couple of times he jerked awake and knew from the songs on the radio he'd nodded off for a few minutes.

She glanced over at him the third or fourth time it happened. "Why don't you drop the seat back and sleep?"

"I'm okay."

He wasn't, but she was tired, too. She had the air-conditioning on, her window cracked and was singing along with the songs, all tactics he'd used to keep himself awake behind the wheel. It was a long ride and he wanted to make sure she didn't nod off herself.

"Matt."

She touched his arm and he looked over at her. Awareness hit all at once. The car wasn't moving. His eyes had been closed and his eyelids felt heavy and gritty. And his neck was stiff as hell. He'd slept, and slept hard.

"We're home," she said quietly.

He tried to straighten his body out, cursing himself for apparently falling asleep with his head cradled sideways against the seat belt instead of just reclining the seat when she suggested it. He undid his seat belt, but sat for a minute, trying to shake off the grogginess.

"It's too late to go get Bear."

He nodded. "House is quiet without him. Lonely."

"Then come in with me."

It was too dark to read anything from her expression, but he heard nothing but sincerity in her voice. "I wasn't angling for an invitation. I'm just tired and my filter's running behind my mouth, I guess."

"Do you want to be alone right now?"

"No." He snorted. "See? Filter's busted."

"Come inside, Matt."

He nodded, his sense of good judgment obviously lagging as far behind as his *don't say that out loud* filter. But it was the truth. He didn't want to be alone. He wanted to be with her.

TWENTY

HAILEY WASN'T SURE what to do with a man who was bone-tired, emotionally tapped and not in the mood to talk about it, so she made him hot cocoa. Matt didn't say a word while she microwaved a mug of water, then added the cocoa mix and half and half, and she didn't push it. If he wanted to talk, he'd talk.

When she set the mug on the table in front of him, he wrapped his hands around it as if they were freezing and he was trying to suck the heat out of the ceramic. "Thank you."

"Do you want me to make you something to eat? I know you didn't have any dinner."

"I'm not hungry, but thanks."

He took a few sips of the hot cocoa, then he just held the mug and stared at the brown liquid. She rested her hands on his shoulders in a gesture of comfort, but the muscles were tight, so she started kneading them. Using her fingers and the heel of her hand, she massaged his neck and shoulders, trying to ease some of the tension.

Matt moaned and lowered his head, totally exposing his neck to her touch. "That feels amazing."

"I'm sorry I sent your dog on a sleepover. You'd probably be curled up in bed with Bear already."

His shoulders shook when he chuckled. "Bear has his own bed. We don't snuggle."

"That's too bad. Sometimes you just need a hug."

"Sometimes." He grasped her wrists and pulled until her chest was against his back and her arms were wrapped around him.

She stayed like that for a while, but after hours in the car, her back started protesting the position. And, as hugs went, it wasn't enough. She wanted to hold him.

Without removing her arms, Hailey walked around the chair and lifted her leg over his so she straddled his lap. The edge of the table pressed against her back, but it was a minor nuisance compared to the pain she saw in Matt's eyes.

Tightening her arms around his shoulders, she rested her cheek on his shoulder and hugged him tight.

His arms wrapped around her waist and he buried his face against her neck. "Thank you for waiting for me."

"I'm sorry about your friend's accident, but I'm glad he'll be okay."

"I've been shot at. I've rolled a truck so bad it took them an hour to cut me out of it. But I've never been so scared as I was giving Pete CPR. His daughter calls me Uncle Matt, you know. She's five."

"And he's going to go home to her in a few days. That's what you need to focus on."

His fingertips bit into her skin. "I know that, but… I'm trying to shake it off, but I'm so damn tired."

Hailey pulled back and cupped his face in her hands. "Let's go to bed. Bear's being spoiled rotten at the Northern Star and nobody's going to expect you to be at work first thing in the morning."

She slid off his lap and nudged him sideways until she could crouch in front of him to unlace his boots. Once she had the laces loosened all the way down each, he toed them off and she pushed them aside. But when she took his hands to pull him to his feet, he resisted.

"Maybe I should go home."

"You really should have made that decision before we got your boots off."

He didn't smile. "We're a bad idea."

She sighed and squeezed his hands. "Yeah. But we're friends, you need some comfort and, to be honest, I could use some, too. We can go back to being a bad idea tomorrow."

After only a moment's hesitation, he stood and let her lead him through the house. When he stumbled slightly on the stairs, she realized just how tired he was and tightened her hand around his. Whatever adrenaline rush had come with the day's events and kept him going had definitely left his system

When they reached her room, Matt balked again.

He took a couple of steps inside and then stopped, though he didn't let go of her hand. "I'm exhausted, Hailey. I've been sweaty all day, I probably smell like hell. I'm grubby."

Starting at the top, she undid each of the buttons of his uniform shirt, yanking it out of his pants to undo the bottom few. "Take care of your belt."

Exhaustion made his hands shake a little as he took care of his gun, setting it on her dresser, and then laying the belt with the rest of its accouterments across the armchair in the corner. When he was done, she slid the shirt off his shoulders to reveal the T-shirt underneath.

"Arms up," she told him.

"Hailey, I—"

"Yeah, I get it. You're grubby. I'm going to hold you and I'll be grubby, too. And then we'll get the sheets grubby." She lifted his arms up and then pulled off his T-shirt. "In the morning, we can take showers and I'll throw the sheets in the washer."

She bent to pull his pants off, offering her shoulder for support as she removed each sock and pant leg in return. Then she turned down the blanket and sheet.

Hailey figured by the time she turned off the lights and stripped down to her underwear, he'd be snoring, but when she slid into bed, he threw his arm over her and pulled her close.

"You have soft sheets," he murmured. "I'm sorry I'm getting them dirty."

She nestled against him, so almost every part of their bodies were touching. The feel of him, so warm and strong, crumbled the foundation of the emotional walls she'd been trying to maintain. "I like you more than I like my sheets."

"I like you, too, Hailey. More than…"

The mumbling faded away and he was out. She waited, holding her breath, but all that came out of him was a long, soft snore.

Hailey closed her eyes, trying to will her muscles to release the stress of the day, but sleep didn't come right away. He liked her more than what?

MATT WOKE SLOWLY, not wanting to open his eyes. For a few seconds, he wondered why Bear hadn't nuzzled him to unlock the dog door, but then he remembered.

He was in Hailey's bed, with her soft, sweet-smelling sheets. He was on his back, while she was on her side, her butt pressed against his hip, but he remembered holding her tightly as he drifted off to sleep.

Emotions churned in his gut, and he sighed as he stared at her ceiling. The last couple days had been an emotional rollercoaster and he wanted off the ride. Thursday night had sucked. He'd let what had happened with Ciara screw with his head and he'd treated Hailey like crap.

Yesterday had been one of his worst days on the job and he'd almost lost a good friend, but then he'd seen Hailey. And being with her—taking her into his arms for comfort—had felt so right.

Now that he'd felt that, he couldn't stand the thought of her walking away from him again. When she woke up, with the emergency over, she'd remember what an asshole he'd been and throw him out. She'd said herself they could go back to being a bad idea in the morning, and now morning had come.

Sliding out of bed, he gathered his belongings and went down the stairs, trying to be as quiet as possible. In the half bathroom off her kitchen, he took a leak and, after splashing cold water on his face, debated on getting dressed.

In the end he stayed in his boxer briefs. The idea—or more accurately, the *need*—to get away and take refuge at camp took hold in his mind. He needed time to let his feelings settle so he could take a good look at them and figure out just what he wanted going forward and that's where he'd always done his heavy thinking. He wouldn't be able to do that here. Not with Hailey so close.

He brewed a pot of coffee for her, then found a junk mail envelope in a pile on her counter and a pen. He wrote her a note and then, feeling like a coward even though he felt it was the right thing to do, he gathered his stuff and let himself out, walking to his house in his boxer briefs.

After taking a shower and getting dressed, he grabbed his keys and jumped in his truck. He knew they were early risers at the Northern Star, so he wasn't surprised to see Josh and Bear outside when he pulled up the long drive.

Bear ran in excited circles, waiting for Matt to get out of his truck. He crouched down and let the dog give him a few happy licks to the face. "Hi, buddy. I'm glad to see you, too."

He walked over to Josh and shook his hand. "Thanks for taking care of Bear. It was nice to know he was in good hands."

"The most important thing is that you're okay. And the other guy? I heard he'll recover?"

"Yeah. He's going to have to take it slow for a while. Not only did he have the heart attack, but his arm's broken and he fractured his foot. But he'll bounce back." Bear jumped up, something he rarely did, and put his front paws on Matt's chest. He staggered back a step, then ruffled the dog's fur. He figured the dog was picking up on the turmoil he felt inside. "Down, boy."

"By the way, the women in this house have now decided we need a dog. I'm not sure when or what, but there will be payback, my friend."

Matt laughed. "Sorry. He has that effect on people sometimes."

"How's Hailey?"

"Probably still sleeping. She did a lot of driving

last night, but I'm glad she was there. Sleeping on cots in the ER sucks, though I've done it before."

Josh looked at him for a few seconds, as though he could see that Matt had deflected to matters of practicality when he knew Josh wanted to know her emotional state. "Yeah, she left town in a hurry."

"Speaking of leaving town, Bear and I are going to head to camp, so I'll be out of town. Maybe through the weekend."

"Heading out of town while she's still sleeping?" Josh shook his head. "You *want* her pissed off?"

"It might be easier that way. It's…complicated. But hey, thanks again for taking Bear."

"We've got some airtight containers we use for storage in the cellar and the barns, so I'll probably hold on to the bag of dog food I got from Fran. That way if you get in a jam again, we'll already have some. And no, I don't want your money. You can pay for lunch sometime."

"Sounds like a deal, though I hope you having to rescue my dog won't become a habit."

"We don't mind and chances are, at some point we'll need a favor from you. This way you can't say no." He grinned, then patted Bear's haunches. "Rosie's making breakfast. You want to stay?"

"I'm going to hit the road, but I appreciate it."

He let Bear into the truck, but Josh said his name before he could climb in himself. "Did I forget something?"

"No matter what happens between you two when you get back, make it right with Hailey. Whether it's over or not, you need to own it and talk to her. She deserves that."

"Yeah. She does."

He got in the truck and headed back toward his house. Reaching over to scratch Bear's head, he turned his options over in his head, but he kept coming back to the same one. "Hey, buddy, you want to go to camp?"

HAILEY OPENED HER eyes, trying to focus on the clock. At first she thought it said six o'clock, but then she realized it was an eight. The realization she had to open the library in two hours made her close them again.

She stretched her leg out and her foot eventually reached the other side of the mattress. Matt was already up, which surprised her. He'd been as beat as she'd ever seen another person.

Maybe he was making coffee. She inhaled deeply, but didn't smell fresh brew. But, then again, she probably wouldn't be able to smell it all the way up the stairs and in her room, anyway.

When she heard Bear barking, she opened her eyes. Bear was supposed to be at the Northern Star. She slid out of bed and pulled back the curtains, but she couldn't see what was going on.

After pulling on a pair of sweats and a hoodie,

she went downstairs, the aroma of coffee hitting her about halfway down the stairs. There was a note next to the coffeemaker.

Thank you for coming after me last night and for letting me stay. I'm going to camp to get my head on straight. I hope. Matt. P.S.—I made you a pot of coffee. It was the least I could do.

She wasn't sure what the hell that was supposed to mean, but she didn't like it. He was running. Whether from her or from what had happened, she didn't know. But this smacked of a man who didn't want to stand up and face feelings that had gotten messy when he wasn't looking.

Since he was right about it being the least he could do, she poured a cup of the coffee he'd brewed and added some milk and sugar. She wouldn't chase after him. If he wanted to run, he was free to go.

But as the caffeine kicked in, so did her annoyance. He was free to go, but that didn't mean she was going to give him a pass or make it easy. She topped off her mug and took it outside. Sitting on her front step, she could see everything that went on next door.

Bear spotted her and ran over to say good morning. She gave him a good scratch and his tail thumped in happiness. "He went and picked you up early, huh? Guess he must have missed you."

Matt walked out and tossed a duffel bag into the backseat of his truck, then went back into the house. A couple minutes later, he reappeared carrying a bag of Bear's food and a cooler. Those went in the bed of the truck, and he used bungee cords to secure the cooler.

Bear seemed to know they were going to the cabin. He was almost quivering with excitement and he stared at Hailey, his tongue hanging out, as though he was willing her to be excited, too. "Sorry, buddy. I'm not invited."

Matt looked over at her house, no doubt looking for his dog, and his gaze zeroed in on her. She just looked back, not giving him anything to go on if he was trying to gauge her emotional temperature. Obviously when he wrote the note, he'd intended to get out of town before she woke up.

Since she wasn't doing anything interesting, Bear left her and went running back to Matt. Then he ran to the truck door and did a couple of tight circles. Obviously the Lab loved going out in the woods and he was ready to hit the road.

And so was Matt, judging by the fact he wasn't carrying anything else and had his keys in his hand. She saw his hesitation, but in the end he walked slowly across the yards to talk to her.

"Heading to camp, huh?"

He nodded slowly, his mouth set in a grim line. "I need to think. Get my feet back under me."

"Good luck with that."

"I figured after you did all the driving last night

and getting in so late, I'd let you sleep in, so I tried not to wake you."

She smiled then, but it wasn't a happy smile. "That's what you're going with? Rather than, I don't know…emotional chickenshit?"

"I'm afraid if I don't go off by myself and figure out what's going on in my head, I might say or do something even more stupid than I already have and make things worse."

It was an admission, she supposed. An admission he'd done and said stupid things and that he didn't want it to happen again. It wasn't an apology and it said nothing about his feelings for her, but it eased the pain in her heart a little knowing he wasn't leaving just to avoid a really awkward morning after scenario.

But she didn't think running away was ever a good solution to a problem. "I wish you'd stay, Matt. We need to have a conversation."

"I'm sorry. I'm not ready for that yet. I don't know what to say."

She stood and opened her door. "Have a nice time."

He didn't call after her, but she wouldn't have turned back if he did. If he didn't want to talk, she wasn't going to waste her time. She was going to take a shower, throw her sheets in the washer, and then get ready for work.

Saturdays weren't often very busy, but she knew

today would be unusually so as people came in hoping for details about the accident. She would simply smile and assure them their game warden was unhurt and his partner would recover. Nobody, not even Fran, would guess her heart was breaking.

TWENTY-ONE

MATT WASN'T SURPRISED to hear the crunch of tires coming up the narrow dirt road to the cabin. It was his dad, by the sound of the engine. Again, not a surprise. His mom had been shaken up by Pete's accident and had called him several times, so they knew he'd been at camp almost two days now.

He stayed in his chair and waited, though Bear couldn't stand the anticipation and ran off to meet their company. A few minutes later, a chair thumped down next to his and his old man sank into it with a groan. He popped the top on two beers, setting one in his cup holder and handing the other to Matt.

"Catching anything?"

Matt lifted a shoulder. "I'm not sure I even put a worm on the hook, to be honest."

"Did that once, when your mom and I were going through a rough patch. Couldn't even stand the sight of each other. I came up here and probably sat here for five or six hours without ever baiting the hook."

"I'm only at two hours today. Got a ways to go yet. Caught a few yesterday, though, so I must have used bait."

"I heard your friend's going to be okay. That's good."

"Yeah, I called a little while ago and spoke to his wife. He's doing great, actually, considering. And I didn't get too much grief about taking a couple of sick days." Bear finally settled between the chairs and Matt reached down to scratch the top of his head. "Long drive just to check on me. Did Mom put you up to it?"

"Let's just say she thinks it was her idea, but I was coming anyway. So, son, is this about the accident, or is there a woman?"

He could lie, but his dad had driven two hours to offer a shoulder. The least Matt could do was lean on it. "Little bit about the accident. A lot about the woman."

"Hailey?"

"I think I started falling for her when I found her breaking into my house through the doggy door to make sure Bear was okay." It felt good to say that out loud. Scary, but good.

"But, being you, you made sure she didn't know it, right?"

"We're different, Dad. Like *really* different. And right now we can joke about it a little, but over time I don't think we'll joke about it any more."

"You and Hailey have been dancing around this for quite a while now. What happened? What drove you up here this weekend?"

Matt took a long sip of beer and then told his dad how Hailey had rushed to the hospital after making sure Bear was taken care of. And how she'd waited for him, brought him home and took him to bed. "She was just…there. She didn't care that I didn't take my boots off at the door or that I smelled like dry stress sweat and who knows what else. She made me hot cocoa and then let me hold her until I went to sleep. I don't know what to do with that."

"I'll tell it to you straight. Walking out and coming up here was the *wrong* thing to do with it." His dad shook his head. "She doesn't strike me as the kind of woman who makes a four-hour round trip to a hospital and hangs out in the waiting room to bring a guy home and into her bed just because she's a nice girl. She has feelings for you, which means right now she's probably the most pissed off woman in a hundred mile radius."

"I have a knack for ticking her off, for sure."

"This one's a doozie, son. But I guess that just sets up the make-up sex to be all the sweeter."

Matt almost choked on his beer, and it went down hard when he managed to swallow. "Thanks, *Dad*."

"Hey, good sex has a way of soothing a woman's ruffled feathers."

"If I have sex with Hailey again, it has to mean she's willing to go all in." Matt took a deep breath and blew it out in a rush. "I can't do casual anymore. If she doesn't want me, I'll have to walk away."

"Why wouldn't she want you?"

The words stuck in his throat, giving Matt time to figure out a way to spit them out that didn't make him feel stupid. "She likes finer things. She has nice sheets and likes to dress up and go out. She wants a guy who…you know, like a magazine ad guy."

"You know I love you, right?"

"You're about to tell me I'm an idiot, aren't you?"

His dad nodded. "If you walk away from a woman you love because she has nice sheets, then goddamn right you're an idiot."

"I didn't say anything about love." Matt's stomach churned and he set the beer can in the cupholder.

"You know I love you, right?"

"You're a real comedian today. And of course it's not about the sheets. Just like I know she's not writing me off because I had a scruffy beard when we met. All of those are the little things that add up to the fact we're really different."

"Of course you are. So are your mother and I. You think she doesn't like to dress up and go out sometimes? I go, because she puts up with me smelling like fish guts and disappearing for hunting season. You're not looking at the big picture."

The big picture scared the crap out of him, that's why. "I just want to make her happy, and I'm not sure if I can."

"She's not going to be happy with you every minute of the day, son. You'll argue. I've been married forty years and there's a lot of arguing. She yells at you when you track mud through the house. You yell at her when she buys a black pocketbook that doesn't look any different from the three black pocketbooks she already owns. Sometimes you can't stand the sound of her voice and other times you wonder how you'd even breathe if she wasn't there. That's marriage, and she'll feel the same way. But when you've got a good woman who loves you, your back's never truly against the wall because she's there. She's got your back."

Hailey would have his back. He knew that, deep in his gut. Even though he'd been an asshole, she'd taken care of his dog and rushed to get to him. No questions, no recriminations. He'd needed somebody and she'd been there. It was that simple.

His dad sighed, his gaze fixed somewhere beyond the pond. "That's what's important, son. When you're knocked down and on your knees, you want a woman who'll help you up. And, if you're not ready to get up yet, she'll wrap her arms around you and not let anything or anybody kick you while you're down."

He'd had a glimpse of what that felt like the other night. The fear and general shittiness of the day hadn't been able to withstand the comfort of Hailey's arms around him. "What if she doesn't want me, Dad?"

"Then she's the idiot." The certainty in his dad's

voice made Matt smile. "Worst case, you nurse a broken heart and start looking for a different place to live so you don't have to see her every day."

"I can't imagine not seeing her every day."

"And there you go." His dad stood up and squeezed Matt's shoulder. "I'm going to take a leak and see if you left any cans of beef stew in the cupboard. If you're smart, you'll get in your truck and haul ass back to Whitford before she gets too worked up."

Two DAYS. Two days Matt Barnett had been gone and Hailey wanted to strangle him. Or hug him. Maybe she'd just hug him really, really tightly and fulfill both urges at the same time.

While he'd gone off to hide, she'd worked. She'd smiled and told everybody who'd asked that he was just fine. She'd told Tori and Paige and anybody else who was worried about her that she was fine, despite the fact she'd cried more tears than she'd thought a body could hold.

When she heard his truck pulling into the driveway, she was torn between wanting to march over and demand to know what his problem was, and wanting to hide in her room and pretend she wasn't home.

Assuming he'd care, of course. Nothing said he had any intention of darkening her doorstep.

But she couldn't stop herself from looking out

the window. He was wearing that damn red flannel shirt, unbuttoned over a T-shirt, and a hat that had seen better days, though it wasn't the really gross hat he'd been wearing the day they met.

She wasn't on her game, though, and when he turned to look her way, she didn't close the curtain in time. They made eye contact and he held it until she turned away from the window.

Jerk.

When the loud knock echoed through her house, she wasn't surprised. The doors were locked. An unusual occurrence during daylight hours, but she didn't want him to think everything was okay and he could come on in. It wasn't business as usual.

Then the doorbell rang and made her jump. She'd honestly forgotten the thing worked because nobody ever used it. She didn't jump the second time, and the third time just pissed her off.

She yanked open the door and it must have been obvious she wasn't happy to see him because Bear stopped wagging his tail and sat down next to Matt's feet. "What do you want?"

"I'm sorry."

"Thank you for your apology." She started to close the door, but he put up his hand to stop it.

If he'd actually made contact with the door and prevented her from closing it, she probably would have lost her temper. But he stopped short of it, his hand turning into a pleading gesture.

"Please hear me out, Hailey. Let me explain."

"I asked you to talk to me two days ago. You ran away."

"Because I was scared. I got scared of what I feel for you, so I tried to drive you away by being an asshole. But then Pete's accident happened and you came for me. It hurts that I can't be the kind of guy you want."

Her heart clenched, but she clung to the anger she'd been nursing since he took off. "How could you still think I didn't want you?"

"To sleep with, yeah. But I think we've already established I'm not your Prince Charming. I mean, look at me. I'm a guy who hasn't shaved in two days and smells like woods and bug spray and the inside of a tackle box, with a dog who may have rolled in something questionable."

"And I still wanted you." Bear's tail thumped against the ground. "Both of you."

"Wanted. Past tense."

The look in his eyes tore at her, but she wasn't giving him a pass. "I deserve better than this, Matt. I asked you to stay and talk to me, but you ran away."

"I needed to think."

"Great. You got what you needed. Now I need to focus on what I need, and it's a man who knows how to compromise and talk things out."

"Please don't do this, Hailey." She could hear the strain in his voice and Bear must have picked up on it because he made a whimpering sound and thumped his tail some more.

"You said yourself we're a bad idea. I don't have a cabin in the woods to run off to, so you need to respect that I need some space." She closed the door before he could say anything else, then rested her forehead against it.

This wasn't going to work. Even if he stayed in his own yard, she couldn't even begin to heal her broken heart with him so close. She needed to pack a bag and go stay with somebody else. Her mother, preferably, but she couldn't exactly commute from Massachusetts. And Mitch was home with Paige and Sarah, so she could either throw herself on Rose's mercy and beg a room at the lodge, or she could go to Tori's.

She chose Tori, just because there were too many people at the Northern Star, a couple of whom worked closely with Matt. After packing a couple of tote bags with the bare minimum, she locked her house and threw them in her car.

There was no sign of Matt or Bear, which made it easier to back out of her driveway onto the main road. And she didn't allow herself to look in the rear-view mirror as she drove away.

TWENTY-TWO

FOR ONCE, MATT was thankful to live in a town that thrived on gossip. It hadn't taken him long to hear Hailey was staying with Tori, which put his mind at ease. Of course, he also heard Hailey was staying with Tori because he'd broken her heart and was a horrible jerk, but he didn't blame them for siding with her.

First, because she was born and raised in Whitford, so it was only natural they'd rally around her. And, second, because he deserved it.

The problem was that he had no idea how to prove he could be the man she wanted him to be.

Her house sitting empty was killing him slowly. Knowing she wasn't there made him feel as if there was a void in the pit of his stomach he could never fill. He missed her and it was so painful he was surprised he kept breathing.

It didn't help any that Bear seemed to miss her as much as Matt did. His expectant whines and his sad eyes when he ran next door only to find the pretty lady still wasn't home just made her absence that much harder for Matt to deal with.

By Thursday morning, when he left for work, he

was starting to wonder if she'd come back. He knew how much she loved her house, and the fact he'd driven her away from it just added to the guilt he was carrying around.

He was an idiot. There wasn't really any way to sugarcoat that fact, and he accepted it. He'd lost the best thing that ever happened to him and he had nobody to blame but himself. He'd been so afraid of losing her, he'd driven her away.

Once his workday started, he managed to keep busy enough to not drive himself crazy. Outside of holiday weekends, Tuesday through Thursday tended to be quiet on the Whitford trails, with only a few local riders out, so he was in his truck, patrolling the roads over by the lake. Hailey was never completely out of his thoughts, though. She'd asked him to respect her need for space and he was trying like hell, but he needed to see her. He just wasn't sure if showing up at Tori's apartment was the way to go or not.

When a call to help convince a confused moose to leave town and go back into the woods came and he spotted a florist, he decided it was time to act. Once the animal situation was taken care of and his shift was pretty much over, he popped in and bought a bouquet of red roses. It felt a little cliché, but he was a man with few options.

Then, of course, his radio squawked and his plan had to be delayed. By the time he rolled into Whitford, he was tired and second-guessing himself. It didn't seem like showing up at the place she'd gone to be alone was the way to answer her request for space.

But when he saw her car in her driveway, the frustrations of the day fell away. She'd come home. Whether or not that meant anything where he was concerned remained to be seen, but at least she was back in her own house.

When he got out of his truck, Bear ran around from the back of her house, then stopped. He barked, then headed back toward where Matt presumed Hailey was before stopping again. The dog was obviously ecstatic to have Hailey back and wanted Matt to go say hi.

He clutched the bouquet of roses in his hand, trying not to squeeze them and break the stems. Then, after taking a breath to steady himself, he followed Bear into Hailey's backyard. She was sitting in a chair, a glass of lemonade on the table next to her, and she gave him a sad smile.

"Bear missed me, I guess." The lab was bumping his head against her knee, begging for more attention.

"He's missed you a lot. So have I."

"I was at Tori's. Which I'm sure you already knew since Fran knew."

"I did know, but I was trying to give you that space you asked for." He held out the bouquet, breathing a sigh of relief when she took it and buried her nose in the blooms.

"I've never gotten roses before. They're beautiful. Thank you."

"They'll need water soon. After I bought them, I got a report of an RV being driven erratically. I had to find him and then wait for a drug dog and… whatever. They had to sit in the truck longer than I anticipated."

"They're still beautiful."

"I'd like to take you out to dinner."

She looked at him over the flowers, a wry smile twisting her mouth. "Because it went so well last time."

"I'm sorry for that. I was so nervous and I got defensive and I was an ass. That's why I went to the cabin to think. I was so afraid I'd say something stupid again and I thought if I could just lay it all out in my head, like a script, I'd get it right."

"All I wanted was for you to *talk* to me. Getting called out for emergencies and never knowing exactly when you're going to be home is part of your job. I was learning to adjust to that. But running off to your cabin because you don't want to have a conversation? I'm not dealing with that."

"I know that, and I'll never ask you to again. I've never felt what I felt that morning. I realized I was in love with you and I was so afraid I'd ruined everything, so I ran. I should have stayed."

Tears glistened in her eyes, and she shook her

head. "Don't tell me you're in love with me when I'm mad at you."

"Okay." He wasn't sure he understood that, but he was prepared to do anything she asked of him. "I'd still like to take you out to dinner. A nice dinner, tomorrow night. I've missed you. You became my best friend and, even if I've ruined any chance we had of being together, I'd like to at least try to save our friendship. Please."

Her sigh was heavy, shuddering a little with unshed tears, and Matt watched Bear drop his head on her lap, wondering why she was sad. She scratched his ears idly, then nodded slowly. "Dinner tomorrow sounds okay."

"Thank you."

It was a second chance—or maybe third—and he intended to make the best of it. He had twenty-four hours to figure out how to convince her he could make her happy.

HAILEY SMOOTHED HER dress over her hips and faced her reflection in the mirror. It wasn't a sexy dress like last time, but the dark blue fabric and more modest cut suited the occasion. It wasn't meant to be a fun date this time. Matt obviously had things he needed to say and one way or another, nothing could be settled until he'd said them.

I realized I was in love with you...

If only he'd stayed in her bed the morning after

the accident and told her that instead of sneaking out while she was still asleep.

She was ready when he rang the doorbell, which was jarring in its formality. She wasn't prepared for the sight of him in a suit and tie. It was obviously one he'd had for a long time, though the classic cut wasn't really out of style. His face was smooth and he smelled delicious.

"You're wearing a suit."

His smile was tentative rather than the cocky grin she loved so much. "I knew you'd look gorgeous tonight."

She drove, since they were taking her car and they weren't a couple anymore—official or otherwise—and when he gave her the final few directions which led to a restaurant so fine she didn't know anybody personally who'd been there, she softened a little. He'd obviously put a lot of thought into this dinner out.

They were seated at a very private and romantically set table, almost as if he'd prearranged it, and she tried not to hold her breath as the waiter handed Matt the wine menu.

"We'll have a bottle of Sauvignon Blanc, please."

When the waiter left, Hailey couldn't help smiling at him across the table. "You've been holding back on me."

"I'm a man of many skills. It's best not to reveal them all at once." When she arched an eyebrow at him, he laughed. "Okay, I called my brother-in-law. My sister likes wine so I figured he's had to order it a time or two."

"And you came up with the Sauvignon Blanc?"

"Well, I know you like seafood, chicken and pasta more than beef, so white was the obvious choice. Then he told me the top three most likely to be on the menu, and then I made him call my voice mail and say them all so I could practice." His grin returned in full force. "If you order the prime rib, I'm going to look bad now."

She laughed, and felt herself softening inside. Though it seemed a small thing, she knew asking his brother-in-law to teach him how to pronounce wine names was a big deal. And yet he looked relaxed, without the shadows in his eyes that suggested he felt judged and found wanting. It was progress.

Dinner was delicious and they talked about inconsequential things. His work. Her work. Paige and Mitch's argument because Mitch was convinced Sarah smiled at him first, while Paige said it was gas. Hailey found herself relaxing, enjoying the evening more than she'd anticipated. This was the Matt she'd fallen for, and she'd missed him.

"I love the way the candlelight reflects in your eyes," he told her while they waited for their dessert and coffee to be brought out.

"This has been a lovely evening. I know you don't care for this kind of restaurant."

"Sitting across from you, listening to you laugh, makes this my favorite kind of restaurant. I'm pretty sure no matter where I am, as long as you're as happy as you look right now, it'll be my favorite place."

Tears stung her eyes and she forced herself to look away from his gaze. "What's changed, Matt? What changed between the last dinner and this one?"

"I lost you. I've changed because between the last dinner and this one, I've felt how much it hurts to not have you in my life every day." He reached across the table and took her hand, his thumb brushing over her knuckles. "I screwed up, Hailey. I know I hurt you, but I love you and I want to make you happy. I want serious. I want real. And forever."

She believed him. Looking into his eyes, she knew without a doubt he loved her and meant every word he was saying. "I want serious, too. I've loved you for a while now. I tried not to at first, but you're the man I want."

The waiter chose that moment to appear, but Matt didn't let go of her hand. Once the coffees and the cheesecake they'd decided to share were on the table and the waiter was gone again, he squeezed her fingers.

"Sometimes my laundry's pretty ripe."

She smiled. "And sometimes I like to make the drive to Portland and spend hours at the Maine Mall, window shopping."

He winced, but she could see the humor in his

eyes. "I'm almost afraid to ask what the payback for camp will be."

"I think camp will be fun. I'll read my book while you fish and, when you catch one, I'll clap and ooh and ah over how big it is."

He gave her a crooked grin. "That sounds awesome, but you don't have to clap. There's not really any applause in fishing. They do need to be cleaned, though."

"I'm not going to clean your fish. That's never going to happen. But I do promise I'll never contradict you when you're telling somebody it was *this big*." She pulled her hand free so she could hold it up about a foot from her other one.

"I knew you were my kind of woman." He winked, but then he turned serious again. "I know my job requires a lot of me, but when I'm with you, I'll be with you one hundred percent. And I want to come home to you."

"I want that, too. Whether it's five-fifteen or seven or three in the morning, I'll be there. What you do is important and it's a part of who you are. I can handle it."

"We'll handle it together." He looked around for the waiter. "I feel a sudden need to pay the check and get you home."

She laughed and picked up her fork as she slid the plate toward her side of the table. "If you think I'm leaving this cheesecake uneaten, you're crazy."

"Half of that's mine," he protested. "And take your time. I have forever with you now."

"Thank goodness I bought brand-new hiking boots for that stupid adventure tour. Otherwise, I might never have gotten lost and you wouldn't have found me."

"I think I still would have found you." His gaze captured hers over the flickering candles. "I didn't know it, but I'd been looking for you a long time. And we both know I have an impeccable sense of direction."

Three months later...

"GOT A BITE!"

Hailey looked up from her book to watch Matt reeling in his line. Sure enough, there was a fish on the end. While he picked up a net with one hand to secure it, she set her book in her lap and clapped.

His laughter echoed through the trees. "There's still no applause in fishing."

"I'm making new traditions. And your dad thinks it's adorable."

"He thinks *you're* adorable. Especially when you beat my five-year-old nephew at cards and did a victory lap around the cabin in your flannel pajamas."

She snorted. "I earned that victory lap. Caleb's no slouch at Go Fish, my friend."

Matt dropped the fish into a bucket with the other

two he'd caught and then leaned in for a kiss. "I think you're adorable, too."

She put her hand on his chest to hold him back. "You know the rules. No kissing while you're wearing that hat."

"But it's my lucky hat."

"Maybe, but it ain't your *get* lucky hat."

She loved that his expression no longer turned cloudy when she wrinkled her nose and held him at bay. Over time he'd grown to trust the fact making him take his boots off outside meant she didn't like muddy floors, not that she didn't like him. The same went for really disgusting lucky fishing hats.

"Oh, I think I'll get lucky later," he said, which she didn't think was likely as they were bunking with his entire family. "I have a surprise for you."

She narrowed her eyes. "What kind of surprise?"

"We're going on a road trip."

He started gathering his fishing gear, so Hailey stood, tucked her book under her arm and folded her chair. "To where?"

"That's the surprise."

She followed him back toward the cabin, where the sounds of his family filtered out through the open windows. It was definitely a full house with everybody there, but Hailey liked his family and they liked her. When she and Matt had both managed to grab a four-day weekend, she hadn't minded at all the suggestion they get out of Whitford.

They'd arrived yesterday morning and spent the day doing the things they usually did at camp. Fishing. Card games. Walks in the woods. A campfire when the sun went down, with lots of stories, laughter and s'mores.

Today, after lunch had been cleared, Matt decided he wanted to fish for a while. Hailey always packed books, so she had no complaints. She wasn't one to turn down quiet reading time. But the idea of a road trip was intriguing.

"Is Bear going with us?" she asked, hoping to weasel a clue out of him.

"Nope. He's going to hang out here."

"Do I need to bring anything with me?"

"Nope." And he refused to say anything more.

After saying goodbye to the family, they got in her car and she wondered if this road trip was the reason they weren't in his truck. They almost never brought her car to the cabin because driving it meant Matt had to slow down on the back roads.

When he finally, after over an hour of driving without so much as a hint, slowed and took a right turn at a sign for a luxury resort Hailey had only ever seen pictures of, she looked at him with wide eyes. "Are we lost?"

He gave her an indignant look. "I'm never lost."

When they reached the end of the long, winding drive and the resort came into view, she sucked in a breath. It was even more gorgeous in person. The sprawling, historical resort, with its deep porches and gables was more massive than it looked in photographs. With immaculate grounds surrounded by woods, the photos didn't do it justice.

Matt pulled up in front of the grand front entrance and an attendant appeared with a luggage cart. Hailey looked down at her jeans and sweatshirt, wincing. It wouldn't surprise her at all if the guy pointed them to the service entrance. Then Matt popped the trunk. There were two garment bags and a suitcase in there.

"When did you put those in there?" She remembered leaving her house and she remembered him carrying in their duffel bags when they got to camp. She didn't remember a suitcase and two garment bags.

He grinned. "You may not know this about yourself, but you're remarkably easy to distract."

She might have been offended if he wasn't leading her through the front doors. The lobby alone was breathtaking, and she hoped she'd get a chance to look around the hotel. She wasn't even sure why they were there, but she was going to soak in every bit she could.

It seemed a little surreal when Matt gave his name to the woman at the desk and Hailey realized he had a reservation for the remainder of their mini-vacation. "We're staying here? Really?"

"Really."

"You were right earlier. You're totally getting lucky tonight."

He led her to the elevator and, once the doors had closed, he squeezed her hand. "I bet this place has a great fishing pond."

"Tell me you're kidding."

"No, I bet it really *does* have a great fishing pond, but you'll notice I didn't bring my pole."

"There wasn't room with the suitcase and garment bags. What's in them?"

"I know what I put in them. What Paige packed for you, I have no idea."

"Paige was in on this?"

He shrugged. "I was going to do it myself, but then I opened your closet and panicked."

The elevator stopped and he held her hand as they went down the hallway to the room they'd been given. After sliding the key card through the slot, he stepped back and let her go in first.

The room screamed expensive romance, from the wine chilling in a bucket to the luxurious-looking bed linens just begging to be rumpled. Their suitcase was sitting on a rack and their garment bags were in the closet. She kicked off her flip-flops to walk barefoot across the thick carpet to the window. The view of the grounds, with woods and distant mountains in the background, was breathtaking and she sighed as Matt wrapped his arms around her from behind.

"This is the most beautiful place I've ever been."

He kissed the back of her neck, making her shiver. "The bathtub is enormous and has the same view. We'll check that out later, but right now I'm going to take a shower and get dressed."

"We could check out the shower together."

Growling, he nipped at her neck. "As good as that sounds, we have early dinner reservations and they take those very seriously."

When Matt disappeared into the bathroom, Hailey went to the closet and took out the garment bag that had a tag with her name on it. After spreading it on the bed, she unzipped it and smiled. Paige had packed her favorite little black dress—the one she'd spent too much money on after convincing herself it could be worn for any occasion with the right accessories. After rummaging through the suitcase, she saw Paige had packed the right ones. Black heels, a silvery pashmina shot through with metallic threads, and her pearls. It was all very Audrey Hepburn when Hailey wore it with her hair up.

And, of course, her friend had packed her sexiest underwear. Hailey hung the dress back in the closet until it was time to put it on, and she was about to go through her makeup bag when the bathroom door opened.

With a towel around his waist, his naked chest still glistening with water, and his jaw freshly shaven, Matt grinned and she wanted to sweep everything from the bed to the floor and have her way with him.

"Just how soon are those dinner reservations?"

"We don't have time for you to keep looking at me like that." He held the towel around his waist as if she was going rip it off and jump him. Which was tempting, she had to admit. "You need to get ready."

By the time Hailey had showered, blown her hair out and pinned it up, dabbed on a minimum of makeup and put on the sexy underwear, she was half-afraid Matt would be asleep. But when she opened the bathroom door and stepped out, her heart skipped a beat.

He was wearing a suit. A *nice* suit, obviously new, with black dress shoes and a very sexy tie, and her mouth went dry. He'd worn an older suit when he took her out to dinner after their break-up, and twice a month they went into the city for dinner and he always wore a button shirt with nice pants, but this wasn't a Matt she'd seen before. He didn't fidget or tug at the tie. He just stood and let her get her fill of this magazine cover version of him.

"You look amazing," she said finally.

His gaze raked over the small amount of black lace barely keeping her decent. "So do you."

"I can't believe you did all this. I can't believe we're here."

"I'm going to go have some prime rib prepared by one of the best chefs in the state with the most beautiful woman in the world. There's no place else I'd rather be."

The sincerity in his voice made her eyes tear up and the last thing she wanted was raccoon eyes. "I should get dressed."

He helped her zip her dress and, when it was time for the pearl necklace, he stood behind her and took it from her hand. Before doing the clasp, he ran his fingertip down the nape of her neck. "Every man in that restaurant's going to envy me tonight."

"There will be other men there? I'm sure I won't notice."

"We need to get out of this room before I forget I'm supposed to be helping you into your clothes and not out of them."

Once they'd ridden the elevator back down to the lobby, they followed the discreet signs guiding them toward the restaurant. Hailey was glad they weren't running late because she kept stopping to admire some bit of architecture or art. Matt just smiled patiently and let her explore.

Then they reached the arched glass walkway that connected the main hotel to the restaurant and she stopped halfway across. It was the most beautiful scenery she'd ever seen and she turned in a circle, taking it all in. But it was looking over the gazebo by the lake and over the woods to the mountains that took her breath away.

"Look at that view. It's stunning."

"It's one of the prettiest spots in the state. I wanted us to see it together."

She smiled, warmed by the heat in his eyes. "Thank you for this weekend, Matt."

"It's barely started."

"I know, but this spot… This moment, with the view and us looking amazing and surrounded by this romantic atmosphere. It's so special."

He squeezed her hand. "This spot right here, huh?"

"Yes." She breathed deeply, looking through the glass and trying to absorb it all. She would never forget this moment.

"Hailey."

He said her name quietly, his voice serious, and she looked away from the window. First at his face, and then at the velvet box he had in the hand not holding hers. Her breath caught in her throat and tears threatened to blur her vision.

"I love you, Hailey. I love the you that crawled through the doggy door and let me get your sheets dirty when I needed you. I love the you that runs around in flannel pajamas with the kids and the you that looks like a movie star right now." He let go of her hand to open the box, and the diamond sparkled at her in the golden light from the chandeliers. "I wanted this moment to be extra special for you because every moment with you is special to me. No matter where we are or what we're doing, all that matters is that I'm with you. Will you marry me?"

"Yes," she whispered, but she wasn't sure any

sound came out because her throat felt choked with tears, so she tried again. "Yes!"

When he slid the ring onto her finger, she had to blink back tears to see it sparkling in the sunlit hallway. Then she threw her arms around his neck and kissed him until she could hardly breathe, not caring who might see.

"I love you," she whispered against his mouth.

"I love you, too. More than you can imagine."

"We could go try out that huge tub and order room service."

"Oh no, you don't, future Mrs. Barnett. There's a very expensive bottle of champagne in that dining room just waiting for me to pop the question."

She laughed. "A diamond ring *and* champagne? You're going to spoil me, you know."

"And I'll love every minute of it. Because I love you."

"I'm glad I waited my whole life for you."

He lifted her hand, kissing her knuckles just above the ring. "Me, too. Now let's go drink some champagne and live happily ever after."

* * * * *

New York Times bestselling author Shannon Stacey brings you an irresistible new Kowalskis story.

Liz Kowalski is heading home to Whitford, Maine—this time for good. Eager for her family, a fresh start and some fun, she doesn't count on being rescued by the chief of police her very first night back in town. Drew is everything she's *not* looking for…so why is she still so attracted to him?

After a brief, forbidden rendezvous at her brother's wedding, Drew Miller expects Liz to return to New Mexico and stay there. But when they're stuck together on the annual Kowalski camping trip, things start going a little *sideways.* Keeping their hands off each other proves just as impossible as keeping their secret from becoming public knowledge.

Amid family, mud and melted marshmallow, Liz and Drew try to fight what's growing between them. But a little time alone, a lot of chemistry and too many opinions might be just what it takes to bring together two people so determined not to fall in love.

Love a Little Sideways

Available now wherever books are sold!

CAR00225

New York Times Bestselling Author

MARIE FORCE

Another scandal at Watergate, only this time it's murder…

Detective Sergeant Sam Holland of the Washington, D.C.,
Metro Police needs a big win to salvage her career—and her
confidence—after a disastrous investigation. A perfect opportunity
arises when Senator John O'Connor is found brutally murdered,
and Sam is assigned to the case.

Matters get complicated when Sam has to team up with
Nick Cappuano, O'Connor's friend and chief of staff…and the man
Sam had a memorable one-night stand with years earlier.
Their sexual chemistry still sizzles, and Sam has to fight to stay focused
on the case. Sleeping with a material witness is a mistake she can't
afford—especially when the bodies keep piling up.

Fatal Affair

Available wherever books are sold!

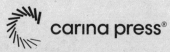

www.CarinaPress.com

CAR00221

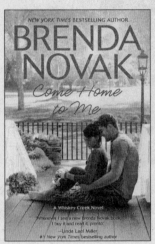

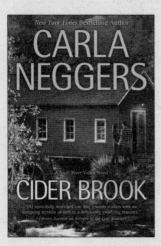